Safe Word

Safe Word

by

Molly Weatherfield

CLEIS
PRESS

Published in the United States by Cleis Press Inc., P.O. Box 14684, San Francisco, California 94114.
Printed in the United States.
Cover design: Scott Idleman
Book design: Karen Quigg
Cleis Press logo art: Juana Alicia
First Cleis Press Edition
10 9 8 7 6 5 4 3 2

Permission to quote from "Mr. Tambourine Man" by Bob Dylan granted by Special Rider Music.

To my husband, with love

ACKNOWLEDGMENTS

I'm grateful to be writing pornography in its most expansive era in two centuries—and to have received encouragement and criticism from three of the era's prime movers: Susie Bright, Pat Califia, and Carol Queen. Thanks to all of them, and to the staffs of Good Vibrations and Modern Times, where I've read from early versions of this book. Excerpts from this book, in somewhat different form, have been published in *Pucker Up* and in *Sex Spoken Here*, edited by Carol Queen and Jack Davis. Thanks also to the editors of *Black Sheets,* and to Gareth Branwyn, Tristan Taormino, Grant Antrewes, Richard Kasak, and Jennifer Reut.

I also want to thank Thaisa Frank for her provocative questions about what I think I'm doing. And I need to acknowledge that Carrie's comments about *Clarissa* and *Justine* are based on Angela Carter's argument in *The Sadean Woman*.

The next set of acknowledgments is necessarily more anonymous, but no less heartfelt. Thanks to Ellen, Jeff, Roz, Barbara, Jim, and Ellie, meticulous readers of the second draft, who pointed out the dull spots and inconsistencies with such good humor and enthusiasm that I didn't doubt that I could fix them. Not to speak of my assorted errors, linguistic, culinary, and typographic.

My husband slogged through every draft, including some truly awful stuff at the beginning. He kept his cool when I got defensive, was right more times than I have ever admitted, and hung in through waves of soul-searching and revision. He's a gifted, loving, and stubborn reader. And he knows where the stories come from, too.

Contents

Prologue

Dear Carrie,

You will continue brave and beautiful, I know.
In a year, you'll be much more so than you are now.

I sold you at this auction because I wanted to
see if I—and you—could pull it off. But I also did it
because if I hadn't done it, I would have wanted to
call the whole game off and see if we could become
friends. Or lovers. Or something. Go to the movies
together and see if we liked the same ones. I still
want to, and this is both surprising and disturbing.

I'll be at the Place d'Horloge in Avignon next
March 15. That's two weeks after your term of service ends. Come if you want to....

The First Day

*B*efore the French revolution, the family of the Marquis de
Sade owned half of Provence. They'd begun getting rich in
the middle ages. The first family member to have his name offi-
cially recorded, Louis de Sade, provost of Avignon, financed the
building of the St-Bénézet bridge—the famous pont d'Avignon—
in 1177, and the family coat of arms can still be seen on the
bridge's first arch.

The Sade family made its money in textiles, lumber, brew-
ing, and ropemaking, as well as from collecting the tolls on
the pont St-Bénézet. It was possible, in those days, for a rich
merchant, banker, or shipper to obtain a title. The family consol-
idated its position by a series of marriages to the oldest nobility
of the region, and by its services to Avignon's wealthy and cor-
rupt exiled Papal court. Italian functionaries at court detested
Avignon and longed for Rome: The brilliant young courtier
Petrarch wrote that the winter mistral winds turned the area into
"a sewer where all the muck of the universe collects."

Avignon's medieval walls still stand today, though half of
the bridge was washed away when the Rhône flooded in the
seventeenth century. The huge Palais des Papes—its interior

wrecked and ransacked when the French National Assembly annexed it in 1791—is populated only by the echoes of a century of intrigue, excess, and debauchery. The city itself is heavily touristed, like much of Provence, and a bit pricey. And in the summer, the central Place d'Horloge is packed.

On this particular day in mid-March, however, it was sunny and lively without being oppressively crowded. An American man was sitting at one of the cafés that line the square, drinking coffee and frowning as he tried to read a French architectural journal. Trendy, he thought, trendy and pretentious. Not that he was sure of that assessment. His French wasn't great, and his concentration, right then, quite minimal. He'd placed himself so that he could see down the rue Jean-Jaures, toward the train station, and he'd been glancing up eagerly whenever a slender young woman, especially one with close-cropped hair, came from that direction.

Lots of attractive people were strolling across the Place that day, lots of women he liked looking at, the Provençal sunlight shining through the plane trees on their little French breasts and big French educations. And since he was extraordinarily good-looking (his gray hair merely signaling an elegant way of approaching forty), none of this was going unnoticed. Once one of the young women he'd been watching turned back to him and smiled. "Would," she said, "that I were she." It took him a moment to negotiate the French grammatical construction in his mind before he returned the smile, shrugging apologetically. He got up and went to a tabac. My first pack in six months, he thought, damn her anyway.

There were ten Gitanes stubbed into the ashtray when, early in the afternoon, a slender young woman, with very short brown hair, walked quickly into the Place. She was pale and

3

pretty, and she wore a leather jacket, big white shirt and little black miniskirt, black stockings and cowboy boots, dark wire-rimmed glasses. She had a backpack made of soft red leather slung over her shoulder, and she carried one of those little note-books they sell in papeteries, *its satiny pages marked by faint purple grids.*

Pas mal, *thought the woman who'd smiled at him earlier. Not bad. Not so fantastic as he is, but a good body, anyway. And a bit of style—gamine in very expensive leather. The haircut is good—not quite shaved, but close enough. It makes her look poignant, vulnerable. And young—Jean Seberg selling the* Herald Tribune *on the Champs-Elysées. Oh, but she is that young, I can see that, now that she's turned her head a little. She's very young, isn't she, twenty-three, twenty-four, perhaps?* Tiens, Monsieur, *not very original of you.*

She sniffed disapprovingly, ready to pay her waiter and move on. But there was something about the tableau that held her attention. She watched the man straighten up in his chair, his nervousness rolling off him like beads of water, his face falling into confident, authoritative lines. And—almost in response— the girl slowed her pace as she approached him, still vulnerable, but increasingly knowing and deliberate in her movements. The woman felt her face grow warm, as though she'd been peeking through a keyhole.

Enough, *she chided herself—enough of this pair and their slightly indecent game. And as she drifted out of the square, she muttered to herself (in English, for she admired the American cinema),* Fasten your seatbelts. It's gonna be a bumpy ride.

The man smiled appreciatively as the girl in boots slipped into the cane-backed chair next to him.

4

"Well," he said.

She giggled a little. "Well."

It seemed that neither of them had prepared any other opener. He stubbed out his cigarette while she took off her sunglasses—her gray eyes were mutable, surrounded by shadows—and put her notebook into her pack. They exchanged dazed, slightly ironic smiles: *How do we get beyond this ridiculous moment?* A waiter came by and she turned to him gratefully, ordering a kir in offhand, fluent French. A kir, and—yes, he nodded—another coffee for Monsieur.

"I'd forgotten," Monsieur dutifully pitched her a second opening line, "how good your French is. You lived here when you were a kid, right?"

"Pretty close," she nodded, "Montpellier. The year I was twelve. My whole family. I didn't want to go home at the end of the year. I cried for a week and I moped for like a year afterward. And I was determined not to forget a word of French. Funny thing is that I didn't."

"Well, it's a very strong kind of energy, adolescence," he said. "When I was in my teens, Kate's family went to Venezuela for a year. Talk about energetic—I got straight A's, was president of my class, captain of the soccer team. My parents were ecstatic. I built seventy-six balsa wood model airplanes. And the day before Kate came back, I burned them all. It was an impressive fire. And two days after that, I—we—well, it was our first time."

Her eyes clouded over. Storm warnings. He watched her closely. *She needs to get used to hearing that sort of thing,* he thought, the pleasure of ritual sternness flooding his body like very strong coffee. She recoiled slightly, but surprised him by steadying herself a few ragged beats later, shrugging, exhaling sharply, a rueful smile playing at the corners of her mouth.

5

She pulled a cigarette from the pack on the table, fumbling with the plastic lighter.

"Here," he said, doing something mysterious to the side of the lighter, "they've got those child-proofing switches on them now."

"But you don't smoke," he added, a bit reproachfully, as she took a timid drag.

She stubbed it out, scattering ashes on the table.

"Sorry." She managed a wobbly smile through weakly exhaled smoke. "I'm nervous."

He was patient, affectionate. "We're both nervous." He smiled, nodding at the overflowing ashtray, while he scanned her expression carefully. Actually, she's a lot more self-possessed than I imagined she'd be. Less readable, too. Less of a kid. And she's taking my measure as carefully as I've been taking hers. Slow down, he told himself.

And to her, "Look, I've got lunch reservations. A nice place, we can just make it if we hurry." He'd chosen a dim, comfortable setting for telling her what he wanted from her—she has to want to do this. To understand. Fully. What she can expect. He'd imagined her, sitting very straight against an upholstered banquette, listening carefully to him as haughty waiters came and went with plates of legendary food. A formal venue for pulling off the big deal, the intricately leveraged buyout, at once hostile takeover and entente cordiale. He liked formality; he'd have hired the Hall of Mirrors at Versailles if it had been available.

But you need a certain timbre of concentration for deal-making, and the truth was, he wasn't in the mood. He was—it took him a moment to frame it—curious about her. About certain specifics (though he knew he could demand that she answer those questions), but also about, well, he wasn't sure what. But she had spent a year away, in demanding circumstances, and, at her age, people change....

Cool it, he told himself, willing himself to detachment, a flaneur's aestheticized attentiveness. He watched the shifting points of leafshadow on her pale cheek, almost the color of (but greener than) the dark, delicate, skin below her eyes. He made no move to get up, lazily aware that they probably couldn't get there on time now, even if they did hurry.

She shrugged again, warier now. "I'm not very hungry."

"A walk, then," he said. "Okay? And then maybe a picnic in that park up on the hill—the Rochers des Doms. Next to the Popes' Palace. So I can keep looking at you in the sunlight, Carrie." And scope you out a little.

He'd regained the advantage. Relax, Jonathan, he thought contentedly. There's plenty of time for everything.

CARRIE

It could be a photo spread, "Win a Dream Date in Provence," with shots of him smiling as he leads me up the wide stone steps to this park, or frowning comically at the whimsical sculptures set among early roses. The packages—food, baguette, and wine bottle—tucked just so under his arm, for our *pique-nique*, as he'd confided to the lady back there in the *charcuterie*. Oh, and be sure to include a shot of her as well, beaming at him as she wipes her hands on her apron, insisting that he taste all the *spécialités de la région* before he chooses. As though pâté were really what she wanted to give him a taste of.

People try to please him, everybody becoming a merchant or purveyor, obsequious, deferential. He hardly notices, smiling absentmindedly, choosing the best, drifting on. And I've only got myself to offer—sounding quite ridiculous, too, babbling idiotically about the view of the Rhône, the bridge, the neighboring walled city across the river. The grass always greener in the other medieval walled city.

Petrarch first saw Laura here in Avignon, at mass in the Church of St. Claire. The Sade family claimed that the girl who inspired the poet was Laure de Noves, wife of Hugues de Sade, who bequeathed two thousand gold florins for the bridge's repair, in 1355.

That's when the family coat of arms was added to the bridge, seven years after Laure had died of the plague. She'd had eleven children, and belonged to a court of learned ladies who wrote Provençal verse; both of these facts are more interesting to me than whether or not she truly was Petrarch's blond, bloodless Laura. Of course the Sade family insisted passionately on the connection, but it's never conclusively been proven.

You can't see the coat of arms from here, though, and you can't walk down any closer—there's a locked gate blocking the path during off season. Pretty name, Laure. I read about her the morning before I first went to Jonathan's house. Which is probably why I memorized all those dates and details of her life so obsessively—to distract me from what I knew he and I would be talking about that afternoon. The arrangements and negotiations. Ground rules, bylaws, and administrative details, simplified for the novice I was then. Three afternoons a week. Come to the side door, undress, kneel in an assigned spot, tethered and waiting. Ready—*that's the easy part,* he'd joked—to do absolutely everything he commanded.

He told me to ask him whatever I thought I needed to know. And after that (except for the occasional time-out period, when he'd explain how he was making the rules tougher and more challenging, and did I have any questions?) I spoke only when spoken to. *Yes, Jonathan,* mostly. Or, through tears, *I'm sorry, Jonathan,* promising to do better next time, to respond more quickly, anticipate his desires. Sometimes there would be interrogations—I'd blush, stammer, distort my mouth to voice unspeakable responses to his impossible questions: *How does that make you feel? Describe it for me.* And later, when he'd taken to sharing me, packing me off to a friend or associate for an afternoon or a weekend, he'd demand that I render full, and entertaining, account of the interludes. *Tell me a story,* he'd say. *Tell me everything.*

I wonder if he'll want to know about this last year away from him—the patient, painful succession of days under the hands, the whip, of a professional trainer. Although perhaps there's more to show than to tell: I feel myself performing for him already, in little ways, just to give him a glimpse of what I've learned on my junior year abroad. Body language. New fluency, inflection of bone, and muscle. Nuanced—remarkable, given the decidedly non-nuanced manner in which it was drilled into me—controlled, even contrapuntal. I can hear my treble voice chattering about a learned lady of the fourteenth century, but it's really the bass voice that's pulling out all the stops: melodic line from hip to neck, play of unvoiced signifiers as perfect as my French *R*, but subtler, more elusive, like the way the tongue hits the teeth, the top of the mouth.

JONATHAN

Oh, yes, this is nice. Just watching her, that new quality she's got—experience, I guess you'd have to say. I wasn't sure I liked it at first, but it's growing on me, confusing me a little maybe, but hey. We should open the bottle of wine, I suppose, get a little more confused. Soon, soon.

It's corny, coming up to this park, but it's what I imagined when I wrote the note, remembering the night we met. We'd talked about the south of France—she was studying the poetry; I told her a little about the buildings and bridges.

It hadn't been easy putting her at ease. Or listening to everything she had to say, once I did. I suppose it's how smart college students talk nowadays—a few solid insights floating in a sea of deconstructionist jargon. Except that she had lots of those insights—fleets, flotillas of them, whole armadas of ideas steaming into port. Oh well, I thought, I can always gag her. Or—even better—forbid her to speak. Because, of course, I'd have better uses for that mouth.

I liked watching her, though—all the neurons firing, a jittery lightshow pinball machine behind her big, scared eyes. It would be fun to have all that intensity beamed onto me. Talk? Only when I permit you to. Think? Try thinking about how to please me. To entertain me, anticipate what I'll want next. What I'll want you to be. Object, servant, victim, toy? Footstool, coffee table, ashtray? What about performer? Or private dancer, perhaps? Housepet. Pissoir. Slave.

It had been a boring party, before I noticed her. Great ass, I'd thought absentmindedly. Pretty girl, I'd supposed too, but not as interesting from the front. Still, I found myself keeping tabs on her, following her around from a distance. I'd chat with friends, while some third eye kept track of her whereabouts. She didn't know anybody except a friend who didn't want to be bothered with her. She was doing shy, bored things, fiddling with her beer, trying to keep out of her friend's way. She was sweet and shaggy-looking, graceful and a little lost and dreamy, I think I remember thinking—to the extent I was thinking of anything at all, besides keeping her little black jeans within my line of sight.

I followed them into the library, where people were watching videos. Fuck—she sat down on the floor, hugging her knees. So much for that, I thought, this is stupid anyway, I'd be better off at home with a book. But the room had crowded up, and I would have had to trip over people to get out. And then they started the bondage video. It was messy and amateurish, and people hooted, which bothered me a little. Because there was also passion on the screen—clumsy and graceless, to be sure, but authentic and obsessive too. Which was probably why everybody in the room was so noisy and giddy, to avoid facing up to that. I cast my eyes idly over the laughing crowd, trying to imagine what they were thinking.

Well, I'll be damned. The girl with the ass was gazing up at the screen as though it were telling her the meaning of life. Flushed face, parted mouth—quivering, guilty, enthralled, spectacular. Her face was the real porn show, and I could gladly have watched it all evening. I'd hear sounds from the TV speakers, a whip's crack, a groan of pain, and I'd watch the show she was putting on, her troubled, clouded, smudgy eyes reflecting the flickering light of the screen. It was a voyeur's dream. In the midst of a noisy, unconscious crowd, too—she was the only one in the room really seeing the movie, and I

11

was the only one really seeing her. She'll look like that for me, I thought. She'll do anything and everything I want.

She did, too. For a year and a half. She took everything I dished out, meekly and silently challenging me to raise the ante. And never letting me forget the critical consciousness beneath her compliance. I wondered about that consciousness. I found myself thinking about her, at times when I would rather not have.

I needed a break. She was more than I'd bargained for, more than my life, which has its own complexities and eccentricities—not to speak of affinities and obligations— could readily absorb.

The auction was a good solution to the problem. It would be a challenge for her, and for me, too. They don't take just anybody; I'd have to work her hard to train her for the entrance trials. It would be an excuse to keep dreaming up new stuff—full-time, too. She'd move into my house for a few very intense months, and then she'd be gone, giving me a year to decide what I really wanted. Fine. And then at the last minute—after she'd been auctioned off but before they signed the final papers—I lost my nerve. Suppose she didn't want to come back after a year (absurdly, I'd never even considered the possibility). So I wrote a ridiculous little letter—which didn't feel so ridiculous when I was writing it.

Embarrassing to think about. Well, don't think, then. Look at her instead, her neck in the golden afternoon light— the year's discipline outlining her gestures, like a narrow stroke of cobalt pigment. The skin over her spine's top bump is paler than her cheek. She must have worn a collar all year, her neck looks startled by its freedom.

They'd drifted into silence, leaning against a stone railing over-looking the bridge. He opened his mouth to speak, at the same time as she began to say something. They both laughed nervously.

"You go ahead," he said.

"You know," she began, "when I got here this morning, I really had no idea what to expect from you. Well, I mean there was that letter you wrote, in 'Passionate Shepherd' mode...."

He raised his eyebrows, searching for the reference. Passionate who? Oh, right, as in "Come live with me and be my...." Terrific road map, poetry, for steering around the unsayable patches in a conversation.

"Yeah," she nodded. "But, of course I could see right off that that wasn't really what you wanted, so then I thought you'd go straight for the hard core. Read me my rights, you know. Oh, that was sort of a joke they had in the place where they prepared me for the auction—you know, if you think you have any rights, you're in the wrong place...."

She turned away from him. Valiant, he thought, the poetry, the sort of joke.

And yes, he had been planning to read her her rights, in that highly esteemed restaurant. It would have been just about now, too. A done deal, instead of...whatever free-form nonsense they'd gotten themselves into.

"Which scenario," he asked carefully, "would you have preferred?"

"Well," she lifted her eyes to him, "either one would have given us a clear script to follow."

Fair enough, Jonathan thought. Neither of us ready to fold yet.

"You don't like just hanging out with me?"

They both smiled at the hurt tone of his voice.

"It's difficult," she answered, "with all the open questions sort of hanging in the air between us. I mean, I get the sense that you still want me, but I don't get at all what you've got in mind."

"I want you profoundly," he said quickly. "Complexly," he added. "And quite against my better judgment." He grinned. Elision through allusion. The movies as good as the Norton Anthology for a game of hide-and-seek.

But we could play this way forever.

He made a decision.

"And I do have something pretty, uh, structured in mind. But it'll take some explaining, and arranging. If you agree to it, of course."

She nodded. Almost submissively.

"But" (oh, don't go away yet!), "I've been thinking that we need this unscripted time together, before all that comes down. Kind of a vacation. Time out, you know? I think we need to talk. Catch up."

"Vacation..." she repeated. "You mean, seriously with no rules, no punishments, no, uh, hardware for a while...."

"If you think you can handle it a little longer."

He smiled at the look she threw him.

"Yeah," she said, "I can handle it."

CARRIE

But I think I might have preferred being read my rights. Because time out sounds fair, even scrupulous, I guess, but dangerous, too.

Well, I do like to hang out with him. Talk, laugh, reveal trivial things about myself. Share my own meanings for words—

here, let me draw you a map of the territory, it'll be so much easier for you that way, when you're ready to roll your troops over the border and take over. When you've decoded all my messages, satisfied yourself that I have no private meanings, no safe words, left.

Still, he's right, this is the way to do it. Think of it as an experiment. My science education seems to have ended in third grade, but I used to love it when we'd shake iron filings over a piece of paper and watch them line up in the magnetic field, positive and negative poles. Test the strength of the attraction, the lines of force. I'll leave when I know I can, and I'll stay if I know I must. And I'll know which is true—well, as I told my seatmate on the train this morning, I'll know it when I know it.

We shook hands on that, an hour later, when we left the train. Clasping hands, for want of a more appropriate gesture, to seal our compact, our brief intimacy between Paris and Avignon, the unlikelihood of our meeting again. He was a good, sympathetic listener, quiet and surprisingly unflappable, like someone who's read the book before he's seen the movie. Call him a perfect stranger, absent a more suitable term, bidding me a formal, reluctant farewell at the frontier. And daring me to be as brave as I need to be. Get it right, he urged me with his eyes. Be certain.

"Okay," I said, goaded to boldness by the memory of the handshake this morning. "Sure."

And laughing suddenly now, at the two of us—well, were we going to stand here exchanging coded messages forever? When the next step was so idiotically simple? "A vacation sounds great, Jonathan. But it begins in your hotel room. In bed. Right now."

JONATHAN

Part of me wanted to laugh too, especially at the look on her face—or looks, since she couldn't quite make up her mind between smug and terrified. I nodded cordially, as though she'd praised the view or the weather, endeavoring not to betray my surprise. Or the more immediate discomfort—forget the part of me that wanted to laugh; how long had I been ignoring those other, dangerously urgent, signals?

We sat quietly in the taxi, a little space between us, both of us equally astonished by her move. Hardly touching each other—I mean, not *not* touching; every so often one of our hands would creep over that little space. But hardly touching. Waiting. The hotel didn't have an elevator—just as well, it wouldn't have worked very well to jam ourselves into one of those little French cages right then.

We climbed the three flights of stairs doggedly, entering the room silently. She wandered to the window, opening it out wide, and looked out into the courtyard, the geraniums in pots, deep red and pale purple. You could hear birds, and you could see two young women taking in the fragrant, billowy sheets they'd hung out to dry that morning. "Nice," she said.

I stood next to her and closed the curtains. She turned toward me and I looked down at her neck, rising from the crisp, oversized white shirt under her leather jacket. She didn't have a bra on—the shirt was loose and opaque enough so that wouldn't immediately be apparent. But, trust me, I knew. I looked at the inverted triangle of chest above her shirt's top button, the shadow at the apex where her breasts began. I almost reached to undo the button. And then...I had a better idea.

I took off my own jacket instead, tossing it on a chair. Sweater and shirt, too. T-shirt. Her mouth twitched a little at the corners, and I kicked off my shoes, reached down, and pulled off my socks.

She put her hand on my belly, and I knew she could feel it tremble. I leaned over to kiss her, lightly, quickly, just grazing her lower lip with my teeth.

She sighed, and then she backed up a step and folded her arms across her chest. Well, she'd certainly gotten into the spirit of this vacation thing. She was smiling now, full out, looking tough in her leather jacket. Her eyes were on my belt buckle. Hungry, amused, challenging. If she'd ever, during the time we'd been together, if she had ever *dared* look at me that way...well, it would have been unthinkable—she'd have gone off the chart, that informal and arbitrary matrix of transgressions and punishments I'd worked out as our arrangement progressed. Arrive late at my house, five strokes with the rattan cane, forget to address me by name, ten....

Well, if I'd wanted to guarantee her (hey, and *me*) a monster erection, I guess I'd succeeded. Probably it was the memory of those punishments—clashing deliciously with her unaccustomed boldness today. I unhooked my belt, using those memories to keep myself focused. Tossing aside my pants, pulling off my shorts. The moment off balance as each foot pulls through its leg hole. And then...nothing to do but stand there and submit to her appraising gaze.

"Well," she murmured, "you're still a very beautiful man, Jonathan. And you're right—it's crazy how little I know about you some ways. Like, how old are you anyway?"

"Thirty-eight," I answered, trying to sound casual. *Still*...the word had a cold edge to it.

She nodded noncommittally. "Help me with my boots, please?"

She sat on the bed and I knelt to take off the stiff, pretty new boots with their intricate, multicolor stitching. She took off her jacket but sat still. I pushed her skirt up. She had on long black stockings, a black garter belt, no panties. Slender, very white thighs. Her pubic hair was short, like the hair on her head; they'd shaved her cunt, the hair was just now growing back. The black stripes of the unadorned garter belt drew the stockings up very high, very taut. The whole effect was so ambiguously situated between whorish and conventlike— after a year, did she really remember so precisely what I liked? Or maybe it was just what Constant liked.

I undid the garters. And then I put my head down and caught the embroidered edge of a stocking in my teeth. I could feel her thigh under my lips and I slowly pulled the stocking down, my mouth sliding over her knee, her calf, her foot. I kissed her instep. And then I repeated the whole business—for the other stocking, the other leg, the other foot. She had just the slightest, heartstopping trace of a purple welt on that second thigh, not quite healed—I lingered on it. It made me want to eat her alive.

I reached for the hook of the garter belt, pulled it softly, and it fell away. The little black miniskirt was made of some stretchy fabric. It was easy to pull off, and she helped me, lifting her ass slightly. I pushed her back on the bed, very gently, so that she was still sitting up, and straddled her. And, much more slowly than I wanted to, I unbuttoned her shirt, while she kissed my neck, my shoulders.

And there she finally was, and I stopped caring about what she might want. I fell on her, grabbing her ass, tonguing her breasts, moving her up to the pillows. Forget the sensitive lover thing; at that moment all I wanted was to get as much of her into my hands as possible, before I got as much of me as possible into her. She moved against me, wrapping her arms around me, arching her back. I felt the hard points of her nipples against my chest. I moved into her, too quickly, really, to savor the familiarity, but I would, later, next time. I tried to work carefully, moving in long, slow strokes. I wanted to last forever, I was afraid I wasn't going to last at all, I guess I lasted long enough—to hear her cry out, anyway, roughly, from the dark bottom of her voice.

And afterward, after I felt her come one last time—just a little internal flutter—I heard, or maybe felt, a low laugh bubbling up from her belly. I'd forgotten that laugh, but now I remembered it—her laugh that caught the ridiculous edge of sex so exactly.

I'd punished her, of course, the first time I'd heard that laugh. I'd been charmed by it, but I couldn't let her get away with such flagrant disrespect. I gave her four, I think, or maybe six. It was early on in our time together, and she was still pretty awkward in most ways, but she surprised me by how gracefully she took those strokes. Funny what you remember. And what pushes you forward. I wondered how long until I'd be disciplining her again. But for now, it was enough that she was here, under me. For now.

CARRIE

We must have fallen asleep. Because the next thing I remember was the sun coming through the curtains. It was low, and the light was pink. Sunset.

I was lying on my side. Jonathan was behind me, one arm flung across me, his hand on my breast. Long, tapering fingers, beautifully articulated bones spreading out from his wrists. My skin looked pink in the light, pale pink against the olive of the back of his hand. I could probably bend my head down to kiss his hand if I tried, I thought.

I wanted to, a little. To show him how good I was feeling. Not that I'd exactly been keeping it to myself, but still. It was all so luxurious, so warm and indolent. During the past year I'd occasionally thought of his hands, the bones in his wrists. Their images would drift, unbidden, into my thoughts, late at night, perhaps when the day's challenges had overwhelmed my defenses. I'd remember their weight on my body, their elegant curve around my breasts. And I'd remembered correctly, too, as it turned out. I'll move, I'll do something soon, I kept promising myself. But right at that moment I didn't want to do anything but lie there with the slanted light of the sunset lengthening against us on the bed. Well, perhaps I could shift backward a little, a little closer to his hip....

His hand tightened. He was beginning to wake up. I lifted my head and licked his fingers. I inched my ass closer to him. He turned a little, and I could feel his cock—still a little moist, but not yet hard—jumping a little against me.

I turned a little more so that my ass was directly against his cock, and he moved his other hand under me, reaching for my other breast. He kissed the back of my neck. I arched my back, stroking his belly, his stiffening cock, with my ass until I felt him move into its furrow. Slowly now. I moved back and forth—teeny movements really, stomach contractions, rotate an inch forward, an inch back—while he grew against me.

20

"Okay," he whispered, and we moved onto our knees, him on top of me.

The bed had a headboard. I grasped it. I didn't want him to have to balance on his hands. I didn't want him ever to take his hands off my breasts. He spread his fingers a little, enough to catch my nipples between them, and then tightened. And while I gasped at the pinch, while I lost a beat in thralldom to that sensation and he felt me lose that beat, he moved his cock against my asshole.

I wasn't ready for him, quite. He knew that, he'd been looking for that moment. He wanted to feel me yielding to him. He pushed slowly and I gave way, arching my back, opening to him, forgetting everything except that yielding, that always frightening letting-loose.

It hurt a little on every thrust. (It always does. I hope it always will.) I pushed back against him. He moved more deeply into me, and I teased myself a little. It hurts too much, I thought, I have to ask him to stop. Yeah, right. I felt myself opening my mouth and trying to shape some words—*please,* or *slower,* or something—and all I could hear was the sound of myself coming.

He moved his hands from my breasts to the wall above the headboard, leaning heavily forward, surrendering to his own orgasm. Somehow we slid down together to the bed, my sweaty back plastered to him while I felt him shrink slowly in me.

I began to believe, for the first time that day, that I was actually here. With Jonathan in a small hotel with faded blue shutters at the windows and geraniums in the courtyard. Lavender and lemon vervaine in a vase on the dresser; the sheets of our bed still distantly smelling of sun and fresh air, underneath our darker, saltier smells. Vacation: You know you're on holiday when the smells, the colors, begin to take on this sort of painterly solidity. And when the other stuff—the rules, the plans—become vaguer, hazier. Yes, really a vacation, time out from rules and plans, from fantasies, and from reciting his letter to myself as though it were a mantra. No need for romantic endings, or for any endings at all, just yet. Only this lovely, wonderful, all-enveloping lust, in the sweet, simple, declarative present. It would do for now. It would do quite nicely.

JONATHAN

It was dark outside now. I didn't want to get out of bed, but finally I had to untangle myself from her to pee. Use the bidet too. Nice. Always a surprise how nice, how sensible.

"We never did have that picnic," she called from the bedroom. "I'm starving. Where's that food you bought?" I heard paper rustling.

When I came back in, I found her cross-legged on the bed, munching a piece of bread.

"Crumbs in bed," I said. Surprising myself by how compulsive I sounded—like a bad parody of myself in a more commanding persona. Still, there was a perfectly good table in the corner of the room, with two perfectly good chairs standing beside it—was it really so impossibly middle-aged to want to use it? I opened a bag of food, began setting it out. She shrugged, giggled, watching me search my pockets for my Swiss Army knife. I cut pieces of cheese, spread pâté on bread, opened the bottle of wine. I set everything out on paper, found the napkins and plastic wine glasses I'd remembered to get.

"In return," I said, "you're responsible for entertainment. I want a story from your year." Surprising myself again, this time by my eagerness to hear, to know, everything. Insults, punishments, humiliations: all the ways she'd been used, forced, bound, whipped, punished—how, and (trickier business) by whom. So that I could lay claim, begin to possess the experiences she'd had this past year. *Droit du seigneur.* My right to demand that she spin the straw of experience into the gold of narrative, for my entertainment. For the edification and delectation of the gentleman in the audience.

She looked thoughtful for a moment. "Well, okay," she said slowly, "if you want to. But when we're done eating. And back in bed."

Fair enough. We were both so ravenous that the food disappeared pretty quickly, and the night air was chilly enough to drive us under the covers.

"Okay then..." she began, snuggling against me. "Well, I think I'd better begin at the beginning...."

CARRIE'S STORY CONTINUES

So there I was, less than an hour after being auctioned off, kneeling on the floor of a limousine in front of my new master. I could feel the car's suspension under my knees—we were driving over cobblestones. We picked up speed on the paved streets; perhaps the driver had turned onto one of those small highways they sometimes build around the perimeters of ancient cities. I was naked, under a rough black cloak, except for tightly laced high boots. I'd been taught some new rules during my stay in the warehouse: I had to keep my eyes lowered, instead of maintaining eye contact, as you'd insisted. It was difficult for me—fixing my gaze on his very neat suede shoes, the thickly carpeted floor, while his hands methodically probed, opened, examined me. I wanted to know what he looked like. All I'd ever really seen of him were gray-tinted glasses.

He took his hands away now, reaching for a small package next to him on the seat. I could hear the faint clink of metal. Buckles, I thought. He tore open the wrapping paper and I could smell the leather—I think he was rubbing it between his fingers, to check its thickness. I relaxed my shoulder blades, lengthened my neck for him. The collar was tall and stiff— I would have to get used to holding my head very high. And in front, dangling down over the gap between the bones of my clavicle, I felt a heavy iron ring. Was it three inches in diameter? Four? Big enough for him to grasp in his hand.

Yes. He used it to pull me down to his crotch, quickly unbuttoning his fly with his other hand, filling my mouth with a swollen cock that reached insistently for my throat. It took some effort to move my head back and forth over him, with my neck so cruelly bound. I think he sensed that, and I think he enjoyed it, too, pulling me closer with the ring, and holding me down firmly while I swallowed.

And then—well, that's easy. Put him gently, humbly, back in his pants. Straighten out his clothes, with light, deft hands. And then lean back on my knees—back straight, head high, eyes down, tits out, waiting at attention in case he wanted me again. He reached over me to a magazine rack, and selected a newspaper, opening a *Wall Street Journal* and relaxing behind it, and I realized that he hadn't said a word to me since...well, he'd never said anything to me at all. I wondered if he ever would.

It was becoming difficult to stay still. Not just the aches at my knees or having to keep my balance as the car sped up and slowed down, but the silence, the poverty of images. I scanned my memory for stray glances I'd caught of him. I didn't think he was tall. His hands were large—I had the impression that he was squarely built, broad for his height. In good shape for his age—late forties, maybe? I'd heard his voice, at the auction, when he'd come over to where I'd been displayed on my little carpeted pedestal. He'd parted my ass with blunt, dry fingers, and commented to an assistant about my "pure passion for obedience." His English was precise, accentless; I suspected it wasn't his first language. He'd laughed a little, when he'd seen how jolted—how summoned to attention—I'd been by his fingers in me. He was right; I did want to obey him. Although maybe he'd meant that I want to obey everybody.

Only now, maddeningly, I didn't. I felt fidgety. I needed to hear his voice. I could happily obey him, if he'd tell me to do something, but I was having a difficult time doing the most important thing of all—which was waiting. I realized (tacky, obvious, but there it was) that I'd expected him to give me a little discourse on himself—how tough he'd be—Sir Stephen informing O of his fondness for habits and rituals. He wouldn't have had to say a lot; just something to give it, you know, a story line.

Yeah, I told myself, as the limo's wheels rolled over smooth road and sunlight flickered through the tinted windows, that's you all over, Carrie—life's only real when you've made it into a story. But the more I scolded myself, the more I found that I wanted to lift my eyes and peek at him. One peek, I told myself. Just to see what kind of a mouth he had.

Wide. Determined. The cheeks lined, the jaw squarish. That was all I allowed myself, through my eyelashes. A little something to go on, to settle me down for the rest of the ride. To allow me to imagine what sort of person might have those hands, that taste and smell. He was very rich, the assistant had told me. And he liked a bargain.

The car finally stopped in front of a hotel, and he stepped out and turned, to allow someone to drape a topcoat around his shoulders. I caught a glimpse of black cowboy boots—Stefan, the assistant from the auction, respectfully murmuring assent to Mr. Constant's instructions: Get her ready, after she's fed and bathed and rested. "I'll be back for her at eight," Mr. Constant concluded, in his mild, accentless voice. "Oh, and give her two strokes, won't you, to remind her to keep her eyes where they belong."

The strokes had been swift and furious, the first making me gasp, the second wrenching tears and a few gurgled sobs from me. And neatly placed, I thought now, examining myself in the mirror while I waited for the large bathtub to fill.

It was taking a while, even with water pouring full force out of the taps into the square tub, its deep bottom sunk below the bathroom floor. Black marble. Ugly, expensive. Black tiles on the walls with a sort of water lily design etched into them to echo the metallic faux-Monet wallpaper on the ceiling and upper part of the walls. And too much light. Too many mirrors, also, in front of me and behind me:

I stared curiously at the infinite parade of pale naked girls in cruel black collars, angry red stripes neatly X'ed across their infinite parade of asses. It was like seeing the year I'd signed on for, spread out before me.

I looked tired, my eyes much more deeply shadowed than usual. I'd been woken up early that morning, to get me ready for the auction. And I'd stood for I don't know how long, chained to my pedestal while the buyers had examined me. I was glad I'd get some time to rest. I just hoped, as I stepped carefully into the tub, that I wouldn't fall asleep in there.

The hot water felt great, the tingly buttermilk bath salts soothing my ass. But—no need to worry about falling asleep—the collar felt even tighter that it had on dry land. I couldn't dangle my head back as I wanted. And the leather would stiffen, too, as it dried. Get used to it, I told myself, as I experimented with how to dunk my head under the water to rinse my hair. Get used to it; you'll be wearing it all year.

And when the makeup lady woke me later that afternoon, I wondered if I had fallen asleep in the bathtub after all. But no— I remembered then, through an enormous yawn, that after I'd finished my bath I'd been fed small cubes of cheese, fruit, and raw vegetables on a heavy white china plate on the floor near the bed. And given water too, in a big bright yellow plastic dog's bowl—I remembered feeling grateful that it was the big kind of bowl, for German shepherds or Akitas, because I'd been so thirsty. And glad that the pallet, which Stefan had prodded me down to for my nap, was soft, covered with a sheepskin, and placed near the floor vent, in the warm air currents.

I was lying on my side, my hands behind my back. Stefan had buckled a pair of leather cuffs around my wrists, and attached my hands behind my back—I'd had to dip from the waist to get to the food and water—and he'd also tethered me in place at the end of a long chain leash. But I must have slept well, I thought, because I felt a lot better, and amused to hear the makeup lady—a small, cheerful woman with bronzey dyed flyaway hair and rouged pink cheeks—imperiously telling me in French that I must wake up and sit *au delà,* at the vanity table across the room, my leash dangling between my legs.

She worked cheerfully and carefully, humming to herself, chattering about what a sweet little boy I looked like in my haircut, entirely unperturbed, it seemed, by my chain and nakedness. Was this something she saw every day in this hotel? I wondered. Or did Mr. Constant's money override people's usual expectations? I gazed at myself in the mirror. I looked better after my nap—my eyes huge and startled above pale pink and ivory cheeks, mouth carefully painted the color of a purplish bruise—while she rubbed a little more of the purplish lip gloss on my nipples.

Stand up, she told me. Turn around slowly, while she considered what else to do with me. She brushed and trimmed my pubic hair a bit, used a little more of the lip gloss at my cunt, but that was about all she could come up with, since I'd been manicured and depilated within an inch of my life that morning, for the auction. She stroked my ass pensively, and then she quickly packed up her makeup kit, tossing away used Q-tips and cotton balls, gently prodding me back down to the bench, this time facing away from the mirror. "Be good, *petite,*" she called to me, clattering out of the room on high, slightly broken-down, platform shoes, the room suddenly becoming very quiet, the wrought iron vanity table bench cold and hard under me.

Next act, I thought, hearing a sound at the door a few minutes later. Opening acts for my own performance in this *commedia*, all the characters sketched in broad strokes. The dressmaker was thin, with features as sharp as the pins and needles stuck into the front of her dress, her eyes glittering gray behind spectacles. Her assistant, a bored, chunky teenager with lots of black eyeliner and a nose ring, grimaced under the burden of the big garment bag and various other packages, and chewed bubble gum to the rhythm of the Discman plugged into her ears. I could hear the tinny ghost of a back beat when she bent to smooth long black stockings up my legs.

No garter belt—the stockings went high up my thighs and seemed to cling there. The shoes had very high, straight heels, straps at the ankle, and an inch of platform sole. The back beat from the Discman changed slightly as I stood up— a new cut, reggae-inspired, perhaps—and I swayed a bit to its distracting rhythm, my hands still bound behind me.

They let me sway until I got my balance, freeing my hands then, and unhooking the chain from my collar, to put the dress on me. It was really two pieces. The top was dull, matte black, a boned corset with cups for my breasts—a bustier, but with laces in the back so that you could tighten it. And the bottom was a skirt made of many layers of white tulle or organdy, one of those tired, old-fashioned-looking sheer fabrics that prom dresses—the good kind, that you get in thrift stores—are made of. The hemline was uneven, sometimes above my knees, sometimes below it. And above the organdy was a layer of what felt like thin, transparent vinyl— well, more like cellophane really—stiff, iridescent, unnatural.

I heard the skirt's odd rustle as the assistant slipped it over my head. The dressmaker tugged it here and there, turning it a bit, putting in a few clever stitches near the hem to make it less even, more raffish. The bustier, now—the assistant hooked it up the front, pulling at the laces behind me, and then indicating, with a nod and a little shove, that I should walk around the room, so that her boss could see the effect.

"The darts aren't right." Stefan must have come in from the adjoining room. The dressmaker murmured what sounded like grudging agreement, and the assistant rolled her eyes in exasperation as she struggled to undo the hooks and hand the corset to her boss for alteration.

Oh, yes, much better, they all agreed, after the adjustments had been made and the garment was hooked up again and relaced. Even Ms. Discman's eyes widened and her mouth slowed as she watched my second circuit around the room. I was still a little tentative; I'd mastered the shoes but I was dizzy from how tightly I'd been laced—the dressmaker had pulled them a full inch tighter than before. And when I passed the mirror, I saw that her alterations had transformed the dress entirely. Or had I just been too stupid to notice, my first time around? The tight lacing, the billowing skirt, the bare, vulnerable expanse of chest below the cruel collar. This was the Roissy dress, updated as expensive trash, a nouveau-punk pastiche. Involuntarily, I felt around the skirt, front and back, for the strings, the hooks, that I knew had to be there.

"Yeah, sure, try that part," Stefan said in a bored tone. And it wasn't very difficult to hook the little tabs of cloth in place, so that the skirt was lifted, front and back, to expose my ass and cunt.

"Keep it rolled up while you wait for him," Stefan added. He'd been thanking the dressmaker, tipping her, perhaps. I heard the door shut behind her, while he turned off some lamps. "You can sit on that bench until fifteen minutes before he comes for you—I'll let you know when that is."

I thanked him. No need for him to expand on those instructions. I knew he meant that fifteen minutes before Mr. Constant was due, I'd move down to the floor, in the center of the room, to wait for him on my knees. And that there was no need for me to know what time it was now, or how long it would be before that happened.

They're not exactly boring, those long stretches spent waiting for a master. You're hyperconscious of your body—you hope it will be pleasing, after all the preparation and grooming it's had. You breathe with your whole body, which is so open and displayed and ready. You're a little afraid of the moment when you'll be judged, examined. You're afraid but you also can't wait—to be seen, to be touched, to be commanded, forced, used.

I don't know how much time passed while I sat on the iron bench in the darkening room. There was a clock ticking on the mantle, but Stefan must have turned it around while I was asleep, so that I couldn't see the time. I watched stars appear in the evening sky, and I looked down at my body, and at my dress. The bustier felt even tighter than when I'd been standing, and my breasts swelled, plump and white, over the bra that barely covered the rouged areolas of my nipples. The odd, synthetic material of the skirt billowed to either side of my waist, iridescent as insect wings, crinkly as gift wrap, surrounding my pale thighs and dark naked cunt. Even with the skirt unhooked, so that my cunt and ass would no longer be visible, so that we could go out—and I knew we'd be going out, this was a dress for going out—this was a dress for announcing precisely what I was. In some ways it was simply a setting for the collar and cuffs—the way some black velvet evening gowns are settings for fabulous diamond jewelry. I swallowed, resolving to wear my restraints proudly. And then I snorted, wondering where I'd copped that pretentious thought.

I quickly stifled the snort, though, at the sound of Stefan's footsteps. Down to the floor now—he pointed out the spot with his toe, training a reading lamp at it, and dimming a few more of the other lamps. And perhaps because he'd told me I'd wait fifteen minutes, it felt like an eternity until he led Mr. Constant into the room. I was surprised by the edginess in the air; it was the first time, all afternoon, that I'd wondered what Stefan might be feeling about any of this. I could feel how relieved he was when Mr. Constant commended him on the dress and chuckled appreciatively at how my ass had been marked. Stand up, turn slowly, Stefan commanded me. Let down her skirt and get her cloak, Mr. Constant told him, before leading me quickly and silently to the elevator and outside the hotel, down a few crowded, brightly lit downtown streets to a restaurant. Showtime.

I followed the maitre d' across the floor, the big ring in my collar catching the light of candles on tables, Mr. Constant walking close behind me like an impresario, my cloak over his arm. I could hear murmurs. I blushed, but kept my chin lifted, even higher than the collar forced me to. I could feel my nipples stiffen, my cunt get wet, my whole body open and swell under the stares directed at me.

An image floated into my mind. I guess I thought of it because we were going to Greece the next day, but it was from an old fantasy, one I'd played over and over again, late in bed at night, during high school. I was naked, chained from a collar much like the one I was wearing now, the chain tugging me along behind a chariot. Booty of war, a slave captured at Troy, following barefoot behind the warrior who'd loaded me on his ship. He'd also got a wagon full of pottery and weavings, and some sheep and goats. The little Greek island kings had squabbled, had even come to blows once, over how to divide the spoils, especially the pottery. It had been raucous, cruel, violent, petty—like the rest of the war. They'd enjoyed it. And now, ship safely in harbor, we were marching through the gates of his city in a victory parade. The crowd lining the road seemed huge to me—I tried not to look at them, but I could hear, I could feel them—drunk, laughing, jeering. I thought I could hear them that night in the restaurant, though it was really just the tinkle of silver and china and crystal, and perhaps a few polite gasps.

Chill, people, I thought. If I can deal with it, so can you. But it's probably easier for me. Because I have to concentrate on walking in these shoes, and breathing in this dress, while you can hang out at your tables feeling…well, what *are* you feeling? Shamed curiosity, self-shielding contempt, outraged desire? Or envy, which is what Mr. Constant is really hoping for. He wants you to desire me, and to envy him terribly. And I know this because it's what I want too.

It couldn't have taken more than two minutes for the maitre d' to guide us across the restaurant. But it felt like an hour, with that Technicolor epic running in my head. And its coda, when everything caught up with me.

As we entered the private dining room at the back of the restaurant, Mr. Constant whispered, "Bravo." I smiled. It was the first thing he'd said to me.

A waiter held a chair for me. I lifted the stiff, oddly smooth, and crinkly skirt when I sat down—it wasn't exactly something you'd sit on. The seat cushion tickled my bare ass. My cunt was moist; I was going to leave a sticky little wet spot on the dusty-rose velvet. I sat as straight as I could while the waiter fussed with the flowers and glassware.

"And pull her dress down," Mr. Constant added, "so that I can see her breasts."

The waiter's hands were deft, circumspect. He used a finger to lift each of my breasts out of the bra cup that held it, and to fold the stiff cloth below it. My breasts rose under Mr. Constant's gaze, their painted nipples standing at obedient attention. I kept my eyes down while the waiter answered all of Mr. Constant's questions about the menu, and disappeared silently.

Mr. Constant and I looked at each other across the table. That is, I looked at the flowers, the silverware, his hands, everywhere but his face. And I felt him looking at me all over, sternly, while I struggled to manage my body, my eyes. I realized that he was speaking to me.

"...Much better," he seemed to be saying. "I'm glad you take instruction so well. You'll have to learn a great deal of patience and control. But you seem to be making a good start.

"You can look at me tonight," he continued. "I know you've been waiting for me to tell you a little about what you can expect. And you can ask me some questions."

I raised my eyes, slowly, past his wide chest and shoulders, the aggressive set of his short neck. He had salt-and-pepper hair, in a brush cut. Large, blunt, decided features, ruddy skin, large pores. And the glinting gray glasses. I was glad to be able to look at his face, but I was disappointed by how little it revealed, with the glasses hiding his eyes.

"You like being publicly displayed, don't you?" he asked.

"You like it much more than you thought you would."

"Yes, Mr. Constant."

He nodded. "I thought you'd respond that way," he said, "but it was just a guess. It's a relief to know that my buyer's instincts were correct. Because I intend to show you, on the dressage circuit."

I'd seen dressage shows, of course. You'd taken me to some, Jonathan, to show me how much I had to learn about submissiveness. I thought of the participants, offering their open, vulnerable bodies to an enthusiastic crowd, to judges who would decide which of them had presented the most appealing and comprehensive tableau of availability and obedience. I knew how much control it took, and I didn't think anybody in their right mind would enter me in a difficult competitive event like that.

"I employ an excellent trainer," Mr. Constant was saying. "You'll receive a lot of instruction. Of course, it will take a lot of work, but I think you'll try hard for me. I think you'll want to present your body in all the difficult, painful modes we'll teach you."

I found that I didn't quite have the breath to give sound to my assent, but I mouthed the words, whispering that yes, Mr. Constant, I would try very, very hard.

"But ultimately," he said, "I see you as a racing pony. I find pony races very entertaining. Have you ever seen one?"

"Uh, no, Mr. Constant."

"We'll take you to one, so you can see. They're loud, fast, a little dangerous. And people bet large amounts of money."

"But Mr. Constant," I said, "I've only had a week of beginning pony training, and I've never raced or competed at all...."

"Yes," he nodded, his glasses opaque in the candlelight, "the odds will be stupendous."

I thought of protesting, but of course I couldn't do that. I giggled instead, nervously.

He didn't seem to mind. His body spread out a little in his chair, his neck relaxed a bit. "I'm rather an *arriviste*," he confided. "I wasn't born so wealthy—I've just perfected a few tricks that seem to work very well in the current financial environment. We work from my place in Greece, mostly, except when I have to go to New York from time to time. But the way we approach the market—it takes very good satellite technology and lots of time and concentration. So my only amusements, really, on the island, are the occasional party and checking in on your training—yours and Tony's. And then attending the races and competitions where you're shown.

"I suppose," he said slowly, "that outside of my work— outside of the risks and quick decisions and high stakes— what I most enjoy is a disciplined body, painfully bound and displayed for my entertainment, either at a public competition, or at night, in my room."

"Will it be very painful, Mr. Constant?" I felt my voice wobble.

"Painful enough to entertain me," he said somberly. "You can buy slaves, you know, whose specialty is pain. But I know you're not one of those. And neither is Tony. I prefer material like you, it turns out—fast, eager learners who can be taught to bear what they have to, but who never quite get used to it."

He seemed to have scoped it out pretty well.

And then he added, laughing a little, "Oh, and don't waste your time wondering whether I'm really one of those tycoons whose dearest wish is to be tied down and beaten. I've met a few of those gentlemen, but we don't seem to have much in common."

"Well, uh, it all seems very, uh, *simple,* Mr. Constant." It scared me a little. I didn't know if I'd be good at simple.

"You'd like a bit more mystery," he nodded. "Hidden motivations, complex revelations. Ah, yes, like your Jonathan."

How did he know this about me? I didn't know how much information the auction people collect, in the folder that's available to interested buyers. But I guessed there would be some pretty elaborate psychological profiles in there. And, oh shit, of course—he'd read your note, Jonathan. Well, after all, I thought, Stefan wouldn't have given it to me without routing it by his boss first. He'd read it and he seemed to find it amusing. Or perhaps not so amusing. A hint of rancor crept into his voice.

"Oh, yes," he said, "I've met him…he puts in an occasional appearance at a party or exhibition. I think Ms. Kate Clarke must have introduced him to me a year or two ago."

He grimaced slightly.

"Quite the master," he said, "for a girl who's read so many books. Fancy bastard. Handsome, too. And he seems to have had all the time in the world to amuse himself by playing at being in love with you. Kept you guessing, I expect. Was he really in control of things?, you wondered—or was he secretly pining, no, what's the word? oh, *languishing,* yes, that's it, was he languishing for your little soul?

"He wants you to guess about it all this year," he added, "on my time. Well, you have my permission. As long as your body is obedient. I'm less concerned about your soul, I guess, than he supposes he is.

37

"He spoiled you terribly," he concluded, "but he didn't ruin your good instincts. I think a little *simplicity,* as you put it, will improve you tremendously."

"Avignon," he chuckled, as the waiter came back into the room with the first course, "Avignon, March 15 next year—well, the Place d'Horloge is a nice venue for a reunion. And we'll keep you too busy to fret much about it in the meantime. But," he trained his glasses at me, "it's rather an old story, don't you think, Carrie?"

"Yes," I said softly. "Yes, thank you, Mr. Constant."

And then we both turned our attention to the food that the polite waiter was setting out. Oysters. Very cold, with a peppery sauce. Lots of them, too, piles of them. I'd never had oysters where you didn't have to count how many you could have. The waiter opened a bottle of wine. He didn't make a big deal of staring at my breasts, but he didn't look away either. I dipped an oyster into the sauce and swallowed it slowly.

"It's very good, Mr. Constant," I said.

"Yes," he answered placidly, the rancor drained from his voice, "and it's nice to watch you, Carrie."

"Thank you, Mr. Constant," I breathed, trembling.

"What else did you talk about?" Jonathan asked sourly. Well, it's no fun being dissected so neatly by someone you have absolutely no memory of meeting. Still, he enjoyed thinking of her, eating oysters in her pretentious collar, bare, painted breasts above the punk Roissy dress.

Carrie scanned his face.

"He didn't say anything else about you," she assured him, a small, opaque smile on her lips.

CARRIE

A girl who's read so many books. I didn't usually associate the bookish side of myself with the outrageously got-up girl who'd allowed herself to be sold to the highest bidder. But maybe there was a connection. Enthrallment to narrative, the joy of being ravished by the text. Interesting. And interesting that he knew it about me. It gave me the courage, during dessert, to check up on something. It was in my contract, but you couldn't be too sure.

"Mr. Constant, I will get some time to read, won't I?"

"An hour or so," he answered, "most afternoons. There's a small library, and we can download books from Project Gutenberg."

"Thank you, Mr. Constant. And will Stefan be training me?"

He laughed. "Stefan? What gave you that idea? Oh, the punishment today. Nice job, don't you think? But no, he's my secretary. He works for me on the financial end—well, that's what I hired him for. But he also does chores for me, when I don't have time for them. Bright boy." He shrugged, bored with the question, pausing before he added, "You've never had a trainer, so you don't really understand what it's about."

I hoped he might describe it. But he just sipped his coffee, leaning back comfortably in his chair, and smiling at my respectful posture and bare breasts. And at my eagerness, my ignorance, my naïveté, I thought.

The polite waiter asked if we'd like more coffee. Mr. Constant shook his head. He stood up, and told me to stand up, too.

"Pull up your skirt," he added. "That's right, all the way up, and bend over the table."

He pushed my waist down, so that my ass was in the air and my breasts were crushed against the table beneath me. They felt sticky—raspberry sauce, perhaps. I heard the waiter draw in his breath and mumble something.

"Have them add the upholstery costs to my bill," Mr. Constant added, chuckling at the stain I'd left on my chair.

"Yes, of course, go ahead," he continued hospitably, and I felt a hand, I guess the waiter's, tracing my butt, following the red lines from Stefan's switch. Mr. Constant explained why I'd been punished, and how well I had responded. I wasn't much now, he continued, while I felt a deliberate finger move up into my cunt, but he was confident of my potential, and of my ability to learn. The finger slid delicately over my wet, sensitive insides and then moved slowly out again. I bit my lip.

Mr. Constant grasped my shoulders and turned me over, so that I was lying on the table, the light shining in my eyes, the two men darkly silhouetted against it.

"Just bought her today, after all," Mr. Constant concluded. "So she's got a long way to go. Well, you'll see—I'll let you have her next time, as a tip. But tonight, well, here, the service was excellent."

As my eyes adjusted to the light shining into them, I began to make out details. The waiter was about my age. He was slight, with wavy black hair, a delicate, aquiline nose, and gold-rimmed glasses, cute in a nerdy sort of way. Studious-looking, like somebody I might have hung out with in Berkeley. And he was looking at me intently, his lips parted, so that I could see the little gap between his front teeth. I couldn't help wondering whether there would really *be* a next time.

He helped me up, deftly brushing crumbs off me and wiping off my sticky tits, and then regretfully (or did I imagine that?) putting them back into my dress. He picked up my cloak and I could see that he wasn't sure whom to give it to.

"Mr. Constant," I said, very softly. He turned, surprised and almost angry, and I could see him wondering if I were up to this after all.

"Please, Mr. Constant," I said, "may I carry my own cloak?"

He nodded, and the waiter handed it to me, and as we walked back through the restaurant, past the staring diners at their tables, I swept it behind me, like a train, feeling myself grow proud of and almost intoxicated by the spectacle I knew I was creating. You once asked me whether I liked to be looked at, Jonathan. Well, I guess you knew, even if I didn't really, until that evening.

He smiled. "Of course I knew."

He'd shut the door of the hotel room behind us and cut the laces of my dress with a pocket knife. I was kneeling now, at his feet, wearing only my shoes and stockings. The leash I'd worn that afternoon was a shiny pile of links under a bright lamp on the table at his elbow, next to an old leather casket that looked like it might originally have held jewels or coins.

I watched his large hands select items—shiny metal, dark leather, matte rubber—from the casket, arranging them on the table's lacquered top as though he were preparing for surgery. Finally a riding crop, next to a slender whip coiled like a watchful black snake at the table's edge. He buckled the casket shut and put it on the floor.

He considered the hardware he'd chosen for a minute, then picked out a brass clamp to bind my cuffs together behind my back. And now a pair of nipple clips. They were pretty, actually, shaped like silvery little seashells.

"Good," he murmured, fingering my right nipple, which had stiffened when he'd run the palm of his hand lightly across it, "very good, very obedient little body." He opened a clip and closed it painfully on me. I kept silent, as tears started their mascaraed paths down my cheeks. I breathed hard, leaning into the pain, as it bit into my other nipple, tugged at my other breast.

The clips were attached by a silver chain. He tugged at the chain, lightly, this way and that. My breathing became tremulous, sobbing moans bubbling out of me, ebbing and flowing with the awful pulling at my breasts. He kissed me—light kisses on my cheeks, my eyelids, the underside of my chin near the collar. He picked up another of the shiny objects from the table and hung it from the chain between my nipples. A weight. No, not just a weight, a bell. It tinkled gaily. He took it off, substituted a heavier one, with a deeper sound, and unhooked my wrists.

"Hands and knees," he said, slapping my ass lightly. "Head up," he continued, "and crawl around the perimeter of the room. Quickly. I want to hear the bell jingle loudly."

I bet he did. He knew the pure chiming sound made the pain seem rougher. I circled the room, hoping he'd tell me to stop, and then I just started around again. "Head up, Carrie," he called. "Keep that bell visible, or I'll hide it inside of you. And then you'd have to work much harder to make it jingle, wouldn't you?"

So I arched my back as I crawled, leading with my

breasts, like the figurehead of a ship.

"Better," he said, as I finished the second circuit of the room, staying on my hands and knees at his feet, "but you need a little help."

"Turn around," he continued, "stand up and show me your ass." I obeyed, bending slightly at the waist, opening for the dildo that I knew was coming, shivering at its hardness, moaning at the feel of his hands on my hips as he belted it into place. He pushed me back onto my hands and knees, still facing away from him, and I felt something cold running down the center of my back. A chain. It went from the ring at the back of the collar to what I guessed was another ring, at the back of the dildo. He pulled it tightly, so that I had to hold my head even higher, showing more of my breasts. It pulled at the tightly wedged dildo, too.

He told me to turn around again and face him; I shuffled around on my knees. He considered me for a minute— I could tell he enjoyed these little decision points—before he hung another bell between my breasts. He picked up the whip.

"Around again," he said, cracking it against my ass, "quickly."

It was more painful this time, keeping my back arched so extremely, pain now coming from my asshole as well as my nipples, the bells discordant with each other. I had to figure out a new, twisting motion to keep both bells sounding, even though every twist pulled the chains tighter. And when I didn't move fast enough, the whip would catch me, while he tugged at the leash. When I'd completed that circuit of the room, he pulled me to him by the ring in my collar and stroked my face. I kissed his hand.

He tapped the bells, making them ring again. He traced the outline of my mouth with the riding crop. "I look forward," he said, "to coming by and watching them work you in the corral."

Yes, I thought, come and watch. Please.

"And just the mouth, too," he mused, "for a bit and bridle. And next time...hmmm, perhaps I'll attach a leash to your nipples, and direct you from there. Or your labia." He stroked my belly and squeezed my ass. And then he yawned contentedly.

"The possibilities," he said, "are not infinite. One comes to the end of them in about a year's time. But at the beginning, it's always a great pleasure to contemplate them, in their variety. Undress me."

I was a little dazed, though, I guess by the variety of possibilities ahead of us, and I hesitated for a moment. He laughed and hit my thigh with the crop. "You can use your hands," he said, a rough edge to his voice cutting through his amusement. "And hurry up," adding another stripe to my thigh.

He leaned back while I fumbled with buttons, zippers. He was patient, as I suppose people who always have things done for them must be. And I did hurry, because I wanted to see him. He had a broad chest, slightly short legs. Muscular shoulders that his suit had emphasized, and a slight curve outward at the belly, which it had hidden.

He stood up, naked, his cock erect. "On the bed," he said, "hands and knees." He examined the whip marks on me ("Good, good," I heard him murmur again). And then he took the dildo out of me and fucked me up the ass. Deeply, but almost pulling out from time to time, repeating the moment of entry as many times as he could. He ran a blunt hand over my front, my neck and throat, slapping my breasts to keep the bells jingling.

And then he did pull out, leaving me empty and gasping. "Come on," he whispered, leading me by the hand to the bathroom, where he sat down on a marble bench that made one of the sides of the sunken bathtub.

"Wash me," he said, nodding to the piles of snowy towels and washcloths. I knelt before him; his cock was shiny, purple, the skin stretched taut. I was very careful, very gentle, very thorough. I felt like I was performing a ritual from some early half-forgotten Mediterranean religion. My belly trembled, my breath was shallow.

I put down the towel and took the tip of his cock into my mouth. Then I licked the seam along its back, my lips reaching his balls....

He pulled me up so that I was kneeling between his legs, his bent knees tight around my torso. He took the clips off my nipples, and I blinked, in the bright white light, while he kissed my face, my neck, waiting for the pain to subside. He picked up another of the washcloths and carefully cleaned the runny makeup off my face. And then he led me back to bed, gently pushing me back onto it, kissing me all over, and licking my bruised nipples. He took off my shoes and stockings, which, of course, were down around my ankles by now. And he took off his glasses for the first time. His eyes, I just had time to notice, were large and hooded, a light, greenish hazel in the dark. I looked at him for a moment as he raised his head, shifting his weight, pushing his cock into me. And then it was pure indulgence, just the lovely simple hard stroking, a treat for me, the only treat I'd ever get from him. I accepted it happily—kicking and coming until I was

45

exhausted. He raised himself higher on his knees then, lifting my ass in his hands, coming and fucking me deeply.

I wondered if I should slip out of bed, to sleep on the pallet on the floor. But his arms were tight around my waist.

"It won't be like this after tonight," he said, his voice sounding loud in the darkness. "Not at all." I moved a little closer to him. To show him that I understood what he was saying.

"But tonight I wanted to make love to the girl I spoke to at dinner. That nice, eager…" His voice trailed off into a yawn.

Clueless, I thought, as he turned onto his back and fell serenely to sleep. Clueless is the word I believe you're looking for, Mr. Constant, to describe me. The cold metal ring dangling from the front of my collar bumped against my breastbone as I curled up into a more comfortable position. I crossed my arms lightly across my chest, being careful not to touch the ring. He hadn't forbidden me to, but I didn't think it was mine to touch.

She took a deep breath and stopped.

"Oh, yes," *Jonathan said happily,* "I've missed your stories."

He lay on his back, pleasantly buzzed, his mind's eye reviewing the procession of images. Unpleasant guy, Constant, but hardly stupid. Nouveau riche, *a little crude perhaps, but there was substance there—well, he'd chosen* her *at the auction, hadn't he? Tacky though, showing her off to that kid, that waiter, like that—and I would have punished her for so evidently enjoying his hand on her. And* in *her, too, jeez. I like the hotel part though, lovely, all the fetishes, the tears. I look forward to watching them work you. Oh, yes, please.*

I'll make love to her now, or in a moment, he thought. She deserves it. Although usually he masturbated to her stories. Or

46

thrust himself into her mouth, sometimes just before she finished the last words. But he was feeling pleasantly affectionate at the moment—and anyway, they'd fucked so hard earlier that this time he'd been able to let the buzz build slowly, free of urgency. But it was getting on time, now, he thought lazily....

So he didn't comprehend at first when she informed him that now she'd like a story in return, please.

He sputtered a bit in amazement.

"You heard me," she said.

"But you're the storyteller," he protested, weakly.

"And just where," she demanded, "is that written?"

He sighed. A story? My god, what was she going to ask for next? Still, he couldn't very well wimp out on it. And after all, there was a lot he needed to tell her. But making a story out of it—deciding what counted as beginning, middle, and end. The exposure—one thing to lay your body on the line, but to lay out your sentences, your sensibility, to scrutiny like that—well, he'd do it, but just this once.

"Okay," he laughed. "Just give me a minute."

JONATHAN TELLS A STORY

There were parties to go to, the nights before the auction. During the days, I wandered around the city—it had a few good buildings to look at. Kate had accompanied me on a few of these walks, when she'd had time for me—when she didn't have meetings to attend, appointments to keep. She wasn't going to have any time for me today, though; the governing board of the auction association would be voting on the coming year's budget. I was envious of how seriously she took it all.

I shivered as she pulled away from me, chilly air rushing in to replace the warm, rosy flesh that had engulfed my body. I sighed, looking out the window at the lead-colored sky. A freezing rain was beginning to fall.

"There's nothing I want to see at the cinematheque today," I said. "And the museums are closed. Good thing I've still got a few crappy novels to plow through."

"You'll get cranky, reading in here all day." She sat back on her haunches as my cock dropped out of her. Her knees were still tight around my thighs. "I'll send somebody over to keep you occupied this afternoon."

"Thanks," I said, holding onto her ass, trying to keep her in bed, "but I'm already cranky. Do you have to go?"

I could see the little vertical line peeking out below the red-gold bangs falling down her forehead. She gets that line there when I act spoiled, babyish. I sighed again, letting just a little too much time go by before I said anything.

"I'm sorry," I said then, reaching up to trace that line with my finger, and then tracing her profile, her pure jawline, the silky curtain of bobbed hair bending against the back of my hand. "Of course you have to go," I said.

She swung a leg over me and sat on the side of the bed, elbows on her knees, letting herself hang for a moment, her flesh taking on bluish tones, the cynical sag of a Degas whore squatting over a washbasin. My chest tightened—she doesn't usually let me see her that way; I'd be insanely jealous if I thought she allowed anybody else that intimacy. And then she stood up quickly, belly concave, everything suddenly tight and pumped and in place. She was pretty pissed at me.

She seemed to have cheered up, though, after her shower. She kept the bathroom door open, letting in fragrant steamy air, and chattered about the silly characters she'd have to argue down at the meeting. She wouldn't tell me what they'd be arguing about, though.

"I mean, it is a 'secret society,' after all," she said, her eyes glittering green in the mirror as she carefully outlined them. I was drinking coffee and eating toast in bed.

"Want a slice?" I asked. "You'll need energy, to fight the good fight for all us parasites who'll be staying in bed today."

"They serve bacon and eggs," she said, "and strong tea in glasses. Very good schnapps, too. Anyway, I argue better when I'm hungry. I'll eat after I win." I watched her pull on some intricate new underwear, pour herself into one of her little power suits, zip up formidable high boots. A reverse striptease: She began to look tall—amazing that she can pull off that illusion—and I felt myself getting hard again. She glanced at me and smiled.

"I'll send somebody for early afternoon," she murmured, tossing a fur-lined raincoat over her shoulders and shutting the door behind her.

I didn't ask whom she'd send over. She was traveling with an entourage—her three personal slaves and a trainer to attend to them, for those times when she was attending meetings, or coping with me. Fine with me, whichever one she chose. Surprise me, I thought. They were all pretty spectacular.

It was the boy, Randy. Good choice, I thought, as dusk gathered, late that day. He'd been very accommodating, all in all, though there had been a point, midafternoon, where he'd needed a spanking with my slipper. Right now he was kneeling at my feet, energetically polishing my shoes, his bare hands buffed shiny black as he rubbed the cakey polish into the leather. He used his tongue from time to time, too, neatly, like a cat. He was very decorative, curved over my feet like that. And it was a lot better shine than I would have gotten in the hotel lobby.

I was sitting in the armchair, across from the full-length mirror, so that I could also see his butt. Nice. But he was finishing up now, I realized, because he was getting a little hypnotized by his reflection in the toes of my shoes.

"Hey," I said, smacking him lightly on the shoulder, "kneel up, Narcissus. You're done."

I wouldn't discipline him for it. He'd put in a good afternoon, amusing me and keeping boredom at bay, and if he liked to look at himself once in a while—well, he really was awfully pretty. He raised his head, big amber eyes veiled under long black lashes, shy smile on his face.

"Let me see your hands," I said. Mmmm, a few little blisters on the fleshy part of the palm, under the black shoe polish.

"How will you clean them?" I asked.

"Steve's got some kind of solvent, Jonathan," he said. Steve was Kate's lead trainer. "It works very well, but it kind of hurts the blisters."

I bent and kissed him. "Yeah, but you need clean hands, after all."

"Oh, yes, Jonathan," he agreed.

Narcissus. Kate's boy slaves always looked a little like I had, in my late teens. I wondered if Randy knew that. Probably not—probably he wouldn't be able to discern a trace of resemblance between his perfect little self and a guy in his late thirties. Which gave it a touch of elegant melancholy, for me. *It's a long rainy afternoon—play with your pretty former self, sweetheart. Your unconscious former self.* Although of course I'd never been anywhere near as unconscious as he seemed to be. And certainly not as eager to please.

I looked down at him, kneeling easily at attention. Polishing my shoes had aroused him—his cock was stiffening under my gaze. I lifted it with my foot, rubbing my instep against the bottom side, nudging the base of his balls with a shiny polished toe. His face remained impassive, but his breathing became just a little ragged.

I stroked his cheekbone, and then the graceful sweep of his eyelid—lightly, with one of my fingers—while I continued to probe him, below, with the toe of my shoe.

"You've been a good boy today," I said softly, "even with your one little lapse. But now it looks like you're in some danger of blowing the whole thing, doesn't it? I mean, it would be pretty disgraceful if you came all over my shoes, wouldn't it?"

He was struggling to breathe evenly.

"Wouldn't it?" I repeated sternly, jerking his chin up.

"Yes, Jonathan," he whispered, "it would be disgraceful." I could feel his balls tightening, his hips contracting.

"I could let you fuck me," I said thoughtfully, jerking his head up a little further. "Hey, look at me, kid, we've got some serious problem-solving to do here." His eyes flew open, the pupils big and black, distended with fear and desire.

"See, here's the problem," I said. His cock was swollen, like a mushroom after a summer rainstorm. "If you fuck me, you'll get shoe polish on my nice white cotton T-shirt, or on those bedsheets, hey, even on the headboard of the bed or something. I mean, you'd leave nasty little black fingerprints somewhere, wouldn't you? Wouldn't you, kid?"

"Oh, no, Jonathan," he gasped, "I'd keep my hands

behind my neck...uh, no, clasped at the small of my back, I think, and I'd keep my balance."

I glanced down at the neat muscles in his belly. "Yes, I suppose you could do that. But how do you intend to grease my asshole? Not with those fingers."

"With my tongue, Jonathan," he whispered urgently. "It's, uh, unusually long."

"Really." I had to laugh, pressing my fingers into the corners of his mouth to open it up. "Show me."

And it was, too. Long, pink, strong, a semicircle of even white teeth beneath it. Kate must have opened up his mouth like this, I thought, when she'd examined him, in some auction hall somewhere.

I dropped my foot, let his chin go, stood up, and stepped over him to get a small jar of grease from the top of the dresser. I opened it, put it down on the floor in front of him.

We were still in front of the mirror, facing sideways now. I took off my shorts, keeping my eyes on him as he bent gracefully from the waist, dipping his tongue into the jar. His back straightened—a flower unfolding—as he carried his little wad of grease up to my ass.

Ah. He pushed it in, patiently, insistently. Not too deeply at first. I could feel his nose, between the cheeks of my ass, his chin below. He dipped down again. And yeah, his hands were folded at the small of his back, like a skater. He held his body elegantly. And his mouth and chin were shiny with grease and saliva. I liked the contrast.

A bigger cargo of grease this time. Perhaps I'd opened up more, while I'd been watching him. Oh, yes, he really could use that tongue. He pushed it upward, wiggling it a little, too. Breathing hard, straining the muscles at its root—muscles I hadn't really given much thought to until this moment, the more fool me. I felt my belly clutch a little, tremble, as he made another trip downward. I didn't want him to finish this part.

No, scratch that. I got a glimpse of his cock, springing out from him, dark and shiny, but with a kind of downiness, too, and a drop of precum at its tip. I knelt on the bed, spreading my legs. Sighing, opening.... "Oh, and kid...I want you to make this last a while."

A deep intake of breath, and a clenched-sounding "Yes, Jonathan."

And he did make it last, opening me, filling me—filleting me—enthusiastically, but respectfully, too, drilling into me like a docile little machine, never forgetting who was boss. I came all over those sheets that I'd been so solicitous to protect from his fingerprints. And then he finally let go—screaming, almost, with relief. I could feel his hard belly muscles relax as he allowed himself to drop lightly on top of me. But his hands were still behind him.

He kissed the back of my neck, softly, and then he rolled off and slid off the bed, to his knees. Waiting for me to pay him a little attention. I took my time.

And then—first things first. Nope, no smudges, no fingerprints. Not on the sheets, the pillows, not anywhere on the bed. And not on my T-shirt either. I turned slowly in front of the mirror, to get a full view of it. Of course, it was pretty sweaty—I needed a shower. I pulled off the shirt, tossed it in his direction. "Good job, kid." He smiled—quickly—swiveling his head to catch the shirt in his teeth. Great reflexes. He dropped it gently on the floor, in front of him, and bent down to kiss it.

I sat down on the bed and had him remove my shoes and

socks—with that talented mouth, of course—and then I kissed him. A long one, holding his curly head in my hands.

"Well," I murmured, nuzzling him, breathing in his smell—and my own, "you didn't blow it after all. So when you go downstairs to Steve, you can tell him I said you were a very, very good boy today."

He thanked me, a goofy, angelic look in his eyes.

I sat back up, folding my arms. "Do you think he'll have any kind of reward for you?" I asked.

He smiled. "Oh, yes, Jonathan," he said, eagerly. "He promised that if I was a good boy, I could give Sylvie and Stephanie their punishments. If they need them."

"Well, you'd just better hope they need them, hadn't you?" I laughed. "What would you use?"

"Oh, well, I know Steffie needs it, Jonathan." He had to work to keep from grinning too widely. "And I'm not sure what I'll use. A buggy whip, I think. Yeah, I think."

I stroked his hair. I hadn't known he was capable of that hungry grin. "Did anybody ever tell you you look a hell of a lot like me?" I asked.

But, "Uh, no, Jonathan," his bewilderment was quite sincere. "Uh, thank you, Jonathan."

I stood up and stretched. I needed that shower. "You can go now, kid," I said.

CARRIE

"Did you like the story?" he asked anxiously.

"Of course," I said. "You know I did." Well, the Randy part, anyway. I decided not to think too hard about the Kate part. Or the fact that he'd had so much to occupy him, so soon after I'd been gone. Dumb, I chided myself. I mean, what did you think he'd be doing? Ridiculously, I'd imagined him bleak, unshaven, alone. Languishing for me, I guessed. Yes, languishing was the word I wanted.

He looked a little shell-shocked now, though, amazed by how much he'd enjoyed telling me everything. He'd really thought that all those times he'd had me tell him stories, I'd been doing it purely for his entertainment. Damn, I thought, another bottom's secret blown.

But he still needed to be reassured that I'd enjoyed hearing it.

"No, really." I laughed, summoning up images of blackened, blistered palms and pristine white T-shirts. I took his hand and dragged it over my breasts, my painfully hard and swollen nipples. He moved his palm back upward, slowly, over my throat, to my face. I kissed his fingers, sucked them. He moved his hands down over me, cupping one of them under my ass in the protected curve where it met the top of my thighs, stroking me there, while his other hand probed my asshole. He kissed me, using his teeth. I came—not tumultuously, but I let myself, I had to—it was still thrilling to come whenever I felt like it. And when I calmed down, I became aware of one of his fingers up inside my ass, the rest of his hand still curved around it. He moved me toward him, as he might have drawn me to him on a leash, and settled back, sighing contentedly, a sovereign exacting tribute.

Not exactly high finance, guessing the currency he wanted to be paid in. But always as mysterious as high finance, discovering that what he wants is exactly what I want most in the world to do. I let the feeling wash over me while he moved his finger a little higher up me. And then I dragged my lips, still achy from when he'd bitten them, down over his chest, the fine black hair on his belly. Down to his cock.

Slowly, slowly, he's getting longer and harder every time I move my mouth over him. Curving up toward the top of my mouth. Stay up near the tip a few times. Treat myself. Roll my tongue around it. But he's not going to wait…he's pushed deeper, over and past the roof of my mouth and back to my throat. He wants me to go fast now, and now it's not just mouth, or lips. It's like it's all of me, and the atmosphere I'm breathing is entirely the smell of him. Hair brushing against my lips. He's got my head in his hand, he wants to move it himself, and my mouth is soft, liquid, and I can feel, I can hear, his little moans and trembles. He's dropped his hand now, he's disappeared, I don't even know where he is anymore, it's all his cock now, and my sucking, and swallowing, inhaling him, he shudders and cries out and comes and comes and comes.

JONATHAN

Ah yes, well. The end of a good day, I thought to myself. She was here beside me, the storytelling had been fun—and useful, it had gotten us talking, comfortable. Oh, and massively turned on, too, and very well taken care of, thank you. I felt terrific, as if I could sleep forever. I hadn't been sleeping well for the last few weeks.

I turned to her, wanting to gather her to me, before I turned off the light. She was lying on her side, her head propped on her elbow, eyes still bright and impatient.

"You're not tired?" I asked.

She shook her head. "Overtired. Wired. Like a kid OD'd on sugar."

And she expected me to do something about that, I realized. Well, good thing I'll be disciplining her again soon, I thought. And I thought of how much I'd enjoy it, knowing what a greedy little self she'd be hiding behind the bowed head, the body meekly offered for punishment.

CARRIE

I'll pay for this later, I thought. He's keeping accounts and I am deeply in the red. He put a finger up my cunt, gently touching my clit, lightly, lightly. Just letting it all build up in me, all the tension and excitement, and when I started coming, I could see his mouth curve, as he watched me writhe at the end of his finger. And even after I finished coming, and was ready to sleep, he kept his finger down there. He moved it to the outside lips, caressing them softly and sweetly and gently. He sat up next to me, looking down at me, and I reached up and touched his mouth, a wide tilde surrounded by little inverted commas. He sucked my finger, bit it gently, while he moved his hand again, put his finger in me again, and then another finger, and another. I could feel the bones, the knuckles in his hand, as it became a fist, and I could feel the movement of his arm, taking me far away, beyond words and almost beyond consciousness. Totally out of control, until finally I had to grab his arm and beg him to stop, gasping and kissing him wherever I could reach.

He turned off the light and curled up into himself, and I put my arms around his back, my cheek against his shoulder blade. Enough rough strife for one day, I thought, time to give it a rest. Tomorrow, though…well, tomorrow, we'd see.

The Second Day

JONATHAN

The rain woke me up just before dawn. It was pounding loudly on the tile roof, dripping down on our little balcony, outside our window, whose faded blue shutters were still open. I remembered the women in the yard taking the sheets off the line yesterday afternoon, and I felt absurdly happy that they hadn't got their laundry wet. I put my arms around her and rubbed my front against her back, my cock against her ass, and fell back to sleep for maybe an hour.

And when next I woke up it was still raining, but the room was filled with pearly gray light, and she was up, she'd turned around and her face, her mouth, were against my chest, her arms around my waist. I remembered how demanding she'd been last night, and how exasperated I'd felt, but all that seemed comic, cartoonish, in the pastel morning, the smell of the rain dripping from the trees in the courtyard.

I detached her arms, and I got up on my knees and crawled down to the bottom of the bed, and "Ummmmmmm," she sighed as I put my head between her legs. It's different, early morning sex. It's something your body does before your mind's quite itself, all the little complexities and annoyances still sweetly blurred. It's kinder. She opened her legs wide and bent her knees, and I—right then what I was feeling was that I wanted to spoil her so terribly that she'd never, never go away. It meant making my mouth, my tongue, move *so* slowly and *so* gently. Being *so* steady and building *so* gradually. I didn't want her to move away from me, I wanted her to move toward my tongue, my breath, to dissolve under my mouth, her cunt and then all of her, helpless with pleasure, melting beneath me.

Tell her now, I thought. She'll agree to anything.

The thought surprised me. That hadn't been why I'd eaten her. I'd truly wanted to make her feel that good. To render her, well—*helpless* with pleasure was the word I think you used, wasn't it, Jonathan? Shit, it was too early in the morning for that sort of conundrum.

No, I wouldn't tell her now. Wouldn't even think about it for a while. I was tired of strategizing, I thought. Maybe I needed a vacation too.

"Let's have breakfast up here," I said. "I'll lick off the croissant crumbs you'll drop all over your tits."

She laughed. "I'm surprised you want to be in the same room with these sheets. They're pretty rank."

"I can handle it," I promised her. "And anyhow, I kind of like the idea of being isolated from the world. Well, at least until the rain lets up a little."

I did like the isolation, the subtle, underwater light—and how easy it would be to grab her right after breakfast for a quick fuck. Except, as it turned out, I didn't have to grab her at all. I did lick some crumbs off her, and she grabbed me, hard, greedily. She pulled me to her, and I pulled her to her feet, and we fucked standing up by the table, leaning against the wall—a happy, noisy, silly-looking fuck where I kept slamming her hips against the wall, and she had a leg oddly propped against the perpendicular wall to keep her balance, and we hoped the people in the rooms upstairs and downstairs and next door were doing the reasonable thing and having their coffee and croissants in the restaurant downstairs.

"Come on back to that smelly bed," I said, "and tell me what happened next.

"Sort of like we were stranded by fire or flood or something, you know, in some old monastery," I continued, straightening the covers a little, "and had to entertain ourselves by telling each other dirty stories."

"Well, if you really want to…" she said. "I mean, it's just your basic, redundant, S/M tropes, in which your eternally clueless innocent gets shown—yet again—which end is up. Which seems to be more or less how it actually happens to me."

I took her hand. Basic, redundant tropes sounded fine to me. "Come on," I said. "You were in bed, and Constant had just fallen asleep.…"

CARRIE'S STORY CONTINUES

I woke up slowly the next morning, alone in bed. I was a little sad, but not surprised. Next time I saw him, it would be completely different. Maybe I'd be harnessed to a pony cart,

I thought, stretching a little. And then I jumped, as the door banged open and Stefan marched in. He stood over the bed, looking at me for a moment, both of us simultaneously recognizing that I hadn't slept on the pallet. It seemed to make him terribly angry. And then he pulled the covers off me.

"Waiting for breakfast in bed?"

I didn't know what the right thing to do was, so I scrambled off the bed to kneel at his feet. He sat on the bed and jerked my head up, looping his fingers through the ring in my collar.

"Uh, no, Stefan," I said, as meekly as I could. "I'm sorry, Stefan." But of course I wasn't sorry, because I figured that if Mr. Constant had wanted me to sleep on the pallet, he would have told me to, and I didn't see what business it was of a mere secretary to get so exercised about it. Even if he *was* a bright boy.

Bright enough to know that I wasn't sorry.

"Yeah, right," he muttered.

And then he just looked at me, in a sneaky, calculating, hostile sort of way.

Oh, shit, I thought. He's going to fuck me—he's been given permission, as a reward for all the little chores he's been doing. Only he wants to fuck me where Mr. Constant fucked me—shit, Carrie, he worships the guy, how slow can you be, figuring that one out? He worships the guy, he'd give anything to be in my place, and he hates my guts, especially because I've been taking him for granted, as a functionary. Oh, and if he can't be in my place, at least he wants to be in the place where his boss's cock was.

And I heard myself say, very softly, almost meditatively, "Well, he did come in my mouth, but that was before dinner, before I ate the oysters, and some sorbet to clear the palate, you know. And after dinner he fucked me a lot up the ass, but he didn't come, I think he was feeling kind of affectionate to me, so he decided to come in my cunt...." Just trying to be helpful. I figured he wasn't allowed to beat me without specific permission, and I didn't think he'd want to tell Mr. Constant about this little conversation. Of course, I thought belatedly, it's not as if he's going to forget this conversation the next time he does get permission to punish me.

But for right now, I'd won—well, the battle, if not the war. Well, maybe a small battle, anyway. Because even if he was going to fuck me, at least he wasn't interested in discussing it any further.

"Shut up," he said, "and turn around. Head on the floor."

This probably had always been Plan A, anyway. Well, it was what would hurt me the most, and after all, he'd so neatly marked the spot for himself yesterday, with his X. And I won one more tiny battle that morning. I didn't cry, though he hurt me a lot and I certainly wanted to.

"Take a shower," he said afterward, standing up and zipping his fly. "There'll be some clothes on the floor for you when you get out, next to your food and water. And hurry up. Our plane leaves in two hours."

The clothes I found on the floor, next to the cut-up banana and rice gruel, were smaller-sized versions of Stefan's: black jeans, black collarless dress shirt, black leather jacket. He'd probably had to buy them for me, and he wanted to make it clear that he hadn't spent any more time than necessary picking them out. They fit, I guess you could say, in an approximate way. Probably Mr. Constant wouldn't be on the flight, and so it wouldn't much matter what I was wearing.

The plane trip was uneventful. I was right about Mr. Constant's not being there—just me and Stefan, looking like your basic bratty rich leather kids in first class. When we got to the security gate, he silently and matter-of-factly took my collar and cuffs off, and sent them through on the conveyor belt, and just as silently and matter-of-factly put them back on me after we'd gone through the metal detectors. Some people stared, but I wasn't bothered by it as much as I would have thought.

He said almost nothing to me the whole way, except to tell me I couldn't have coffee or alcohol. He did hand me my glasses and the book I'd been reading before the auction, and then he buried himself in some terrifyingly abstruse-looking journal, its subject matter seeming to be balanced on the cusp of mathematics and economics. At least that was what I could tell from my occasional peeks at it. As for the runic-looking notes he furiously scribbled on green index cards, they might have been physics or Gaelic or—for that matter—Greek. I was surprised that he let me peek at all, but his concentration was so fierce that he didn't seem to notice. Or maybe he refused to let on that he was noticing. Well, it must be a perpetual humiliation for him to have to shepherd me around like this.

Maybe, I thought, he'd kind of fade from view when we got to the island. But I doubted it. I imagined him lurking in corridors, like one of those infinitely resentful Shakespearean villains in their black velvet doublets—Edmund, Iago, Richard III. He even somewhat looked the part—though more your handsome bastard Edmund than your crippled Richard—tall, with his pointy cowboy boots, hair in a severe little ponytail, and cold, pale blue eyes. Oh, and a surprisingly small, pretty, sensual mouth.

But I was probably pushing my luck, checking him out as openly as I suspected I was. He was starting to look annoyed, so I read a story or two in the book. And then I was dazzled by the bright beautiful sunlight as the plane swung out over the Mediterranean. I pressed my nose against the window. I'd never been to Greece. I knew this wasn't a sight-seeing trip, but I was still getting excited.

And you could see a lot from the smaller plane that took us to Mr. Constant's island. Beautiful, fierce, rocky landscape in the shimmering sea. There was an open four-wheel drive car parked at the airstrip. We drove through a small village— women in black with kerchiefs peering at us as we passed. When we came to a low stone wall, Stefan stopped the car and told me to take off all my clothes except my boots. He clasped my hands behind my back and told me to kneel up on the back seat. He attached the leash to my collar, hooking it to one of the door handles.

He drove quickly on the bumpy gravel roads. People passed on their ways here and there, leading horses, or herds of goats. I guessed they worked for Mr. Constant or used his land. Two teenage boys who were repairing a bit of wall at the side of the road looked up and laughed uproariously, gesturing broadly with their hands. And about five minutes later, the road stopped, and Stefan led me the last bit of way on foot, over a little rise, to a corral.

No one greeted us. A small figure in black and a naked boy were all I could see at first in the glaring sunshine, against the cruel blue of the sky. I was panting a bit; Stefan had been dragging me along quickly. But now he quickly unhooked my leash and shoved me forward. I think he'd hoped that I'd go sprawling, without the use of my hands to break my fall. I cried out, staggered, shifting my balance wildly, calling on all my will to keep me upright, and miraculously succeeding. It all happened very quickly, but it got the momentary attention of the pair in the ring. And just quickly enough for me to catch a detailed glimpse of them.

First, the smaller figure. My trainer, I guessed. But had Mr. Constant ever said it was a woman? Well, I thought, he'd never said it wasn't. No reason for me to have imagined—as I had—some big, hunky guy. But in the moment while I struggled to keep my balance, I watched her lip curl as she watched me frantically shifting my weight. She knew her job. No need for big hunky guys around here.

She was maybe five foot two, pumped, wiry, with sharp black eyes that contrasted with her pale skin and whitish buzz cut. Her jeans and sleeveless T-shirt were black too, and the very abstract tattoos on her impressive deltoids looked like unreadable pre-Columbian designs. The tattoos were all black, except for the red eyes on the narrow, realistically rendered snake that wound around her left wrist.

Stefan pushed me to my knees and looped my leash around a fence post. "I'm leaving, Annie," he called. She turned, grunted, and turned back to the sweaty panting boy.

And I did too. I mean, it was difficult not to want to look at him forever. The muscles bunched with exertion under his tanned skin were long, neat-looking dancer's muscles. He was shining with sweat, his chest rising and falling, but he was also intent on following her instructions, as he pranced and capered to the snaps of the riding crop in her right hand, the tugs at his reins with her left. His cock was erect, you could tell that he liked this. He tossed his head, bowed it, snorted behind the bridle that distorted his mouth. It was pony dressage, and he was very, very good.

But I have to admit that what most fascinated me was the long tail he wore. It was of bright chestnut horsehair, to complement the thick, wavy, bright brown hair that fell around his shoulders. The tail was attached to a dildo up his asshole, which was held in place by narrow leather straps attached to a belt around his waist. Just like the tail I'd worn during my week of pony training. But it wasn't the technology that made me catch my breath, it was the gender coding. Because all the pony slaves I'd been trained with had been girls. I knew boys did this sort of thing, too, of course, but I hadn't seen a lot of them, and I was oddly moved by the long tail streaming out from between the cheeks of his tight, muscular boy's ass. I was glad that my hands were bound behind my back, but I couldn't help rubbing my thighs together, moving my hips in rhythm with his.

Well, I'd have to learn those moves soon enough, after all. But I'd never be nearly as good as he was, I thought. It was discouraging, and frightening: What would they do when they discovered that I was a washout? I reassured myself that it would be a while, anyway, before they gave up on me. And until then, I told myself, at least I'd get to try it—to preen and prance, to snort and toss my head, and to respond, as he was doing, to her small hands, skillfully wielding the reins and riding crop. She almost never gave him a verbal command, doing it all by degrees of touch, laying the whip on him but also, it seemed to me, cajoling him with prods and tugs. I wanted to know what it would feel like.

They seemed to be finished, now, or taking a break. He stood before her and she spoke softly, sternly to him, criticizing his performance, I guessed, though I couldn't hear the words. He hung his head. And then he turned and bent over, presenting his ass to her for punishment. He turned again, straightening up so that she could beat his cock. And then she took off his bridle so that he could kneel and acknowledge his punishment, kissing the riding crop, and then the soft, red, peat-mossy ground at her feet. The slope of his back was unspeakably elegant, I thought, trying to memorize it in my muscles.

She pulled him to his feet by the big ring in his collar, and she slapped his ass and sent him loping toward a small stable a few hundred feet away. And then—gulp, show's over, Carrie, time to show your own unimpressive stuff—she headed toward me.

I knelt at attention, my eyes on the dirt at my feet. And I wasn't entirely surprised at the stinging swipe of the riding crop against my breasts. I didn't know why I was getting it, but I did know that somehow I'd had too good a time watching Tony.

She reached for an odd, harness-like leather contrivance that was hanging on a fence post.

"Stand up, asshole," she said. She had a nasty, nasal little voice. "I thought you might need this," she continued, buckling strong brown leather straps around my thighs. There were clumsy little squares of wood on the inner surfaces. Just wide enough to keep my thighs apart, to deprive me of a small way of pleasuring myself. I hoped they wouldn't make me wear this all the time—it would make me waddle. But I could see where they'd think I might need it.

She freed my hands from behind my back.

"On your knees," she said briefly. "On your knees and present."

Present—the verb in its imperative case, as in "Present your body to me, slave."

She paused for an uncomfortable moment, realizing that I didn't know what part I was supposed to present first. And then she sneered, as though it should have been obvious to anybody, "Ass."

Okay. On my knees, turned around, back arched. She probed, roughly, but I was ready for her. Impatiently, she pushed me through the other stages of the presentation. Cunt. Crawling around to face her, kneeling up, parting my legs, leaning my torso back to show her how wet and open I was. She pinched my labia. She put her fingers up me, way up this time. The difficult part was remembering that this was for her, not for me. I had to be still, controlled, no matter how much I wanted to come. I tried to even out my breathing.

And now my mouth. She took a small blunt whip out from where her old black garrison belt was holding it in place. I leaned back even further, opened, relaxed my throat to let her fuck it with the whip's thick handle, while I caressed it lovingly with my tongue, my lips. And then I bent to kiss her feet, and to kneel up, my eyes cast down. She nodded, grunted noncommittally.

"Hey," she said now, "Stefan seems to hate you even more than he usually hates the new pet. What did you do?"

No question of lying to her. She had my chin in her hand now and was looking at me searchingly. Round black eyes, like marbles.

"Uh, I talked back to him, Mistress," I said.

"Madam," she said idly, flicking the whip against my breasts.

"I talked back to him, Madam."

"Yeah? About what?" Another little flick of the whip. No point drawing this out.

"Well, Madam, I knew he wanted to fuck me where Mr. Constant had fucked me, to, you know, uh, get close to Mr. Constant, and so, I told him, you know, all the places...." This was not, I was realizing, the easiest thing in the world to confess to her.

She laughed. "Get out," she said. "You said that?"

I nodded, my eyes on the ground in front of her Doc Martens.

"Well," she said, "I won't bother to punish you for it. Stefan will, though, first chance he gets. He doesn't get to give out a lot of whippings, but I do have to get a day off once in a while, you know."

She paused, looking me over some more. "Can't have a slave with a fresh mouth around here. Still, you could have fooled me. I thought you were just a nice eager set of open holes. Well, but that's what you will be, for me, won't you?"

I assured Madam of that. Madam! Jeez, all ninety-six pounds of her. Still, she was right, silly nom de guerre notwithstanding. I wanted to please her. I hoped I'd never think of a smart remark anytime when she was around.

"You need some lunch," she said. "And then you can rest. I'll try you out on the trail this afternoon. Come on."

And she led me, waddling behind her in those ugly thigh straps, to the stable where Tony had gone. He'd been washed down, I could see, and his tail had been removed. And he was on his knees, bent over a trough of—oh, shit, pony food.

God, it was absolutely the worst thing about being a pony slave, those horrible little pellets of, well, who knew what they were—vitamins and minerals and complex carbohydrates all rolled out and chopped up to taste like sawdust. They were mixed with chopped-up carrots and celery, just as they'd been on the pony farm where I'd been trained, making them just barely tolerable. I mean, like it would kill whoever mixed the stuff together to maybe chop an onion into it once in a while. And I was hungry, too. I wished, now, that I'd eaten more of the dinner the waiter had spread out in front of us the night before—the lovely, smooth leek soup, the pale veal with its delicate lemony sauce....

Mercifully, though, I stopped myself before I could seriously think about the orange soufflé in its pool of velvety bitter chocolate. Soldier on, Carrie—no point crying over... well, even spilled milk sounded pretty good compared to what was in that trough. I knelt down in the straw next to Tony, folding my hands at the small of my back as he was doing, sighed deeply, and crunched down a few pellets.

And I was so mopey that it took me a moment to realize that he was whispering to me, "Hey, we only have to eat it for lunch."

I must have looked as though he'd just saved me from a burning building, because he laughed softly at my look of blissful relief, after taking a quick look to make sure that Annie was still out of earshot. "Well, except during competitions," he added quickly, turning back to his food at the sound of her footsteps.

I could live with that. And I could more than live, I realized, with how beautiful he was close up. His eyes were blue, I thought at first, but, no, they were green. And it took me a while to realize, chewing thoughtfully, that one was a bluish green, and one a brownish green, the asymmetry making them dance in his tanned face.

Annie slapped our asses and we followed her, on hands and knees, to the water trough. And then she put us to sleep in adjoining stalls, on top of clean straw. I was glad I'd eaten, and I knew that I'd need the rest for my tryout on the trail that afternoon.

"Okay," she said, taking a breath, "your turn. But wait, are there any more croissants in the basket?"

"Maybe a piece of one." He smiled. "Are you still thinking about the pony food?"

She heaped jelly on the inch of croissant, grunted happily as she popped it into her mouth, and climbed back into bed beside him.

"Okay?" she asked, giving him a slightly sticky kiss.

He was ready this time. Perhaps he'd even planned what he might say. Earlier, so as not to be caught short.

He licked the jelly off his upper lip. "Okay," he said.

JONATHAN'S SECOND STORY

The party guests were all a little manic, not bothering to hide the excitement in their eyes. At the auction tomorrow, they'd be cool, appraising all the flesh set out for them, with practiced hands and miserly eyes—as though the hundred thousand and upwards they'd pay was really a lot of money for them. But tonight they were slightly wild, kids the night before Christmas, dreaming of new toys.

I'd been trying unsuccessfully to move on from a conversation with a boring old guy with enormous, bristling eyebrows. Friend of my Uncle Harry's, telling me all about the old days—these old farts always want to tell a polite young fellow like me about the old days. And now he'd launched into a deadly—and dead wrong—harangue on the budget that had been passed this afternoon. Seems he couldn't see why the association needed to continue investing in computer technology. Idiot. And his conversation was a real yawner, too—even the girl at his feet was looking pretty bored, crouching at the end of her leash. I stroked her head sympathetically, while I excused myself. Sounded like Kate had had her way with the association. I imagined her triumphantly attacking a big plate of bacon and eggs, tossing back schnapps as the votes fell into place.

I stubbed out my cigarette and put another in my mouth, inhaling smoke as a naked blond boy appeared from nowhere to light it for me. Well-organized party. And it was a nice apartment to prowl around. You've seen it, Carrie. It was where you'd been examined to see if you'd get into the auction. The party hadn't spread to that very formal room where they'd used and beaten you so politely. At least, I don't think it had—it was a big place, with a slightly disorienting floor plan. Madame Roget had borrowed it, I'd heard, from some cousin, with one of those sick-soul-of-Europe names, Esterhazy or Thurn und Taxis or something.

In a dark hallway, lit with candles in sconces and lined with hideous family portraits in big gilded frames, I caught sight of Kate's little Stephanie, carrying a big basket of fruit. You could hear a metallic clanking sound as she walked. The tokens in the coinbox hanging from her collar, you know.

And she looked very pretty—naked except for the restraints at her throat and wrists—with her hair all down. It cascaded over her back, except for a few locks caught in slender braids, with ribbons and flowers twined into them, that started at the top of her head, falling down in front of her face and over her breasts.

A couple of guys in tuxes were leaning against the wall, talking quietly. One of them nodded curtly to her and she stopped, put down the fruit basket, and knelt to undo his pants. He grabbed her head, bringing it to his cock and mussing her hair a bit, scattering a few flower petals onto the carpet. There were painful-looking, fresh red stripes across her ass. Way to go, Randy, I thought, as she finished up with the guy in her mouth, swallowing his cum and then thanking him gratefully for it.

Another nod, barely discernible, and then a snap of the fingers, from the second guy now. She quickly stood up, bent over from the waist, and arched her back, propping her hands against some wainscoting. He wouldn't have to inconvenience himself by bending down, and she wouldn't get any handprints on the flocked wallpaper. He was a big guy, but she rotated her asshole directly toward his cock. He'd hardly even have to bend his knees, except perhaps for leverage. But he did bend over, before he entered her, to pick up a large, very ripe apricot from the fruit basket. He put it in her mouth, and as he was getting ready to jam his cock into her ass, he warned her not to get any toothmarks on the apricot. And then he leaned over her, keeping his balance by squeezing her breasts with his big hands.

And when he'd finished with her, and she knelt and bent her head to deposit the still-perfect apricot into his outstretched hand, you could see by the candlelight from the wall sconce above her that there were purple bruises on her breasts where his thumbs had been, and a few tears in her long eyelashes.

She thanked the second guy now, remaining on her knees to button his pants and straighten his clothes. And then both men dropped their tokens into the coinbox at her throat, before they moved off, resuming their conversation, the big guy munching on the apricot.

Nice. The tears, the bruises, and especially the polite sound of her voice as she thanked them. Still on her knees, she quickly scooped up the flower petals from the rug. And then she took a careful, housewifely peek at the wainscoting where she'd leaned her hands, to make sure she hadn't left any messy fingerprints. And almost of its own volition, I felt my hand reaching into my pocket to find one of my own tokens.

I felt a hand on my arm.

"Do pay her," I heard an amused voice say. "That little tableau was certainly worth a token. But she needs to go fix her hair right now. And the caterer needs that fruit at the buffet."

Stephanie looked up and I looked around, both of us startled. It was Madame Roget, very elegant in a cherry red satin caftan. She had diamonds at her ears and lots of rings on long, slender hands. Her round black eyes were serene, merry. Isn't this fun, they seemed to say, I love to give parties. She kept that confiding, and proprietary, hand on my arm.

I put the token into Stephanie's coinbox, and heard her clear little "thank you, Jonathan," accompanying the metallic clanking at her throat. Did I imagine it, or was her mouth twitching just a little, that single dimple in her cheek making a shy appearance, her blue violet eyes looking the slightest bit mischievous through their moist lashes? "And thank you, Madame," she added, as she got to her feet in a single motion, picked up the fruit basket, turned, and continued down the hall.

Caught looking. And as I was beginning to wonder how obvious my erection was, Madame Roget added, "and *I* need *you* to come make love to me."

"Thank you, Madame," I said, echoing Stephanie.

"Can it," she said.

"And may I too call you Jonathan?" she asked, leading me down the hallway and through mazes of rooms. She looked happy and hungry. She was a familiar type—like friends of my mother's—her long, delicate neck and slender wrists suggesting that she subsisted most days on Perrier and papayas. But her gestures, her air of jovial anticipation and randy self-satisfaction, suggested some belle époque gourmand draping a damask napkin over his rounded, dazzlingly white shirt front and preparing to down a dozen roasted quail.

"Of course," I answered. I waited for her to ask me to call her by her first name. And then I stopped waiting for it.

"I've always wanted to meet the boy Kate would run home to, between her periods of service," she continued.

I murmured something about not having been a boy for quite a while, Madame, as she ushered me into the bedroom, and poured us glasses of red wine.

It was like a stage set for *Der Rosenkavalier*, all gilt and lace and damask and tapestries. A huge bed, bright brass and white iron, rose up in baroque curlicues like an enormous birdcage or a clipper ship with billowy lace sails. I sat down in an armchair and watched her take off her clothes, revealing long muscles and beautiful little breasts high on her torso, with tiny, pink nipples. I would have liked to look at her a little longer, but she was impatient. I hurried to undress, to let her pull me into that monstrous bed.

I liked the feel of her under me, strong and tuned, selfish and demanding. I liked the sounds she made when I was in her, long arms thrown over her head, deep cries from her long throat, while she thrashed and arched her pelvis against me. I liked myself with her, too, rougher, cruder than I usually am. But each time I rose above her, just before I let myself come, I would see the same slightly amused look. It was as if she was putting me to work, inviting that once-upon-a-time boy home for odd jobs—yard, basement, and bedroom— much as those friends of my mother had done, a couple of decades ago. Sorry, Madame, you're a little late for that boy at his inexhaustible best. But I tried to remember how it had been, that astonishing energy, and I think I summoned up a version of it.

I was just about to dip my head between her legs again when I heard the door open. Who the hell would barge in like that? I was annoyed. And just a tad relieved.

"You missed the token count, Odile," Kate's voice floated over me. "Your guests were amused."

No wonder I was exhausted. They don't empty the coin-boxes until almost the end of the party—count the tokens, to see which slave had been used most. I would have bet on Stephanie, and yeah—now that I'd raised my head a little higher I could see her, crawling behind Kate on a leash. She had her chin way up and her back arched—very elegant, like a greyhound—and she was attached to the leash by the prize they'd awarded her. It looked like the kind of prize Madame would have dreamed up: emeralds and seed pearls set in flexible gold wire, turning Stephanie's breasts into Fabergé eggs, and held on by tight clips at the nipples. The clips were connected by a gold chain, with a larger link at its center, for a leash.

Madame stroked my head, while Kate reined Stephanie in, nodding at her to kneel up at attention, and tugging affectionately at the gold chain as she removed the leash. Kate had on a velvet tuxedo, slim pantlegs draped nicely over the insteps of satin slingback spike heels. And no shirt, just a nice deep V of glowing flesh between narrow satin lapels. Well, she'd had a good day since she'd climbed off me that morning. She'd argued the board into submission, and her slave had been acclaimed the most desirable at the party. "Steffie told me the two of you had met."

Madame nodded. "I thought," she murmured, "that you might come by."

"He's charming," she added, absentmindedly raking the back of my neck with her nails.

"Ummm, quite, yes," Kate agreed softly.

"Take the big armchair, Jon," she said then. And to Stephanie, pulling her to her feet and giving her a little push in my direction, "cuddle him for a while, darling." She took off her jacket, shrugged out of her suspenders, kicked off her pants.

"Well, Odile...." She raised her chin like a young knight riding into battle. I felt one-upped. And then I relaxed. Hey, let her deal with Madame's fathomless appetites. While I watched.

I refilled my wineglass and led Stephanie to the armchair, collapsing into the cushions and pulling her into my lap, sipping wine and running a hand over her warm, bejeweled flesh. And watching the series of tableaux that unfolded: Kate leaning over Madame and taking her head in her hands to kiss her; Madame's elaborate chignon tumbling loose and dark down her back; Madame opening a drawer in one of the bed tables and lifting out a black latex cock on slender leather straps, while Kate fiddled absentmindedly with a china shepherdess from the same table; Madame down on her knees now, strapping the cock around Kate's hips; Kate turning slightly, to give me a better view of this; Madame's jeweled hands cradling Kate's butt, her head buried in her thighs, licking the cock, sucking it, and moving slowly down to the floor, planting worshipful kisses down Kate's legs as she went.

"Are you ready, Odile?" Kate asked coldly. "Nowadays people don't keep me waiting."

"No, Kate," Madame mumbled, rising from the floor, "forgive me. Just a moment, Kate." She reached into the bedside drawer for a jar of grease, rubbed it up herself with her long fingers, and then kneeled on the bed, her head in the pillows, her narrow rich lady's ass spread out for Kate to enter. Again, those magnificent cries of pleasure, this time etched just a little more sharply, pain adding dark overtones. I watched Kate—her supple lower back, the muscles in her ass and thighs—plowing back and forth in powerful arcs, deep contractions. Fucker, I thought. One of Sade's fuckers, stammering brutes from the garden imported into the boudoir for an afternoon's sport with the gentry—though, in Kate's case, there were clearly other dynamics at work as well. Oh, this is nice, I thought. But it could probably be even a little nicer, with Stephanie sucking me.

I looked down at her, curled against my chest, her wide, serious, troubled eyes fixed on the women in bed. I wondered if she were jealous. No, she was afraid of something. Could be interesting. I dipped my fingers in my wine, dribbled little ruby drops on her breasts, and licked them off, my tongue tickled by the fine gold wire, the little pearls that were as warm as her flesh, the cold, faceted, flashing emeralds. I kissed her, my fingers probing the stripes on her butt. "On your knees," I whispered, nudging her off my lap.

"Yes, yes," I heard Madame Roget's voice, "but turn her around to face us." Damn bossy woman, I thought, looking at her and Kate, flushed and panting on the big embroidered pillows. Kate was refilling their wineglasses. "Is there some unfinished business, Odile?" she asked.

"Unhappily," the lady sighed, her honeyed voice sounding anything but unhappy. "A moment of arrogance, earlier, that's gone unpunished. Tell your mistress, Stephanie."

I could feel, rather than see, Stephanie kneeling up to them, her back very straight. I moved to the floor, sitting against the bed, so that I could watch her breasts tilt upward as she lifted her hands to the back of her neck. She parted her knees, rotating her hips to bring her cunt and belly forward. A penitence posture.

"Well?" Kate asked.

Stephanie sighed.

"Well, Kate," she said, "well, um, earlier, when Jonathan wanted to have me, and I could see that Madame wanted to have him, and...oh, Kate...I'm sorry...I didn't mean it, but I couldn't help being a little amused, and, oh...I'm afraid I showed it."

She was weeping now, big slow tears. One splashed onto an emerald, flashing prisms.

"Why didn't you put a demerit token into her box, Odile?" Kate asked. "Your guests would have enjoyed watching her being punished."

"Well, I thought you might bring her to me, you see. And I wanted to keep that punishment all to myself."

Kate frowned. "But she's so delightful right now, marked just as she is. I hate to mess that up. Damn, and I was so pleased she hadn't gotten any demerit tokens."

This of course caused Stephanie to weep full force, but in the most miserable, abject silence.

"Come over here," Kate said in an icy voice. She was sitting on the side of the bed, the shiny black cock rising impressively from her lap. Stephanie quickly crawled over, her hands still at the back of her neck. Kate lifted her chin in her hand, looking at her searchingly.

"So you think your masters are here for your amusement?" she asked, very softly.

"Oh, no, Kate," Stephanie sobbed.

"Or perhaps you'd like to judge us too, award us prizes, hmmm?"

"No, no, Kate, of course not."

"I don't think you really deserve to wear that pretty prize anymore, do you?" Kate took it off, roughly.

"No, Kate," quieter now, but more deeply humiliated, and also adjusting to having the clips off, and the slaps to her breasts that followed.

"I think a spanking," Kate decided. "It will hurt her, but it won't add any more marks, just a nice, deep, velvety pink background for the ones she's already got. Stephanie, ask

Madame Roget if she will honor you by spanking you as you deserve."

But Stephanie had gotten a bit carried away by the proceedings, and pleaded tearfully to be spanked as long and hard as Madame possibly could.

"Tacky, darling," Kate admonished her coldly. "I said, 'as you deserve.' Don't give yourself airs. Madame will decide how long and how hard."

Abashed, Stephanie got the question right this time, and Madame graciously assented, pulling off the lace coverlet and sitting up straight and whippet-like against the pillows.

She added that she would not mind it if Stephanie cried out, and Stephanie thanked her gratefully as she slid into place.

Madame became more contemplative then, stroking Stephanie lovingly for a minute or two, moving her subtly, spreading her out better, probing her a little, until we all heard some timid moans.

Life's a banquet, I thought, at least for Madame. Well, a pretty sumptuous midnight snack, anyway, with me for hors d'oeuvres and Kate the main course. And now she had this delicious little *tarte tatin* to finish off with. If she ever finished.

The first sharp crack of her palm took me by surprise. She was a hard spanker, the blows making much more noise than I'd expected. And they continued to rain down, in intense, concentrated fury, Stephanie crying out but staying still.

I looked up at Kate, standing at the side of the bed. She still had the cock on—and I was hard too, if rather less imposing-looking. "Let's get out of here," I whispered. I supposed that Madame wouldn't have minded it if the two of us rutted around on the floor while she occupied herself in bed. But I was getting tired of Madame.

Kate nodded.

"She'll send her back when she's finished with her," she said with a shrug, and reached to undo the straps around her hips.

I put a hand on her wrist.

"Leave it," I said.

She grinned, and we started digging through the pile of clothes on the floor, sorting out whose suit was whose, pulling on our pants and stuffing our hard-ons into them.

And by the time we were ready to make our disheveled exit, staggering out of there arm in arm like drunken sailors smuggling bazookas in our pants, the blows had subsided, and Stephanie had slid back across the bed, her face now in Madame's crotch. Madame, not bothering to look at us, made a happy, absentminded little wave of a jeweled hand in our general direction, as she began another of her interminably slow triumphal arcs toward climax.

CARRIE

He didn't ask me whether I'd enjoyed the story this time.

"Turn around," he said. He'd been sitting up against the headboard and I'd been sitting between his legs, his hands around my front, his cock growing against my ass. He wanted me on top of him now, to move me up and down, to make me come repeatedly, his hands tight around my hips, my breasts bouncing. He wanted to exhaust me, as Madame had exhausted him. Done, I thought, curling up beside him, panting and breathing out the occasional soundless shudder when he stroked my thighs. I felt a little one-upped, realizing how easy I was—well, especially after a year of not being able to lose myself in my own enjoyment. But it's also because I'm young, I thought then, smiling to imagine myself someday becoming much fussier and more demanding—a middle-aged lady of voluptuous and gourmandizing appetites. It was something to look forward to. Well, depending on how things worked out, I thought, suddenly much more interested in the fact that (speaking of appetites) I was starving again. We'd managed to simplify life in a charmingly utopian way—reducing it to food and sleep, sex and storytelling—and now it was time for food again. The rain had dropped off to a drizzle. So we went exploring, and found a neighborhood restaurant, where they'd listed *tarte tatin* on the blackboard in the window.

"Ahhhh," I breathed an hour later, blissfully downing the last bite of apple and crust and vanilla whipped cream, as he nodded to the waiter to bring our coffees.

"I'm going to tell my next story right here," I announced. I wasn't sure why. Probably because I wanted to make him sprint—or hobble, perhaps—back to the hotel. Well, because I thought I needed some sort of advantage. Because, damn it, was Kate going to be in all his stories?

But I didn't have time to think that one through right then. I had a story to tell, after all.

CARRIE'S STORY CONTINUES

I wish Madame had let them punish Stephanie publicly, for the entertainment of her guests. So you could have told me what nasty rituals she, or her trainers, had dreamed up. Because it's my experience that that's where they really like to get funky, at those punishment ceremonies. At Mr. Constant's parties, for example, if the token master had found any lead demerit markers in your coinbox, you'd have to go line up at a special punishment station. It was a panel of wall-mounted dildos. And for every lead token, you'd have to bugger yourself on one of those dildos for fifteen minutes. You'd have to hold your hands at the back of your neck—part of the punishment was the awkward, exhausting crouching position you'd have to assume, while you ground your hips like a demented go-go dancer. And guests could fondle you, or flog your front, taking turns with the floggers that hung from hooks at the punishment station. It was worse, I thought, for the guys—people wouldn't leave their cocks and balls alone. They looked so "out there," I guess.

But the hosts at other parties had other, equally fiendish, punishment rituals. And since I often got at least one demerit token in my box, I got to know them all, to be a sort of connoisseur, you might say.

Parties like that were a big part of my life. Mr. Constant would give one every six weeks or so, and he'd go to a few—and bring us, of course—during the weeks in between. Parties like that were one of the things that Annie trained me for.

But first—that first day on the island—she showed me the lay of the land. After I'd dozed in the straw for a while, she prodded me awake with her boot, and led me outside. There was a pony cart waiting for me, with a pile of pony gear—harness, bridle, whip, and tail—on the seat. Of course I was familiar with the cart's basic design—shaped more or less like a plow or a big backward wheelbarrow, but with two big spoked wheels on the sides. The spokes were a rich, mellow, brass color, as were the little door handles and tiny lamps at the front (for night rides, I guessed). Otherwise it was matte black, the seats inside a rich buttery chestnut leather. It made the red and black and gold coaches I'd pulled at "Sir Harold's Custom Ponies" seem as tacky as the name of his establishment. I felt absurdly proud that I'd be pulling something this sober and elegant.

Annie put the bridle on my head, jerking the bit far back into my mouth. It was a thick steel bar, and it distended my mouth and made me gag as she buckled it into place, the heavy leather straps meeting at the back of my head. She turned me around and I bent a little so that she could insert the dildo, with the long horse tail connected to it, into my asshole. She pulled the straps of the belt that held it in place, my body welcoming the parallel restraints at my mouth and ass.

I knew how to be a pony. I was even a little vain about being a rather good one, but I was afraid that maybe I was kidding myself, that her standards were so high that she'd be entirely displeased with me. Anyway, I tried really hard to hold myself in a proud pony stance, while she harnessed me to the cart, grunting as she pulled the straps snugly into place. She did it quickly—I remembered how competent her hands had looked, managing Tony that morning. And when she finished, she gave my ass a hard slap, which I chose to interpret as a good sign. And then she came up front, to show me the whip she'd be using, and she doubled it in her hand and caressed my breasts and then my face with it. I arched my back, rubbing up against the worn leather of the whip. I strained my neck, pushed against the bit a little, so that she could see that I wanted to use my mouth, I wanted to kiss the whip, to show her how hard I was going to try. "Save it, ass-hole," she chuckled, getting into the cart and cracking the whip, and signaling with the reins that she wanted me to gallop.

Good. I wanted to go fast, cover ground, see everything. Blue sky, rocky terrain, fluttering silver leaves of olive trees. Downhill from us, a big stone amphitheater or athletic field. I figured I'd see it again, but not today, I guessed, because we started uphill. The high boots they'd given me fit me well, and their soles were thick. I was glad, because I needed all the help I could get. The path wasn't steep, but I knew that the constant effort of running uphill would catch up with me eventually. Still, I didn't want to slow down until I absolutely had to. But hey, I realized as I felt the whip catch me on the ass, she wasn't going to let me slow down anyway. And I didn't know what would happen when I became so exhausted that I'd have to.

Well, I wouldn't worry about that just yet. It was warm and sunny, early afternoon, and a bit of salty sweat was drip-ping into my eyes, bouncing prisms off the dusty colors in the shining light. Her hands at the end of the reins were quiet, eloquently articulating their desires through the tugs I felt at the bit in my mouth. I didn't know if I was crying out against the bit or if it was silencing me, but it didn't matter, because you wouldn't be able to hear my cries—not over the noise of the cart on the road and of my pounding feet. And now we'd rounded the crest of the hill and there was the sea all around me. Some parts sparkled, and some looked still and deep purple, and I could see tiny islands of black rock off the shore: I half expected that Sirens would be sitting on them. Annie didn't use the whip a lot, just when I'd break rhythm, when I'd become dazzled, distracted, by the colors of the sky and sea. She's onto me, I'd think, pulling my eyes away from the landscape; she knows what I need.

We hit some more level ground now, a road through an olive grove. The light and shade dappled the rocky path in front of me. She slowed me to a canter, and then a trot as we came into full sunlight. She began to be more critical of my form. "Shoulders back, knees higher, tits up and out," she cried out, using the whip for emphasis. I concentrated on my center, knowing that my arms and legs and shoulders would become more graceful as well. Just a little extra energy to the legs, to lift the knees.

We circled a meadow, and I got my first view of the house. And I was so curious that I forgot all my good resolutions about focusing my entire attention on my form. I was disappointed at first. It seemed surprisingly small, gray stone and whitewashed stucco. And then we wheeled around to the right, and I could see that it was immense—built down into the cliff, stairs and terraces leading out from many bright expanses of windows, artfully weathered wooden doors. It must storm here sometimes, I thought—I imagined being naked, chained, fucked, beaten, out on one of those terraces in a storm.

A sharp tug to the left on the reins, the sensation at my mouth spreading down my body, answered by the inevitable sting of the whip on my back. She didn't have to yell anything to me. The whip seemed to speak in her voice. "Enough sightseeing, asshole," it seemed to say, "get those knees up. Now!"

And I did. I stopped seeing anything that I didn't have to see—just a bit of path, a slice of sky, a flare of sun refracting through the sweat dripping into my eyes. Just enough to know what came next and how not to lose my footing. I performed for her, following her hands at the reins, at the whip. I tossed my head, wanting to show her how good I was at this. I lost myself in the thunder of the wheels and my feet and heart, and the occasional lightning crack of the whip.

But now I was beginning to get tired; I was sure Annie could tell, too. I could feel my muscles start to tremble but she wouldn't let up. She was using the whip more sparingly, but only because I wasn't giving her reason to use it more. I was aware of every muscle—or perhaps just the ones I needed, the belly muscles to hold me up straight, and the ones in my legs, my ass, to keep my knees rising as elegantly as I could and my feet falling as squarely. No more showing off and head tossing. Just—silently—doing it. No matter how I looked. I knew I was drooling all over the bit—I had to in order to open my mouth widely, to keep breathing deeply and evenly enough.

My god, would she ever stop? I experimented with a slightly slower trot and she flicked me lightly against the ass. I sped back up immediately. Okay, sorry, I'm convinced. Yes, totally.

Don't waste energy hoping to stop. Simpler merely to resign myself to it—we'll do this for the rest of our lives, I thought. It's not interesting and it's not worrisome. It's just what I have to do. Flawlessly. Elegantly. And there was nothing now but the pull of her reins at my mouth and the rhythm of my trot and a dreamlike haze of sun and exhaustion.

So I hadn't even noticed that we'd circled back to the corral. I was shocked to hear her "whoa" and to feel her reining me in. I tried to stop smartly, next to the fence, but it came out a bit ragged, and I realized that I was trembling all over with exhaustion and dripping with sweat. She took off the harness and bridle, but left on the tail. And she rubbed me down hard with a towel—I was afraid I'd get chills, but I was starting to feel better. I closed my eyes for a moment. It would feel good just to lie down in the sun and sleep....

The hard slap against my flank brought me back to consciousness—I opened my eyes. She had her belt unbuckled and her fly unzipped. Uh-oh. How long had I been dozing on my feet? I got down on my knees as she rolled her jeans down over sharp little hipbones, a small cunt covered with silky black hair. An eager, swollen clit, right up front. I focused on her salty, excited smell. I'm in for it, I thought. I'm going to be punished terribly for not realizing that she would want to be eaten. She was dripping onto my chin, as I carefully licked her out. I wondered if she was thinking about the ride or anticipating the punishment to come. My mouth, my jaws, were trembling, it felt as if all my muscles were going to give in to massive exhaustion, and when she came—jabbing her pelvis forward in several sharp thrusts—I finally let myself collapse at her feet.

She gave me about five minutes, and then she kicked me to a standing position so that she could take the tail out, tossing it into a basket, I guessed for an assistant to deal with. She took my leash out of her pocket, reattaching it to my collar.

"You'll get down on your knees when we go into the house," she said.

The good news, she told Mr. Constant, was that I had some talent as a pony. It had taken me a while to find my stride, she added, but she knew how to get to it now, and we could work on that. Yes, maybe even train me to race.

He nodded, pleased, from behind a big, scarred, old wooden desk. It was a small, surprisingly plain office, adjoining a bigger workroom. I'd seen Stefan in the other room, behind a computer, as well as some other youngish people, also at computers, or at phones and faxes. A dark, slender woman with big almond eyes had looked up curiously from her screen for a moment, before Mr. Constant closed the door between the rooms. The only luxurious thing about the office was the French windows behind me, leading to a long deck. We were on the cliff side of the house, Mr. Constant peering down at me against a wide expanse of darkening, late afternoon sky over the sea.

But the bad news, she continued, was that except when I was harnessed up as a pony, I was horribly spoiled.

"I'll show you," she said, and commanded me through the series of presentations I'd done before lunch, but this time with a running commentary to Mr. Constant. I was slow here, she pointed out, self-indulgent there. "And look at this, will you," she continued, "she seems to think she's being touched and examined for her own pleasure." I stopped listening about halfway through, completing the exercise in a haze of shame and a shimmer of tears, kneeling up and hanging my head miserably.

"She practically expects you to say please and thank you," Annie concluded. So any training she could give me would be a waste, on top of those bad habits.

Mr. Constant looked disappointed. "You're not going to let me have her tonight, are you?" he asked.

"Well, you're the boss," she said.

"But you're the professional," he answered. "I rely on your judgment. What do you want to do with her?"

91

"Lend her out for a week to all the people who work around here. The stables, the garage, the kitchen. She doesn't understand any Greek, which is good. Let her figure out what they want from body language, gestures, snaps of the finger. They'll let her know if she gets it right. And if she gets it wrong...."

She picked up a basket from a low shelf, retrieving some hardware from it. I felt her attaching something to the ring at my neck. A slender chain, two chains. And at the end of each, an implement of punishment. From one, a cat-o'-nine-tails, and from the other, a switch made of a bunch of twigs bundled together. The chains were long, perhaps four feet. The whips would dangle on the floor, even if I were standing.

"I want them to be able to get a good swing," she explained to Mr. Constant. She put a leather belt around my waist and tucked the doubled-up chains in it. She nudged me to my feet, so that he could see how well the arrangement worked. The cold, jingling chains wouldn't get in the way of my walking or crawling. And if someone wanted to punish me, the whips were easily accessible, the chains easy to pull out from the belt. She demonstrated, once, with the bunch of twigs against my ass. And yes, she could definitely get a good, painful, stinging swing.

Mr. Constant looked thoughtful.

"You're obviously right," he said. He turned for a moment, looking silently toward the door behind him. "But let's compromise, what do you say?" he continued, turning back to us. "Before I send her away for a week, I'd like to see her thoroughly whipped."

Annie shrugged. "That's cool. Out on the deck? Come on, Carrie."

And I've always wondered if Mr. Constant had actually wanted Stefan to do that whipping, and not Annie. And whether Annie suspected the same thing, dragging me out to the deck as quickly as she did. And whether Mr. Constant was surprised by how eager I seemed to be, since—as he'd observed—I wasn't one of those pain slaves. But I knew that if I had to bear it, I wanted it to be from Annie and not Stefan.

Not that it wasn't completely awful—the most workmanlike whipping I'd ever received, utterly devoid of rancor, or of any emotion, really: pure technique, based on her knowledge of what her boss liked, and her professional sense of how to make me weep and writhe and scream out over the silent, late afternoon sea. And she'd only get better at it, I thought, as she came to understand me better, after I was purged of my bad habits, and she could begin training me in earnest. I thanked her profusely, through my sobs, after she'd detached the rings in my cuffs from a hook thoughtfully mounted in a beam above the deck's railing.

"The stables first, I think," Mr. Constant was saying.

Which was where I began. On my knees that afternoon, in the dirty straw of a real stable, one that held horses. Two men worked there, an older one, in a tweed cap, and a younger one, with curly black hair and stone-washed jeans. They kept me with them on a leash as they fed and watered the horses, and when they got really busy, they'd loop the leash over some nail or hook.

It's a pretty labor-intensive business, taking care of thoroughbred horses, and a very matter-of-fact one. They worked quietly, the older guy whistling tunelessly, the younger one breaking in with a comment or question from time to time. And every once in a while, one of them would break off from his work, and decide he needed to fuck my mouth or my ass. And, no, I couldn't tell very well which they wanted, so I often got pushed or slapped or whipped—they'd usually use a riding crop or something that was hanging around for the horses, but they also liked the bundle of twigs that Annie had provided for them.

They left at dinner time, when a woman in a black dress and kerchief came by with some food in a pail for me. I'd been tethered next to a pile of straw, with a rough blanket on it, and I figured that I was finished for the day. But they each came back after dinner—in fact the younger guy brought a friend, and the older guy a bottle of wine. They laughed to see that they'd both had the same idea, which, I guess, was to try out what they hadn't had time for during the workday. To experiment with how I could be trussed up in the horses' leather harnesses. To take turns fucking my mouth while I raised and lowered my cunt over the pommel of a western saddle. To rig up odd and original ways of suspending me so that both of them could fuck me at the same time. They played until late into the night, finally leaving me exhausted on my blanket, and coming back early the next morning, to get as much out of me as they could, before passing me along to the goatherds.

Well, I guess anybody would have appreciated a quick release from the rigors of the workday. Mr. Constant seemed to be a tough boss; I had to hustle to be available for the quick breaks they allowed themselves between chores. But there'd be sudden bursts of whimsy and humor, ingenuity and inspiration as well. I developed a new view of the world of objects: Big barrels or troughs were good for upending me over; long tools could be thrust up into me, for comic effect.

Anything that tied or buckled would, of course, be used to bind me into clumsy and painful positions. It was all simple physics, I thought: gravity, friction, the collision of bodies in space, the primitive technologies regulating the expenditure of energy. I learned to move quickly, and to be alert for signals—who'd want what next, and how I could keep from getting punished for being too slow on the uptake.

They'd wash out my cunt or mouth or asshole when it was too cruddy for anybody to want to fuck, but otherwise, at least in the stables and goatpens and the garage, I crawled around smeared with shit and motor oil. But of course I had to be scrubbed down when I got to the laundry room (which was a sweaty treasure house of cunning bondage apparatus). At which point I was also passed from men to black-clad women, who were a lot more difficult, with their disapproving looks, and, as it turned out, very exacting standards. They'd spank or fuck me with just about anything, too: mops, brooms, wooden spoons, those wide paddles you use for taking pizza out of the oven. Well, that was in the kitchen, which is where the week ended up, and where there were also a few younger women, in denim skirts and striped T-shirts, who laughed a lot when I made them come, and made the older ladies very angry.

"Let's go back to the hotel," Jonathan said, putting down his coffee cup abruptly and stubbing out his cigarette. Gotcha, she thought.

They'd walked a block or two when he stopped in front of a hardware store. "Wait a minute," he said thoughtfully, studying the window display. "I need to buy something."

"But I thought we agreed...."

He laughed. "Trust me on this one."

CARRIE

And when he came back out, I couldn't tell what was in the small white plastic bag tucked into the pocket of his jacket.

"What *is* it?" I demanded.

"Dessert," he said. "A second dessert. Wipe that speck of whipped cream off the tip of your nose. And come on, hurry up, don't dawdle." He took my hand and set off at a rapid clip, leading me the couple of blocks to our hotel and up the stairs.

Well, I thought, I'd been right—it had definitely been his kind of story. He slammed the door behind him, and we tried to pull our clothes off, as quickly as we could. Which meant, of course, that we kept fumbling, tripping, cursing to ourselves. Finally, though, he stood behind me, running his hands down my front. I leaned back against him and he whispered in my ear, "Tell me again. I like to hear you say it. He lent you to people in the..."

"Stables," I breathed, "the stables." I arched my back so that I could feel his cock against my ass. He had one hand on my cunt, while the other moved up, over my belly, my breasts, my neck, my face. I kissed the palm of his hand.

"And they dragged you through filthy straw," he said, "dragged you after them on a leash and when they snapped their fingers..."

I reached behind me and pulled his hips forward, while I pushed against him as hard as I could. "When they snapped their fingers," I said, "I had to figure out whether they wanted to fuck my mouth or my ass."

"Oh, your ass," he said, kissing my ears and the back of my neck, "no question about it—definitely your ass this afternoon."

He nudged me over to the bed, and I lay down across it,

on my belly. He kissed my neck again, and then he moved his mouth down, tracing my spine, kissing as he went. "Keep talking," he said.

"But it wasn't just the stables," I said, softly, happily. His mouth traveled lower, following the curve of my ass. "It was also the garage, you know, on the greasy concrete floor, my face almost in the oil pan...."

"And the goatpens and gardeners' sheds, and the laundry, and the kitchen," he whispered, "Don't forget the kitchen." He bent his head again, planting kisses on the backs of both my thighs.

"Yes," I said quickly. I figured I'd better talk quickly, to keep him quiet—to keep his mouth where it belonged. "Yes, they were very strict in the kitchen, but, you know, it was in the goat shed where they really fucked my ass a lot...." He was licking the backs of my knees. "And they used to like to whip me with that little bundle of sticks," I continued, "the one that was hanging down from my collar by a chain." He spread my legs apart and kissed the insides of my thighs. And then he got up on his knees behind me.

He snapped his fingers.

I scrambled to my knees, arching my back, my breasts crushed against the bed, my arms in front of me, my hands anchoring me, gripping the edge of the mattress.

He slapped my ass sharply. Each side.

"Oh, yes," he repeated, "most definitely your ass."

And then he bent over me, and oh yes no question most definitely fucked my ass.

We were both pretty comatose afterward, lying sprawled across the bed for quite a while. And then just kissing, idly and luxuriously, for quite a while longer. Our clothes, which we'd pulled off so clumsily, were lying everywhere around the room. Lascivious disarray—the phrase slipped into my head, probably from something I'd read in my early teens. I liked the way it sounded. I drifted contentedly in and out of sleep on it, ignoring Jonathan's increasing fidgetiness. The messiness was making him crazy. He sighed unhappily, ostentatiously, while I pretended not to notice—and finally he gave up, sighed one last huge pitiful sigh, and pulled himself out of bed to hang up our stuff in the armoire.

And when he came back to bed he was holding that package from the hardware store. I'd forgotten about it. What had he said back there? Something about dessert....

He took a little metal whisk out of the bag. Like something you'd use to made an omelet. Did we have a hotplate in the room? I wondered dimwittedly. Were there eggs, milk?

But he was holding it wrong, I thought, my sex-benumbed mind struggling for coherence. He was holding it upside down. That was odd. He held it delicately, his long fingers around the slender loops of wire, his eyes mischievous in his deadpan face. I was still too tired to move, lying stretched out on my back, too dazed and astonished to do anything at all as he moved the handle up my cunt, rested the edge gently against my clit. And then, well, I guess he started hitting the loops of wire with the finger of his other hand. And the whisk's cool, smooth aluminum handle began to vibrate against me, in my cunt, gently and beautifully, playing its music of the spheres, turning me into a glass harp, a tuning fork, for that long, long, timeless instant he kept jingling the wires. Ahhh....

I was embarrassed, a little, after that. "But where...?" I whispered, after kissing him breathlessly for a while, "how....?"

He pretended to be casual about it. "Oh, that," he began. "Oh. Yeah. Well, sometimes I like to go down to Valencia Street and browse the lesbian sex zines. And, well, uh, when you were telling me about your adventures in the kitchen, I remembered something I'd read. See, there's a zine that has kind of a 'Hints from Heloise' column and I always check it out. Well, I figure they'd know, right?" He shrugged, all boyish, charming, phony modesty. I kissed him again.

And when I went to take a bath a little while later, I found that I was singing, softly at first, but happily and ridiculously, a song from deep within my memory. I know lots of old rock songs, you see. They were imprinted on me, when I was very little, by my boomer parents who played their favorite records over and over, constantly. So, as I was running the hot water and dumping in the bath salts I started singing. I got louder, too, warbling unselfconsciously along with the sound of the water and the pipes—with the harmonies of my overworked senses and overwhelmed emotions. And as I lowered myself into the steaming tub I was singing full force.

"In the jingle jangle morning," I sang, *"I'll come followin' you."* And I wondered if I really would, too.

Of course, you always pay for it, don't you? You get out of the bathtub or shower, you see the other person's amused face, and you realize just how loudly you were belting out your song in there.

"Nice selection," he grinned. "A lesser sensibility might have given me 'You Make Me Feel Like a Natural Woman.'"

"Come back to bed," he added. "I lied before. I want your mouth too."

I'd forgotten how devastating I found that little phrase. *I want*. Well, it was more than a phrase, after all—it was, as I could have told you at nine years old, a complete sentence, the verb sweetly agreeing with the subject in number. Number? One. Just him, his declarative, subjective singularity—taut, swollen, urgent. I want. Tense: the present. Oh, yes, very tense, and very present. A simple sentence, wanting to grow, to complexify, its predicate demanding its object—give it its object. Your mouth. And I opened my mouth, and he pulled my head down on him, hard. Oh, and I want you. I want you. To want it. To want me. It. Dissolve. Drown in the ambiguity.

But you don't really drown. After a while you surface. He pulled me up, helping me to swim, like Alice through her tears. And words, phrases—exclamatory, hortatory—odd, ill-assorted forms from languages living and dead, bubbled up in me, as I demanded more, more from him, his hands, his mouth. Onward, I insisted. Onward and upward and downward too, I directed him. And so on. And so forth. Q.E.D. and P.D.Q. I remembered another barely understood favorite song from early childhood. *She comes in colors*—only I don't, I come in words. *Et cetera* and even *und so weiter*. *Aha* and *eureka* and *excelsior*, too. *Semper fidelis* and don't forget *sic semper tyrannis*. I led and he followed, but matching me, teasing me, laughing at my insatiability and goading me on, chasing me through moods and modes, hollow lands and hilly lands, as the twilight deepened and we exhausted ourselves—our abilities, ingenuities, vocabularies. We slept for a while, and it was very dark when we woke up. Ten o'clock, too late to get dinner in a restaurant. "But I'm starving," I wailed, and we went out to find a café that would give us salad, or cassoulet, or anything.

Over coffee, our elbows on the crowded little café table, our hands linked, I wondered how I could make this moment last, just a little longer. Because out of the happy haze that had surrounded us that long, drizzly afternoon, certain details were beginning to emerge, islands in the sea of memory, the tides of events swirling around them. Things were going to change, I knew. Soon. They were changing now, and I couldn't stop the haze from dissolving, from revealing the new landscape. I looked at him, silently imploring him to help me hold on to the moment, but he shook his head. Damn, I thought, he wants things to move along. He's ready and I'm not. He kissed my fingers, my knuckles that were beginning to clench; he brushed them lightly with his lips. His eyes, peering over the top of my hand, were sympathetic, ironic. He'll be patient, I thought, for a little while longer. Maybe, if I'm lucky, until tomorrow.

Where had it come from, this change in mood, in tempo? Perhaps it had been those slaps. Not that they'd hurt, but they'd lingered, resonating in memory. I was suddenly overwhelmed by memories, images—his hand on his rattan cane, while I sobbed and writhed beneath him. The modeling of the bones in his wrist, the tension of the muscles in his forearm, the heat in his eyes. Was I feeling terror, I wondered, or impatient desire? Was time moving too fast or too slowly?

Back up, I thought. Slow down. This isn't about pain yet. It will be, oh, don't doubt that. But there are other things, important things, protocols and decorum to be put in place first. Those slaps—they're not punishment, after all. They're communication: simple syntax in the pidgin of dominance and submission. Like that snap of his fingers. It's a wakeup call, a warning signal that we're no longer moving through the courtly figures of seduction, flirtation, negotiation.

But it was dangerous to think like that. If you could call it thinking at all. I mean, it was the kind of thinking where thinking makes it so—I was already mainlining his signals, his commands to my wet, open, tremulous, primitive body, feeling the sound of the snap of his fingers.

He shook his head, across the table from me. "You're really something," he said, smiling. And then, looking around him, "I think they'd like to close the café." He gestured for the check, and I tried to compose myself—to get back into real time, to watch the café owner's wife yawning, her reddened hands polishing the espresso machine.

Hurry up please it's time. Time to wrap up the old stories and to make up some frightening, difficult, new ones. Hurry up. Because he won't say "please" tomorrow.

We walked quietly back to the hotel through dark, wet streets. You could see a few stars, but it was still mostly cloudy.

"It's late," he said, opening the door to our room, taking off his jacket and hanging it in the armoire.

I nodded. I pulled off my clothes and tossed them onto the floor.

We got into bed and he snapped off the light.

I snapped it back on. "Not yet," I said. "One more story today."

He raised an eyebrow, and I drew myself into sitting position.

"Okay, Jonathan," I said. I found that I could still conjure up a confident, demanding tone. "A story from you now." But with a subtle weakening at the end, like a boy whose voice is changing. "And one that's not about Kate."

JONATHAN TELLS A STORY THAT'S
(MOSTLY) NOT ABOUT KATE

That letter I wrote to you—I'd given it to Stefan to give to you—got me into trouble. It was definitely an unacceptable thing to do, you see, in the parallel legal universe of the auction association. Stefan should really have refused to let you see it. His story was that he thought I had a right to send it to you, because they hadn't signed the papers yet and you were still my property. But I think he'd passed it on, to you and Constant, just to make trouble for you. And for me.

Because it had definitely been a no-no, and the auction people, the powers that be, felt they had to censure me for it. I'd gotten a phone call from my lawyer, Brewer. Not from his secretary, which is what I would have expected. No, Brewer called me himself, to set up a lunch appointment, to talk about it some more. "What the hell did you think you were doing?" he asked. And when I stammered my apologies—I'd been carried away emotionally, whatever—he sounded serious.

"That letter could get you barred from the association, Jon," he said. "How long have you been a member?"

"Fifteen years," I said. "More, I guess."

"Well, you should know better," he growled. "I'll send you copies of the relevant clauses in the bylaws, so you can see just how entirely out of line you were."

Who reads these things? I never had. Well, but I'd never needed to. I'd always been such a good, well-behaved citizen of the association before. I mean, it was all common sense, basic manners and sensibility, boundaries one wouldn't dream of overstepping. Who would have imagined doing any of what I'd so thoughtlessly done? The bylaws couldn't have been clearer. The prohibitions against declaring love or proposing friendship to a slave, revealing one's own emotions, or phrasing anything as a request rather than a command. Worse, I thought, probably, was the way I'd asked you to meet me in a year. I couldn't specify the exact clause I'd violated, but I knew that Constant had been right to take issue with what I'd done. Because, yeah, I'd definitely wanted you to think about me, on *his* time, across the boundaries of the year he'd paid for.

Constant, Brewer told me over lunch, had really been very decent. He'd known how badly trained you were when he'd bought you—that was why he'd gotten you for less than a hundred K, and he didn't mind that. He liked a bargain and he was depending on his trainer to get you into shape anyhow. So in a sense my sappy letter was just confirmation of what he'd already surmised. "But," his letter to Brewer had concluded, "while I don't mind playing outside the rules once in a while, most of your members would probably not be so forgiving. So I advise you to censure Mr. Keller, and—for the future health of the association—to make every effort to keep your procedures clean and rigorous from now on."

"We'd simply boot you out," Brewer said at lunch, "if you weren't a member of such long standing. And then there's your friendship with Ms. Clarke."

Kate. Oh, shit, Jon, I thought.

"Does she know?" I asked.

He scowled, not dignifying that with an answer. He hadn't spoken to her about it, the scowl implied. He'd find that entirely indecent, embarrassing. But of course she knew. Whom was I kidding?

"You'll come to the office, tomorrow at ten," he said. "I'll draw up some papers and you'll sign them. You'll pay a fine, too. And you'll be disciplined."

I raised my eyebrows. I wasn't used to being bossed around by a man who was, after all, a functionary I paid to keep my affairs in order. And he couldn't mean what it sounded like he meant, could he?

He nodded, his leathery face set in grim lines. "Be there, boy," he said. "And," he looked disapprovingly at the collar-less dress shirt I was wearing, under my jacket, "wear a tie."

"Yes, sir," I said.

Well, I hoped it was a conservative enough tie for him—blue and olive diagonal stripes. Navy blue blazer, gray slacks. I couldn't believe I was dressing this carefully—and shaving this closely. I felt raw.

I got to his office about two minutes late. I'd intended to be early but I'd been held up for twenty minutes while they'd rerouted downtown traffic around a PCB spill. Brewer wasn't very impressed with the excuse, either, when the receptionist led me into his office. "My sciatica's bothering me," he said. "I would have stayed home today, but we've got to get you squared away, you know.

"Thanks, Marilyn," he said now, to the receptionist. "Look, Mr. Keller and I will be busy in conference room H for an hour. You can leave messages on that phone, but don't disturb us otherwise."

She nodded, throwing me a last, wounded look—I hadn't had the energy to flirt with her that morning. I guessed that I usually did—she's always been really nice and helpful to me—but I'd never really thought about it before. And then Brewer led me down the hall.

I'd never been in that conference room before. Odd. It didn't have any of the bland, corporate art they had all over the rest of the place. Nothing on the walls at all. And just a small window facing a blank wall. It was small, for a conference room. And there was only one chair at the oval table, though there was a leather couch against a wall.

I'd thought we'd both sit on the couch, and I headed toward it.

"Hey," he said then, "where do you think you're going, boy?"

I swallowed, turned slowly to face him. He was sitting in the chair at the oval conference table, a manila folder of papers in front of him. He opened a drawer under the table then, and took out a rattan cane, which he put on top of the folder.

"You do want to keep your membership in the association?" he asked.

"Yes, sir," I said.

"Drop your trousers," he said. "Shorts, too. That's right, just let them bunch up around your ankles. And walk over here."

God, I hate that. Hobbling across the room with my pants around my ankles, and then standing there in my gold-buttoned blazer and striped tie, my erection beginning to poke its way through the opening in my shirt. Even as I stared fearfully at the cane. Well, especially as I stared at it.

"Nice tie," he said, and I thanked him. "You can take off the jacket, if you like," he added.

"Okay," he said then, "Twenty strokes, and you'll count them for me, won't you, boy?"

"Yes, sir," I said.

"You can scream all you want. The room is sound-proofed," he added. "We don't want to frighten the secretaries.

Or upset Marilyn. You seem to have upset her enough this morning already."

I apologized, and he nodded. He winced, his posture stiffening—and I realized that his lower back really was pretty painful. And I felt a sudden rush of guilt. Jeez, he was old, he was in pain, and he was taking the trouble to punish me, all to keep me in the fold. This was going to be different from other beatings I'd had from time to time, usually from Kate, or somebody equally delicious. Those had been sport. This was going to be, uh, difficult....

He nodded to me to climb up on the table. "That's it, head down, ass up, spread those knees. And you'd better use your hands to protect your balls, hadn't you, boy?"

And—sciatica or not—he did make me scream. Cry, too, which was much more distressing.

He gave me a few minutes to recover, kneeling by the side of the table, my pants still down around my ankles.

"And now that we've finished with the injury part," he said, "let's move on to the insults, what do you say?"

It was an insulting, degrading letter of apology, detailing the ways I really didn't deserve my membership in the association, and my gratitude that the association, in its mysterious wisdom, was allowing me to stay. I agreed to everything. I signed it, still on my knees.

"You're a nice fellow," he said then. "I've always thought so. I've always liked your uncle too. Well, these things happen sometimes. It'll be all right. But we can't have you acting disrespectfully toward the association anymore, can we?"

"No, sir," I said. "Thank you, sir," I said. "I'll never do it again, sir," I said. "Sorry about your sciatica, sir," I said.

"Oh, you'll be much, much sorrier," he said, "when you get the bill in the mail."

He got to his feet slowly, using both hands to lift himself from his chair. "Pull up your trousers," he said. "And be charming to Marilyn on your way out, won't you? I've got a difficult day ahead of me."

CARRIE

He looked at me curiously and a little nervously, wondering how I'd absorb the images of him being caned, humiliated. Interesting, I thought. And not really so surprising as all that. Because when you think about it, pornography is as often told from the point of view of the victims as history is told from the point of view of the victors. So it made sense to me that the story would have occurred to him. And anyway, it told me something important about his world, his universe.

Well, it reminded me of another story. A whole other kind of story—about a woman who had insisted to a physicist that the earth rested on the back of a giant turtle. And the turtle, the physicist asked, where did the turtle stand? Well, that was easy. On the back of another turtle, of course. And so on and so forth, the woman concluded—turtles, all the way down. Well, Jonathan's cosmos wasn't so different. You'd just have to look in the right direction, which was upward, toward authority. Power and discipline, all the way up.

I shuddered a little and put my arms around him. He kissed my forehead. "Now go to sleep," he said, reaching to turn off the light.

The Third Day

CARRIE

Okay, I thought, opening my eyes to cloudy morning sunshine. Okay, I'm ready. I reached over to Jonathan's side of the bed. I wanted to touch him a little before the day really began. But he wasn't there; he was already up and out of bed, wearing a light blue cotton bathrobe and sitting at the table in the corner with a cigarette and a cup of coffee and a basket of croissants.

"It's getting late," he said.

"Well, I still need breakfast," I said, pulling myself out of bed. And good morning to you too, Jonathan, I thought, while I quickly washed and peed.

I walked behind his chair, leaning over him, my hands creeping into the front of his bathrobe, down over his chest, the muscles in his belly. I kissed his neck, his ears, the top of his head. He smelled nice—soap and coffee, toothpaste and butter and strong French cigarettes. I wanted to fool around a little. But he pulled my hands out, kissed the palms, and put them down by my sides. "Have some coffee," he said.

I shrugged, and put on the T-shirt I'd dropped on the floor the night before. I sat down at the table, munching a croissant, trying to gauge his mood. He looked eager, abstracted, out of patience.

"It looks like it might be a nice day outside," I offered. He mumbled noncommittally, waiting for me to finish the croissant. I fiddled with it, making a million crumbs, scattering them everywhere and then gracelessly picking them up and licking them off my fingers, until I got sick of this nervous, messy routine, guaranteed to make him cringe. I finished my second cup of coffee and wiped my hands.

"Okay," I said, looking at him evenly.

His eyes were opaque, inward-looking, and his voice was soft. "Tell me about becoming a racing pony."

More stories? Not exactly what I'd expected. But okay, I thought, whatever. He nodded toward the bed. I walked over and sat down, drawing my knees up in front of me, propping myself against the pillows.

"Well," I began, "Annie had kept tabs on my progress in the stables and garage and all those other places, and had been reasonably satisfied. So, at the end of the week, they moved me into this white, cave-like room that was carved into the cliff. And a routine gradually unfolded...."

And I told him about mornings in the ring with Annie. I'd stand there in the corral, entirely naked, even barefoot. And she'd touch me here and there. Lightly, just enough to make me want more. I'd follow her fingers, I'd arch and bow my body, thinking of nothing except the signals she was sending me through the nerves in my skin. I'd pose, I'd leap, I'd whirl and caper for her, trying to communicate how much

I wanted her to touch me again—oh, Madam, please, just a little more—miming my desire with every bend and opening of my body. And she might touch me a little more, if she felt like it. But it was just as likely that she'd apply the riding crop. It was a silent business—the idea was to teach my body a sequence of sensations and responses—I felt as though she were tracing a pattern on my senses.

It was only later, when I performed at dressage competitions, that I learned that there were names to the figures I'd learned. I'd repeat them softly to myself: the *pirouette,* a turn on the haunches in four or five strides at a collected canter; the *piaffe,* a trot in place; the *passage,* a very collected, cadenced, high-stepping trot; the *levade,* the *courvet,* and the astonishingly difficult *capriole,* in which the pony jumps straight upward, with its forelegs drawn in, kicking back with its hind legs horizontal, and lands again in the same spot from which it took off.

And there were the simpler presentations, the ones I'd done so poorly on my first day. "Ass!" Annie might cry out, or "Cunt!"—and here again my body would remember all the ways she'd touched me and all the swipes of the riding crop. I'd feel all wet and hot and flushed, but I'd present my ass, calmly, humbly, elegantly, as though that were my mission in life. I'd present my ass, or my cunt, or my mouth. Or I'd kneel up with my back arched, holding my breasts lightly in my hands, at a precise angle, so that she could put stripes across them with a small whip she used only for that purpose. I'd present to Annie, and to Mr. Constant, those mornings he'd come down to watch. And I used what I'd learned that week that I'd been passed around among his employees, too. Because now I knew how it felt to be available to everybody and I knew that was what these postures were really about.

You took me to see presentation competitions, Jonathan, the year I spent with you. I remember how you loved watching them, preferring them to equestrian events, and insisting that I watch carefully. It felt odd, though, the first time I won a ribbon to bring home to Mr. Constant's trophy room, to realize that I was way better than those girls I'd seen performing back in California. It didn't seem right, somehow, but I knew it was true: I was good at this.

Annie would put me and Tony through our paces every morning and early afternoon. And when she'd finished with us, I was happy to eat the tasteless, healthy food in the trough we knelt at, and to collapse for a nap on the straw. We'd clean the stables then, or the outhouse next door, or the brass fittings on the pony cart—we'd have to use our tongues to clean out the little spaces between the spokes of the wheels. And then we'd get an hour or two of free time, on one of the house's terraced patios. The chains leading from our collars wouldn't allow us to touch each other, but we could speak softly from time to time. Tony was a dancer and did graceful and difficult stretching and contracting exercises. I was amazed that he'd want to move at all after the morning's exertions, but he said he needed these exercises for himself, as much as I seemed to need those endless stacks of papers I was always bringing out to the patio.

These were the downloaded books from Project Gutenberg and other e-text sites—reams of paper, printed out on one of Mr. Constant's printers, at my demand, and to Stefan's unfailing annoyance. He'd get even more annoyed because sometimes when I would look up from the text—to watch Tony, or just to think, or to dream—a stray breeze would scatter blizzards of paper out over the sea, and I'd have to ask him to download chapters 2 and 3 of *Pudd'nhead Wilson* again, please, or Act IV of *The Tempest*. I hated reading unbound, downloaded pages, so I ransacked Mr. Constant's library—pulling out a few readable books from among the Grisham and Clancy, the math and economics books, and the books with words like *Excellence* and *Virtual* and *Third Wave* in their titles—just so that I could read something with a cover and a spine.

They were nice, our rest periods, though they'd be cut short those days when the market was extra-volatile. Annie would get a call from Mr. Constant to bring us to the work-room, which was a haze of sweat and adrenaline. And Mr. Constant would take one of us, usually Tony, and hand the other one over to his assistants. And I'd follow the tugs at my collar, crawling under desks and opening my mouth for the eager cocks shoved down it, the quick gushes of cum accompanied by shouts of "Buy," "Sell!" "Did you get it?" and "Aw-*right!* Gimme five!"

Stefan would usually disdain to touch me those days, which was all right with me. But the girl working there, too, the slender, dark, doe-eyed one whom I'd seen the first day, never grabbed my leash either. Or Tony's, for that matter.

At dusk, Annie would take us to prepare for our evenings in Mr. Constant's rooms. We'd be given early dinners in the kitchen, with shallow bowls of resiny wine to lap. And then Annie would bring us to a tiled, steamy little Turkish bath kind of place, where we'd bathe each other, give each other massages. We'd knead each other's muscles until they were warm, pliant, relaxed, our skins burnished with the light, fragrant oil we'd rubbed each other with. I don't know what the smell was, but it reminded me of mown grass. Tony would sit cross-legged, and I'd kneel behind him and brush his hair, stroke it back away from his cheeks, his forehead. Sometimes I'd catch it in a heavy gold clip at the back of his head. And then we'd change places and he'd trim my hair with tiny sharp scissors, and sometimes, if Annie loosened the buckles on my collar, he'd do the back of my neck, with clippers. Those clippers made me shiver—the first time he'd used them, I started to moan and tremble, to come, actually. And Annie beat me for that. Well, actually, she beat us both, silently and ferociously, with the little rubber truncheon that she'd carry during these sessions, because it didn't leave marks.

We outlined each other's eyes with kohl, and darkened each other's lips and nipples, dipping our fingertips into pots of ocher brown rouge. We hung heavy gold rings from each other's ears, put bangles around our ankles. We shared our smells and textures—even, it seemed, our slowed pulse rates and measured breathing. The only other sound was the plashing of a little fountain in the center of the room, which was there, I supposed, to cool the air—keep it from suffocating us. There were no mirrors. If I wanted to see my face while Tony painted it, I had to peer into his eyes—the green eyes of a sleepwalker or an opium junkie, the pupils huge and black, distended in the dim light.

And we'd know that we were finished, that we were ready for Mr. Constant, when we heard the soft, dull sound of the truncheon in Annie's hand—she'd slap her palm with it, twice, a small, tense, watchful figure in black:

lonely, sublimated, subaltern authority. Sometimes I'd fanta-size rebellion: Tony and I joining forces to strip her, bathe her, rub her with oil, and then take greedy turns eating at her cunt with our darkly painted mouths—an orgy of primitive, sibling communism. I pitied her, those evenings, that she couldn't have us that way. Or any way. She was jumpy, impa-tient to get it over with, to snap slender red leather leashes to the rings in our collars, and jerk us along behind her, on our hands and knees, down the corridors to Mr. Constant's sparsely furnished and brilliantly carpeted rooms. (And she'd take it out on us the next day, of course, in the corral, in the open air and blazing sunlight, where she was free to do anything she wanted with us.)

She'd lead us to Mr. Constant's rooms and leave us there, to wait for him if he wasn't there, or to receive his brief nod, if he was. And he'd look us over calmly, and choose one of us, and the other would help. Would kneel there in the flickering light of oil lamps, and help him finish the adornment process, silently handing him the clips and clamps, the straps and buckles and chains, out of his leather casket.

I learned what implements to hand him and in what order, for him to apply to Tony's body, stretched patiently over this or that frame or wheel, or suspended from ropes. I watched Mr. Constant's blunt hands opening little spring mechanisms, twisting tiny screws down on firm, shining bronzed flesh, perhaps bending an arm backward, at some cruel angle, and buckling it into place, until silent tears begin to course down Tony's smoothly painted face—the makeup seemed to be waterproof, tearproof, sweatproof. I learned to recognize Mr. Constant's nod, that we were done, and to fetch a selection of small whips for him to choose from (he liked to take the occasional swipe at us while he fucked us—to keep us present, I think, alert to his rhythms). And then I'd grease Tony's asshole, and back away on my knees, watching quietly. And the next night, perhaps Tony'd do the same for me. I pretended to myself that I hated helping Mr. Constant hurt Tony, but I knew that I was fascinated, that I watched with my mouth hanging helplessly open, my breath coming shallowly. I'd wait eagerly for my turn, fearfully and enviously wishing to be the object of barbarous adornment.

Except for the strokes he'd administer while fucking us, Mr. Constant rarely beat us those nights (though he did enjoy coming to watch us being punished after our training sessions). But once in a while—it seemed to be a special treat he'd only allow himself on rare occasions—he'd summon Stefan, and hand him a whip to use on one or perhaps both of us. It would be an oddly ceremonious event, even punctuated by our screams, and by Stefan's frenzied breathing. "Thank you," Mr. Constant would tell him gravely as he escorted him to the door those evenings, perhaps laying a hand lightly on his shoulder, to steady him. "Thank you. I enjoyed that very much."

"Take off your T-shirt," Jonathan said. He'd dragged his chair over to the side of the bed, and he was sitting backward on it, his chin on his arms. She paused, shrugged, and pulled it off, and she sat up a little straighter, Indian-style, before continuing.

It was a quiet, demanding regime—designed to fit into the spaces of Mr. Constant's work schedule. And then, every few weeks, he'd give a party, a tasteless, Gatsby-like affair, and everything would change. The cliffs would be hung with fairy lights, the island lit with torches. For a week before, you'd see the guests' yachts gathering in the harbor below. Caterers and decorators would have been flown in from—from I don't know where, Athens? Paris? There'd be huge stands of exotic flowers everywhere, marvelous smells drifting up from the kitchen. There'd be a buzz of deliberate, meticulous preparation for the twenty-four hours or so before the guests—as crude and cruel and gorgeous and glittering a bunch as I could imagine—would begin to arrive.

And two hours before party time—well, that's when the human party decorations went up—Tony and I, of course, together with the slaves that the guests would have sent over throughout the day: We'd all have been herded into a holding pen to wait until we were needed, along with the ones that Annie had rented from an agency that specialized in parties like this. Annie was a remarkable organizer—Napoleon deploying her troops. Somehow, she'd look at this mass of obedient flesh and know exactly where to put us. A dozen of us would be pulling the guests from the parking area to the house, in pony carts. Fifteen would be passing hors d'oeuvres, and she'd have chosen ten girls to be suspended upside down, thighs tightly gripping the heavy glass ashtrays balanced at their cunts. The buffet tables would be lit by kowtowing pairs of human candelabra, wax dripping down their arms and backs and thighs from thick candles held in their clasped hands and wedged into their assholes. "Get that bunch strapped under glass tables...those boys get tied to the pillars—make sure they all have leather harnesses on their cocks...and oh, we'll need some more footstools on the main deck...." She'd have assistants for the evening, who would lead us where she directed, and who would apply glittering

117

body makeup to us, paint our faces, attach ornaments to nipples and cocks, harness and bridle us, and hang the inevitable coinboxes from our collars.

The pre-party organization would happen in a blur, but the parties seemed endless. So many cruel hands to pass through, clits to lick, feet to kiss, meticulously polished shoes kicking your butt or prodding your genitals. So much cum to swallow, and all those pinches and pokes and taunts and torments to endure. You'd be assigned a territory—a room, a lawn, a patio. Perhaps the pony cart area—guests liked to race—or the trapeze, ingeniously engineered with slings and pulleys. The worst territory was the games area, near the pool. There were bets, contests—you might have to wrestle, or run a gauntlet, scamper around on your knees fetching things with your mouth—or perhaps not with your mouth. You'd be impaled with unlikely objects, forced into impossible positions, and kicked or slapped if you couldn't maintain your balance or keep up the pace. And you always had to maintain that extra level of awareness, that readiness for the stray nod or snap of the finger. "You there. Put that down and get over here. Now. And open that mouth. Hurry up, what are you waiting for?" And the laughter, after they'd finished with you, especially when they'd made you cry.

I'd never have been able to handle it without that week I spent learning to satisfy the people who worked for Mr. Constant. But then, none of us could really handle the games area, because the people who enjoyed using it were way beyond, hellishly beyond, satisfaction. I thought of it as the Garden of Earthly Delights, only scarier. I was smarting there one night, just about to pick myself up after a raucous game of human croquet, when I heard a voice above me.

"Come on, don't be afraid, Sarah." Where had I heard that voice before? Oh, yeah, "Buy! Sell! Aw-right!" His name was Teddy, I'd picked up from the workroom, and he was big and blond and, yeah, bearish—well, I mean, he looked that way, I don't really know whether he was prone to selling. And she—she was my mystery woman, the dark, dark eyes in the smooth, sad, olive-skinned face. I knew that they were a couple. He was gentle, solicitous with her.

"Just try it," he said to her now. And to me, "Kneel up, stay still."

"Come on," he said softly. He picked up her little hand in his large one, covered with light hair. And he moved it over my breast.

"You see," he said, "you can touch her all you want. That's what she's here for." He grasped the nipple of my other breast, pulling me toward them. I shuffled forward on my knees.

"Stand up," he said.

He showed her the stripes and welts on me—some from Annie, and some from who knew where. He had her touch my collar, so that she'd see how stiff it was, how high I always had to carry my head. He tried to persuade her to put a finger in my cunt, so that she could feel how wet I was, but she refused.

"But you *will* grease her for me, won't you?" he said. "Come on, you promised you would."

"Yes," she said. "I promised."

And she took the tube from him, and timidly began to rub the lubricant up my asshole.

I wished I could see her face, but I tried to content myself with the feel of her little fingers exploring me. And I couldn't help but let out a little wriggle of pleasure.

119

He slapped my breast. "They're not allowed to do that," he explained to her.

"So," he said then, "are you done yet?" I could hear him unzipping his pants.

"I don't know," she murmured. "Did I use enough?"

He laughed, pushing me onto my knees. "I think so, hon. Like enough for a rhinoceros, maybe."

And then he knelt behind me and entered me. I closed my eyes and tried to keep myself open and relaxed. His cock was thick, very hard—the rhinoceros remark didn't seem like such hyperbole right then. And then I felt her fingers on my cheek. She knelt in front of me, and then she sat down on the ground, and she pulled my head into her lap and stroked my face the whole time. Her lap was warm under the cool cotton cloth of her skirt. And I let myself come. I didn't care how much I'd be punished for it. Teddy knew the rules—slaves didn't come while they were being used. I figured he'd put a demerit token in my box after he finished with me—probably two. But, I was beginning to realize now, he'd finished coming, he was withdrawing from me, and he wasn't paying any attention to me at all.

Actually, I don't think they put any tokens of any kind into my coinbox. I think they forgot to—because after he came, he and she just sat there for a while. And then they simply wandered away hand in hand. And I stayed on the ground for maybe five minutes more until I felt cold water dripping on me, and then a kick in my side—somebody who'd just heaved himself out of the pool, standing over me and demanding my mouth.

And I only saw her once after that—later that evening, when I was doing my inevitable turn at the punishment station.

She watched me intently by torchlight, as I bumped and ground my hips and endured the flogging at my breasts.

They left the next day, and I never saw her again. They'd gotten the jobs they'd been hoping for, I heard in the workroom, important jobs at some central bank. So I never found out what—if anything—she'd been thinking that evening at the party, and whether she'd feared or pitied or despised me. She was beautiful, though. Sometimes I dream about her. And when I went to Paris—to get the train for Avignon— I spent a morning at the Musée de Cluny, staring at the unicorn tapestries.

"The pony races," he chided her. "Come on, I want to hear about them."

Why, she wondered. It's not even really his thing. But, come to think about it, she probably knew why he wanted to hear this story. Well, too bad. It wouldn't hurt him to be patient.

"But it didn't happen right away," she answered. "We worked up to it gradually. I had to wait to do it. So it's only right that you should have to wait to hear about it."

It took me a while to get good at the presentations, I told him. And Annie thought my trot and canter could use some work, too—I spent hours just circling a pole in the ring, while she criticized my form, using the riding crop to purify it of wasted motions, to sharpen up my timing. From time to time Mr. Constant would ask when I might be ready to race, and Annie would nod absentmindedly and say something noncommittal. I supposed she had decided I wasn't good enough, and was trying to figure out how to break it to him. But finally, one morning, maybe a week or two after Teddy and

Sarah had left, she led me down the hill to the amphitheater I'd seen my first day, and harnessed me to a racing carriage.

It's more properly called a sulky, though. A light shiny black affair like a bicycle. No brass door handles—well, no doors. It's pure function: just the big, spoked, aluminum wheels, the small, high seat for the driver, at the apex of a long, slender metal *U*-shaped shaft of metal, with a shorter T-bar inside the *U*. It rested casually in the dirt on the tips of the U-bar, waiting for me.

She stood me about three feet in front of it and harnessed me up. Slowly, thoughtfully, she tried different combinations of straps and apparatus that first day. First my pony tail. I opened for the dildo that would hold it into place, and then straightened up so that she could belt the leather straps around me. And then a long, very sturdy strap, running down my back, attaching the ring in the back of my collar to the ring embedded in the base of the dildo. She tightened the buckles, jerking my head back and pulling against the dildo. My back arched like a bow, thrusting my breasts so far out that I could see them, even though my head was angled back so sharply. And I supposed, though I couldn't see it, that my tail jutted straight out behind me as well. Annie moved in front of me, squinting, while she stroked my belly with a finger to gauge its tension.

Not tense enough, I guessed. She took off the tail apparatus. And then she slowly began to push in one with a bigger dildo. Much bigger—it felt like twice the size of the one she'd just removed, traveling up into me like spreading darkness, obliterating all consciousness except my muscles' fearful effort to accept it, to open and reshape myself around it. Oh, yes, that was better. Because now when she tightened the strap running up my back—I could feel a cold drop of sweat beading at the metal rings—not only did my head jerk back, and my breasts and belly thrust out, but my cunt was pushed forward, open and empty in front of me.

Now the studded leather harness, snug around my ribs—I counted half a dozen buckles that she pulled tightly into place in back—anchored in place by thin suspenders over my shoulders and its own little straps between my legs. I'd have thought the business between my legs would be clumsy, but I was so opened out by the dildo that there was plenty of room. She lashed my upper arms tightly together behind me, pulling my shoulders way back, and fastened the cuffs around my wrists to the T-bar. I grasped the rubber handle grips tightly with my hands—it was good to have something to clench my hands around—but I was glad that my wrists were attached to the bar, so that I wouldn't have to worry about losing my grip when my hands got sweaty. Of course, a lot of the pulling would come from my pelvis: She attached the ends of the cart's metal shafts to the belt around my hips.

The bridle, now. The bit widened out my mouth like other bits I'd worn, but it had a high, arched shape as well, with knobs that pressed against the roof of my mouth. I couldn't imagine how it would feel when she'd pull on the reins. And then she demonstrated. Oh.

"It's called a gag-bit," she said. "English animal lovers hated it, but it was very popular in the nineteenth century, because it made the horses foam at the mouth." This was an unusual bit of volubility for her; she must have really liked that detail. The bridle had large blinders at the sides, too. I'd only be able to look straight forward, so when it was time to move to the right or left I'd have to trust the pulls of her hands on the reins, at the gag-bit in my mouth.

She took her time with the lattice of straps at the back of my harness. I knew that this part was important, that it would spread out the weight I'd be pulling, so that I could use all my muscles, arms and shoulders and back and hips and belly. And a final, frivolous touch—she clipped thin, decorative chains from my shoulder suspenders to my nipples.

She didn't make me run full out that first day. She whipped me lightly around the track, both of us concentrating on how to take the curves. She stopped, every so often, to loosen or tighten a strap, fine-tuning the cacophony of sensation she was blasting at my body. She adjusted the bridle, too, so that the blinders would obscure more of my vision. And then she dragged a bunch of obstacles into the track—they looked like big orange plastic garbage cans—and she spent the rest of the day driving me right toward them, zigzagging me around them at the last second with inches to spare.

The zigzagging's really the point of the race, you know. I learned this when they took me to see one a week later. Of course, I wouldn't be allowed to sit in the stands; I crouched at Annie's feet at the edge of the track, getting mud kicked in my face as the boots thundered by. And I realized how narrow a track it was, when you had half a dozen ponies racing on it. It's a Ben Hur setup—you have to run dangerously close to the other ponies, blocking them, cutting them off. Well, the driver makes these decisions; the pony barely sees, with those big blinders at the sides of her face. But she trusts the driver's hand on the reins—and fears the hand on the whip—so completely that she goes wherever she's directed. You'd think there would be more upsets, more collisions, but the ponies are really good. They're pure flesh, pure trust. They hurl themselves into whatever chaotic blur they're directed toward and then swerve delicately to the left or right, following the minutest gradations of pull and pain at their mouths. Well, they do—or I did—after many afternoons out on the track, taking it one more time, tears streaming out from under the bridle. And then, after practice was over, kneeling at Annie's feet to accept punishment for my timidity and clumsiness.

Mr. Constant owned two racing sulkies, so Annie would race me against Tony. And once in a while, as time went on, I'd beat him, too. But it didn't mean much, because while Annie'd be driving one of us, the other one would have to be driven by one of those boys I'd seen my first day. They were light enough—and certainly cruel enough—for the job, but of course they weren't as skillful as Annie. So after a while, naturally I'd win when Annie was driving me, leaning way back in her seat, feet in the stirrups at each side of the U-bar.

Oh, and there's a final wrinkle. You don't just run in a state of physical duress, but of sexual excitement as well. Annie got the young stable guy to help her out here. I didn't know what was going on, that day we first tried this, when he kneeled in front of me at the starting line. I looked at Annie, standing there with her arms crossed and a thoughtful frown on her face, watching me in my bit and bridle, harness and blinders, open and helpless against his mouth on my cunt, his slow, patient tongue on my clit. She watched my belly tremble and my knees start to get weak. And then she prodded him away, quickly swung herself into her seat, and signaled me to begin.

And I couldn't. I just stood there, howling with silent rage behind my bit, until her whip convinced me that I was actually supposed to run in that condition. And when I finally took off, I noticed that everything was just a little more intense, a little more painful, the colors a little brighter, the shadows a little darker than they had been a moment ago. And I ran a lot faster too—to get back around the track to the stable guy's mouth.

"She's a natural pony," Annie said to Mr. Constant that afternoon, when he'd come down to watch my progress. "When I get her the way I want her, she'll run the whole race in that state of terror and arousal. People won't be able to take their eyes off her. Especially after we shave her."

He'd been stroking my face, through my bridle. His hand tightened now, around my jaw, pushing against the gag-bit. "Just so she wins," he said.

Annie laughed. "You'd better consider the first race a freebie, boss," she said. "She needs to get used to the sound of the crowd, you know."

He didn't take his hand off my jaw. He bent my face upward, so that I was looking at him, his glasses reflecting the purple sea. "I don't believe in freebies," he told me.

But of course Annie was right. I don't think anybody could have prepared me for the sound of a crowd at a pony race. It's a formal dress-up event: The crowd in the stands is like a huge flower bed, luxuriant with the ladies' extravagant hats, buzzing with civilized chatter. And when the ponies are paraded out to the starting line, the hats and suits train their high-tech, precision binoculars at them and scream with hysterical, infantile delight. The time I'd watched from the edge of the track, I'd noticed the sound—I mean, you couldn't really not notice it. But you only really hear it when it's directed at you. It's a kind of growl at first—bored, hungry, fractious—while you wait, tensed, to begin. And then, with the first whip crack, it rears up like a furious, demented beast. It sounds insatiable, but it finally spends itself in vicious laughter, crawling back to its den and regathering its strength and spite for the next race.

I wasn't ready for that sound, my first time. I stumbled at the starting line. My timing was off, my feet wouldn't hit the ground squarely. I finished sixth out of seven.

But by the end of that first race, I'd learned how you had to do it. You had to ride the crowd, to get buoyed up by their jeers, pushed along by the waves of lust and scorn and contemptuous admiration. And I knew that Annie wasn't really displeased with me. "There'll be more races, asshole," she said, slapping my butt and sending me to the stocks where losing ponies had to kneel for the rest of the afternoon in the dust behind the stands, available to anybody who might saunter by on their way to get a beer or a lemonade or to use the porta-potties.

Of course, Mr. Constant had me punished for losing. But then, he might have punished me for anything at all, so there was no point getting too upset about this particular obsession. What was important was that I'd figured out this pony racing thing. I can do this, I said calmly to myself. This is just the kind of bent, demonic thing that I can get behind.

And I did. I surprised everybody—except myself and Annie, I think—by winning the next race. Yeah, winning—fuck placing or showing. Blue ribbon winning.

"Interesting," he said. He stood up and loosened the sash of his robe.

He climbed onto the bed and straddled her, pulling her down between his legs and pushing his cock against her mouth, forcing her lips open, moving deeply into her throat, and coming quickly.

He closed the robe and sat back down.

"Go on," he said.

It was in New York—some huge estate near the Hudson River. Mr. Constant had business on Wall Street, and he brought Stefan and Tony and Annie and me along in a private plane. The racing sulky, too—taken apart into pieces and packed in the plane's hold. The estate had huge pony stables for events like this—there were dozens and dozens of stalls, filled with slaves and their trainers. It was busy, noisy, kind of cheerful. This was a much bigger competition than others that I'd been in. It was famous, an institution, really—slaves from all over showing their stuff. It spanned several days, though my pony race was one of the opening events. Trainers looked forward to this competition—it was a chance to see old friends, compare notes, complain about their accommodations, and show off their charges to each other. They chatted companionably, comparing training techniques and pony food (the one Annie was feeding me was predictably awful—pure nutrition).

"She's got a lot of talent," Annie said to a friend, as she shaved my cunt over a bucket the day of the race, "but she's especially got that kind of neediness, you know, that ponies have to have. I mean, you train them by letting them come every time they go around the track, and after that they never seem to learn that only the winner will get the treat at the end."

The friend laughed. "Kate says it's what's most charming about them."

Annie grimaced. "Well, Kate's pony Sylvie is the one to beat in this race," she said. "C'mon, asshole," she added to me, "last time around the track before the race—we'll let the sun dry off your snatch."

Kate? But it wouldn't be the same one, would it? Too unlikely, I thought. But I remembered what Margot, at the auction warehouse, had said. Kate knows everybody in this little world. Maybe it *was* the same Kate. I shuddered a little.

Annie shot a look at me. "Damn Kate," she said to her friend, jerking the ring in my collar as she led me out to the track to practice one last time. "I don't need to be thinking about her right now—and neither does this one."

And so we didn't. Or I didn't, anyway. I ran around the track, getting the feel of the ground under my feet and the angles of the curve at the end of the oval. I looked at the stands. They were big, like at a high school football game, only posher, of course. The crowd's yells would be deafening—Romans at the Coliseum. I took a long, calm breath, imagining it.

Annie stroked my breast. "Okay, Carrie," she said softly—she didn't usually call me Carrie—"I'm going to put everything I have behind my wrist this afternoon."

We had to hurry back to the stable, though, to get me ready, because we could see the first spectators beginning to trickle into the stands. And since mine was only the fourth race that day, we didn't have much time.

We entered the stall, and she kissed my mouth, slowly and deeply. She pushed my shoulders down and I knelt in the straw and kissed the whip she'd be using—she held it, doubled up, in her hand. She caressed my face and breasts with it, and then she put it against my lips again. I kissed it respectfully. I kissed it passionately.

I stood up and she knelt down to relace my boots. To smooth them over my calves and make sure the fine leather thongs were threaded correctly through the eyelets and around the hooks. To pull them tightly, tie them in strong, failproof bowknots. She slapped my ass, and I bent slightly and opened to receive the dildo attached to my tail. The grease on the shaft was cold; the horsehair tail prickled the back of my knees. And there was a new sensation—bits of smooth satin—they'd decorated the tail with ribbons. She harnessed me slowly, methodically, pulling everything tight, double-checking all the buckles, and finishing up by pinching my nipples in their decorative little clips.

I was almost glad to take the gag-bit in my mouth—it had felt empty after her kiss. And as for the blinders at the side of my face—I would have taken the track entirely blindfolded if she'd wanted me to. She stenciled my number across my belly, above my naked cunt. And instead of bringing somebody else in to lick my clit, she knelt down herself, making me tremble so hard that she had to pull away almost immediately. She was right, I was a natural pony—too greedy and stupid to know that I was being tricked. Or to care. "They usually have somebody with a pretty good tongue," she whispered spitefully to me, "at the finish line."

I was ready, I thought—to the extent that I was thinking at all. But not quite. "This is a very fancy race," she said to me, grinning at my helpless excitement. She attached a bright green ribbon cockade to the top of my bridle. "Each pony gets her own color." I guessed the ribbons in my tail were green as well. She pulled off her T-shirt and put on a green satin jacket with my number attached to the back. It looked like something a jockey would wear, except she didn't bother to zip it up. She looked tough, her hard little breasts partly visible through the opening of her jacket. She had a red-eyed lizard tattooed on one of them—it looked ready to skitter diagonally across her chest. I'd never seen that lizard; in fact, I'd never seen her in anything but her black sleeveless T-shirts. The bright green looked good against her pale skin and short white hair, and the lizard, one of its eyes partially obscured by the jacket's open zipper, seemed to wink at me as she moved.

Trumpets blared, and I heard the crowd cheer. They were announcing our race. I trotted out to the track, first parading by the stands, pausing briefly to receive their screams—I could detect the note of scorn, too: They knew I'd stumbled, my first time out. And then I waited, tensed, at the starting line, pulsing, quivering, dancing on my feet. I was aware of other ponies, but I didn't think of them as competition, I thought of them as the bright ribbons decorating their tails. They were the other hues vibrating on the spectrum. Green is in the middle—it's the toughest lane in the race—so there'd be ponies trying to head me off on both sides. I was glad.

And the race itself? Absurdly brief, after all the elaborate preparation. But it was as long as I could stand. And, well—I won, that's all. I mean, sometimes life is like that, you know: no complications, no reversals. Later for the intricacies of dodging and weaving, cutting off the other ponies and being cut off by them. All that would happen in other races, closer races, races I'd win by a nose or a neck or a hair, or not at all.

But not today. Today I was too fast for anybody to cut in front of, and I won, as I'd always known I would. I broke through the tape at the end of the course, and I fell, gasping, to my knees, and I felt hands all over me, roughly taking off my harness, pulling me upright. I felt a mouth on me—I looked down at a sweet curly head at my cunt, that was all I could see, I don't even know if it was a boy or a girl—and I came enormously, sighing and howling behind my bit, almost oblivious to the mocking laughter from the stands. I guess it's a cute moment, the final cruelty of the cruel event, watching the pony get her little yummy at the end. And then they led me to Mr. Constant, waiting with Stefan in the winners' circle.

He was delighted, of course, and the photographers were eager for shots of him with me kneeling at his feet, the blue ribbon pinned to my collar. It was good that I still had the bridle on, because I wanted to grin triumphantly at the cameras, instead of keeping my eyes down and my face impassive. I was feeling so cocky, you know—just controlling my gaze took quite a lot of discipline.

But of course you're never quite disciplined enough for what you'll encounter. A sudden, challenging demand from your master. Or the surprising swoops of your own desire.

Or, something much simpler, that day in New York. A foot, shod in white leather that was softer than my skin, prodding my legs further apart, silently and imperiously demanding that I show more of my naked—and suddenly very moist—cunt.

And a voice—well, first that husky, melodious laugh. "You're doing a good job with her, babe. Too good—I lost a pile of money on this race. But we'll beat you next time."

Kate. And those were Annie's black jeans, weren't they, and her scuffed Doc Martens, so close to Kate's crisp white slacks and soft, backless shoes? And Annie's voice, surprisingly subdued—shy-sounding, even.

"You were right. She's fun to drive."

"And to discipline, I should imagine."

They moved a little closer together, the black jeans pressing up against the white slacks. How far could I raise my eyelids without breaking form? I moved my gaze up Kate's legs, slowly, to the bottom of her white blazer. A little higher, now: Her arm was around Annie's waist. Or maybe her hand was in the back pocket of Annie's jeans—Annie would like that. Could I peek any higher? A little—up to her jacket button, to the pink faille waistcoat the color of the inside of a seashell.... And I knew that that was all I'd be allowed, that I'd never know what sort of hat she was wearing (funny how curious I was about that). And I'd simply have to imagine her cool, pale, limpid, dispassionate green eyes. I was surprised by how precisely I remembered her eyes—I mean, I'd only been in her presence maybe twice before. Briefly, and then only to be prodded a little, to have my form corrected and my progress assessed. Which was probably as much as I could ever expect from her.

She moved her hand over my bridle, tugging here and there to test the tension of the straps, laughing softly as she watched me drop my eyes and concentrate on my breath.

"And you've taught her some manners, I see."

I stared as hard as I could at her white shoes and the dusty ground, fighting the angry, frustrated tears welling up behind my eyelids. I hated Annie right then, with Kate's hand curved around her ass. I hated everybody in the small crowd

133

of people milling around, congratulating Mr. Constant. I hated Stefan, but then, I always did. And I especially hated the photographers, who could look at Kate all they wanted, and who were madly snapping pictures of her. She was talking to Mr. Constant now, congratulating him and also detailing the wonderful job Annie'd done on me. She was charming, and very knowledgeable about the race, almost as though she'd been a driver—or a pony—once herself.

"We got some marvelous footage of her crossing the finish line," she said. "So far in the lead that all you can see is Sylvie's knee and the toe of her boot. We're thinking about an online film clip—maybe a quick cut to her coming at the end. For the racing page."

Logical, I thought. My straining, fetishized body, digitized now, coming soon—and coming ecstatically—to a few thousand very select computer screens worldwide. I couldn't hear Mr. Constant's reply, but I could feel his exhibitionist delight, his hand tightening at my shoulder. Of course I'd been overhearing all the fascinated chatter, at parties and exhibitions, about the new private online system the association was building. Well, but who wasn't fascinated by online porn?

And then—was I hearing correctly?

"Lend her to me, Edouard. For the next two days. I have a scene scheduled and I need an extra girl."

Annie snorted. "And so you want my winning pony. Unbelievable, Kate." Well, I must have heard correctly— either that or I was dreaming.

Kate laughed again. "Look," she persisted, addressing herself to Mr. Constant, "we can do a trade. Take Randy. Annie can drive him and Tony in the boys' pairs race. It's the day after tomorrow, you've still got time to sign them up and she's got all day tomorrow to drill them. They'll be ravishing. Come on."

He stroked my head thoughtfully.

"Boys' pairs," he mused. "That's a nice race. And Stefan and I'll be in Manhattan all day tomorrow anyway." I felt Stefan's hand stroke me too. Surprisingly gently, for him.

Annie whistled through her teeth. "Unbelievable," she repeated, as a guy in khaki pants came over to us.

"Kate," he said, "sorry to bother you, but it's Sylvie. I think she'll cry herself sick."

She moved toward him. "Well, Edouard?" she said to Mr. Constant.

"Why not?" Mr. Constant laughed, and Kate stood on tiptoe to kiss his cheek. She turned to go with the guy in the khakis, first murmuring to Annie, "See you tonight, babe." And I kept my eyes down while the photographers snapped a few more pictures of me and Mr. Constant, this time with a less angry than usual Stefan and a blissful, giddy Annie— who, I noticed later, after they'd hung up the framed pictures on the wall of the trophy room back on the island, looked about sixteen years old at that moment—in her tough green jockey jacket with a happy lizard winking at the camera.

Jonathan grinned.

"I do remember her introducing me to Annie once—she's got a girl in every port, doesn't she? But you didn't actually spend two days with Kate, in New York?"

"Well, a day and a half. We came back in time for her to watch Tony and Randy win boys' pairs."

He grimaced impatiently.

135

"You didn't know?" she asked.

"She never told me. But then, I guess I made a point of not asking."

He looked down at the floor. "I should have known," he said.

She was silent and he concentrated on remaining calm.

"Well," he finally said, "what are you waiting for? Tell me about it."

Funny, she thought, that Kate hadn't told him. She paused a long moment before she continued.

CARRIE TELLS A STORY ABOUT KATE

"She's crazy," Annie said to Mr. Constant, as they promenaded around the lush, leafy estate grounds later that afternoon, leading me by the reins. People would come by to congratulate him on my winning the race. They'd compliment Annie on her driving too, and they'd stroke me, roughly or appreciatively.

"She's such a fucking workaholic," she complained. "I mean, how often do I get to see her, you know?"

He made some distant, sympathetic noises.

"And it's not like she needs the money," she ranted. "She rents this gorgeous house—the back lawn goes straight down to the river—but she can't just party, hang out. Oh, hell no. She's got to schedule scenes, develop accounts three thousand miles away from where she lives...."

She rattled on, blissfully unaware that she was boring him out of his mind. But he was charitable. He loved to win—to win anything at all, really—and an upset, a long shot like my victory, was just about his favorite thing in the world. So he maintained a comfortable silence, enjoying the victory promenade, and tolerating, or perhaps tuning out, her harangue.

While I, on the other hand, was straining to hear what she said. I could see how much she was enjoying it; she'd probably continue for hours if he'd let her. She was affecting this exasperation because she would have been embarrassed to admit how thrilled and delighted she was by that little "see you tonight" and what it promised. Her plaints about Kate's supposed craziness, obsessiveness, were really hymns, hosannas, hallelujahs. Bitching and moaning were ways she could keep talking, savoring her excitement.

And I understood so well, you see, because I was equally excited. *Lend her to me, Edouard.* I had no idea what it promised, but I kept repeating it to myself, hearing it in her voice. She'd said something similar, you know, long ago in San Francisco, when you first showed me to her, Jonathan. She suggested that you send me to her in Napa, if you were too bored or lazy to train me properly. And she laughed to see how excited I got, and how angry you became. You told me later to forget about it, that you'd never send me to her—but I didn't forget. I pranced behind Annie and Mr. Constant in a kind of dream haze, my tail, with its green ribbons, floating in the breeze. And I hardly noticed the hands that stroked and slapped me—everybody, superstitiously, wanting a piece of the winner.

But there was still that night's party to get through. I tried to gather my resources, to be alert to people's signals, as I wandered around my assigned territory, the blue ribbon pinned next to my coinbox. I'd try to focus on the nods and snaps of the finger, the slaps and kicks. But I was slow, dreamy, exhausted from the race and still thinking about Kate. From time to time, I'd hear the dull clanking sound of a lead token in the box at my throat, and my stomach would clench. But really, there wasn't much I could do about it. I would have collected some lead tokens no matter how I'd acted, since some people had lost big money on my race and wanted to take it out on me. And on Sylvie.

I'd never seen Sylvie before that afternoon—she'd been the indigo pony, I realized now. It wasn't hard to pick her out in the party crowd—the red ribbon on her collar was a clue, but mostly it was her beautiful gestures and manners. She bent and opened with the same kind of grace that you'd described Stephanie having. It was a special kind of polish, quite beyond anything I could have done even on a good night. And she was lovely, too, though perhaps less so than Stephanie. Well, not as lush—she looked like a racer, after all, which has its own kind of stripped-down aesthetic. She was slimmer than Stephanie, a tawny, tousled blond, with large gray-blue eyes, and freckles sprinkled over her wide cheekbones and high, very round, little breasts. And she had a subtle, sexy, French overbite. Perhaps it had been that overbite that had made Kate want to put a bit in her mouth in the first place.

I gazed at her curiously, at times when the party guests' demands and desires threw us into proximity. There was a slight blue cast under her eyes, from crying so hard that afternoon, I imagined. But she was quite recovered now, and certainly didn't deserve the harsh treatment she was getting—the commands spat at her, the bruises left on her skin.

She probably wasn't used to treatment like that. Nor to receiving demerit tokens—the hollow lead sounds at her throat must have been hard to bear, not to speak of the token master's affectation of surprise when he held up the lead disks later that evening, for the crowd to see. Or the audience's coarse, drunken, dull-witted shouts of delight. They'd already done a similar number on me, but not so elaborately. It's the elegant, polished slaves like Sylvie or Stephanie that the crowd goes wild about, when they get a chance to see them punished.

There were lots of other slaves up there on the dais that night, and quite a few had gotten demerit tokens. So there were lots of other little dramas to endure as the master went through the line, checking out the contents of everybody's coinbox. They make you wait up there if they've found lead in your coinbox. You kneel up with your hands at the back of your neck, your legs open wide, chest and belly and genitals as completely displayed as possible—the pose that Stephanie had struck in Madame Roget's bedroom. You wait for them to finish the stupid ceremony, the contest. And then they march you off to your punishment.

Except they didn't march me or Sylvie off. We remained kneeling on the dais as everybody else was led to the gauntlet they'd be running. And much of the audience had stayed in their places too.

The token master cleared his throat. What would the gentlemen and ladies say, he asked, to a rematch between these two troublesome ponies? A midnight race? Of course, he added, when the laughs and cheers and applause had subsided, we probably wouldn't be covering much ground this time.

Oh, yes, they loved that. And they all knew what he meant too, chuckling appreciatively as we were attached to whipping frames—two sets of posts set side by side in the ground, each set with a plank between them. We each stood behind a plank, spreading out our arms to be attached by our cuffs. The planks were high off the ground. When they moved my chin into the little valley sanded into the center of the plank—to keep my head still—I had to stand on my toes. I guess we both did, side by side as though we were at the starting line of a race. They strapped bridles to our heads, handing the reins to the punishment masters who'd be whipping us on. And I couldn't see Sylvie, but I knew that she'd be responding exactly as I was doing—as any real racing pony would have done. You feel the whip at your back and the pull at the soft inside of your mouth and you run—you raise your knees in elegant pony gait, and you run as fast as you possibly can. Even on bare feet when you're trussed up too high to land squarely. Even if you're running in place and there's no finish line to head for. You run until the crowd is satisfied and the whipping stops. And then you weep while they jostle to get close up, to poke and slap you, and to comment appreciatively on how nicely you've been marked.

They got bored pretty quickly though, and drifted away. I felt stupid and embarrassed to be left alone with Sylvie there. We listened to each other's sobs until the guy in khakis came and cut her down, kissing her gently, and carrying her off.

I had to wait a little longer for Annie to come get me, and of course she was too small to carry me. She was professional about taking care of me, though—she didn't flaunt the happiness in her eyes. She was sweet to me, too, gently rubbing salve into my wounds, cleaning the makeup off my face, kissing me goodnight as she put me to sleep in my stall. But I could tell that she wanted to get back to Kate. And I couldn't blame her. Anyway, I thought, I should sleep—it had been an exhausting day, and who knew what was going to happen tomorrow? Annie had said she'd tell them to let me sleep through breakfast. Good, I thought, I'd need it. But I was too excited to settle down. I tossed and turned, the straw in the stall tickling the bruises and welts on my ass. And the sky, I could see through the half-open stable door, wasn't entirely dark anymore, whenever it was that I finally drifted off.

So I was pretty wrecked when I woke up the next morning.

And of course I hadn't really been able to sleep through breakfast. The stable was far too noisy, ringing with the clatter of pans of food and galvanized buckets of water, the banging of doors and the creak of hinges, and the brisk, loud voices of grooms and trainers preparing for the day's events. Still, I was glad to be allowed just to lie there for a while. And then it got later and the sun got brighter. And I got a lot hungrier. Hungry and thirsty and tired and thrilled and nervous. But mostly hungry. Had they forgotten me?

I heard Annie's nasal little voice, cutting through the din. "...biting off more than she can chew. I mean, it's really all about him, you know?"

And a lower voice, a man's voice that wasn't as familiar to me. I couldn't make out all the words. "...he's not so bad...."

And Annie, a bit shrill this time, "Yeah, I know, he makes her happy. But he doesn't deserve...." And then, opening the door to my stall, "Oh, shit, she's up already."

I struggled to my knees, catching a glimpse of them before I remembered to lower my eyes. The guy who'd cut Sylvie down looked accusingly at Annie, and then relented a bit. "It's okay," he said, "you didn't really say much."

All of which would normally have inflamed my curiosity. But at that moment I was much too hungry to be curious, so I was soon gratefully—and literally—eating out of Annie's hand. She'd brought me an apple and, even more exciting, a banana, and I was quite beside my self with enjoyment. The guy disappeared, reappearing with a little trough of water for me to lap at, while he and Annie watched me wordlessly.

And after I came back from the latrine, Annie punched me lightly on the arm. "Okay, asshole, go with Steve now," she said. And to Steve, "Well, back to work," hurrying out to Tony and Randy, leaving him to take care of me and me to wonder about him. He had a thick mustache, and he was very muscular, wearing precisely ironed khakis again, and a light blue shirt. I could feel him looking coolly and steadily at me. Perhaps he was still angry at me, I thought, for having won yesterday's race.

I'd be an extra girl in Kate's scene, I thought, as Steve led me to a car with dark-tinted windows, closing the door after me. Which probably meant that Sylvie and Stephanie would be there as well, and probably they weren't going to be any friendlier than Steve. Well, you couldn't blame Sylvie, of course, but I wasn't looking forward to Stephanie either. Because when I'd first gone for pony training, she'd been there, in the same stable. And I'd loathed her, snooty little goody-goody with her flawless manners. My friend Cathy and I used to whisper through a knothole between our stalls at night. We'd giggle and make spiteful fun of Stephanie, like bad kids at summer camp. And Stephanie must have known, I thought. The kids who get made fun of at summer camp always know.

We were driving through the stone gates of an estate now, down a dense, overgrown narrow back road, the dappled sunlight flickering through the trees and the tinted car windows. I stared curiously up at the big story-book house Steve had parked in front of, and followed him up the stairs and through the silent entryway—graceful polished stairway to the right, lace-curtained double doors and large ferny houseplants in front of us and to the left.

"Two flights up," Steve said briefly to me, "first door on the right."

He watched as I walked silently up the thickly carpeted stairway, light from the stained-glass windows painting mottled, vivid designs on my naked skin. I climbed the second flight of stairs. First door on the right. The ceilings were high, the doors at least ten feet tall. I knocked, feeling like a small child.

I had hoped that it would be Kate behind that door, but I wasn't too surprised to find Stephanie, all tumbling black curls and huge blue-violet eyes, peachy skin and single dimple in her cheek. All smiles, too, but not friendly ones. She looked shrewd and calculating, nodding curtly and motioning me into the large room.

It was a nursery. Well, that's what it looked like, anyway—like that enormous Edwardian dormitory where Wendy, John, and Michael Darling had slept, in *Peter Pan*. I guessed that whoever owned the house had hired a decorator to create it for their kids, in a fit of upscale retro Anglophile whimsy. It wasn't a fancy sort of room; it was big and clearly expensive, but the decorator had gone for a sort of shabby, aristocratic, cold-showers-and-beef-tea asceticism. All the more dissonant, then, as a setting for Sylvie and Stephanie and me—naked in our collars and cuffs. Sylvie was lying on her belly on one of the small white iron beds, carefully making up her face in a mirror propped against the pillows. No smiles from her, not even evil ones. Just calm concentration on the mirror, a brief glance at me, and a determined glance at Stephanie, who nodded firmly, shutting the door behind me. The children's hour, I thought, gulping.

The room was full of toys, too, though not the kind the original owners had imagined—these toys were made of leather and latex and brass and iron. There were big wicker baskets filled with whips and restraints of various sizes and shapes. There were high-heeled shoes lined up at the scuffed powder-blue baseboard, and black corsets and garter belts hanging from hooks on the wall that once must have held sweet little smocked pinafores from Laura Ashley and overalls from Baby Gap and OshKosh B'Gosh. There were latex cocks on harnesses, too—a large selection of them, in all the colors of the rainbow. There were two-tone jobs, marbled ones. And some were translucent as well, with glitter embedded in the latex. All sizes and shapes—I mean, besides your traditional naturalistic ones, there were twists and bumps and spirals. I watched warily as Stephanie chose a handful—a bouquet—of them, strapped one on, and tossed another to Sylvie.

"I'll go first," she said to her, blowing her a kiss, "unless you really want to."

"No," Sylvie answered, coolly, "you go ahead."

But first Stephanie just walked around me, critically. "She's really not all that terribly pretty, is she?" she asked.

"Oh no," Sylvie answered, "but, well, she does have something, you know. Even Kate says so."

"Attitude, Kate says. Makes people want to hurt her."

"Umm, well, I can see that, yes. Too bad we only have permission to fuck her."

"Well, her ass is her best feature, after all."

I started to look around nervously, for the grease. I mean, they were going to grease that cock, weren't they, before Stephanie stuck it up my best feature? And I wasn't at all reassured when Stephanie positioned herself squarely in front of me, her voice icy. "Suck it, Carrie," she said.

I hesitated for a heartbeat. Did she mean that the only lubrication I'd get was my own saliva? And then, just before she had to push me down to my knees, I got down quickly, opened my mouth, and inhaled the monster, watching its shaft, in its obscene fuchsia color, disappear down my mouth to my throat.

Sylvie had gotten off the bed and was watching closely. "Deeper," she said to me. She smacked my ass with the cock that she hadn't strapped on yet. "Don't imagine you can hold back on us."

No, I didn't imagine I could. And yes, she was right. I could open my throat a little more widely. I could keep from retching, if I tried, if I gave it everything I had. I felt the latex fill my throat, in hollows that nobody usually touched. My eyes filled with tears, but I kept going down on that cock as though it were my life's work. I was frightened, disoriented. I mean, I'd known I wasn't their favorite person, but this didn't seem like Sylvie or Stephanie at all—more like their evil top twins. It was like getting to see the dark side of the moon. And then they blindfolded me—in soft, thick black velvet—and I couldn't see anything at all.

A hand grabbed the ring in the back of my collar ("silly-looking collar," I heard one of them sneer) and dragged me to one of the beds. I scrambled onto it, banging my shins, and raised myself up on my knees. And I breathed an enormous sigh of relief when one of them shoved some grease up my asshole.

They took turns fucking me—speeding up and slowing down, squeezing and slapping my breasts, and commenting dryly from time to time on my form, my looks, my performance. "Well, she can do this okay, anyway," I think that was Stephanie, very grudgingly—and from Sylvie, a giggled "I should hope so, or I'd lose all my respect for Jonathan." They tried different cocks, commenting on some of the more exotic ones, and giggling about how they looked in them. They kissed and stroked each other, too, I think, though I could only feel and hear it, rather than see it. I began to cry out—it was painful, and it was also arousing—but when I felt the tears soaking the blindfold, I knew I was crying because I was lonely. I wanted one of them to kiss or stroke me.

They didn't, of course. They left me kneeling on the bed and I guessed that they'd gone to one of the other little beds, where I could hear them giggling and kissing, hugging and poking and playing. And then deep moans, and I supposed that they'd taken off the cocks and were happily eating each other, crying out, and then ending with creamy sighs of contentment.

And whispers, then. "Oh, well, she took that pretty well, anyway," and "You can't really blame her for winning, I guess." More ominously, "She's probably not going to have an easy afternoon, after all," and then lots of stuff I couldn't hear, until Stephanie called out to me, "You can come into bed with us if you want, you know."

I tore off the blindfold. It was difficult not to take a

flying leap, and it was delightful to have them touch and kiss me. "Kate lets you make love to each other?" I asked.

Stephanie laughed. "Well," she said, "not all the time. But for treats, yes, she does. Because, you know, Sylvie was so miserable last night, losing to you. We never expected that to happen, after all. Well, nobody did." I forbore to say that I had. I mean, no point messing up this good thing I seemed to have going with them all of a sudden.

She continued, "And, anyhow, Kate says that it's a male thing, that business of being so stingy with a slave's sexuality. Because it seems to us there's always enough to go around—well, we never have any problem with it, anyway."

And Sylvie added, "And neither does Randy."

They giggled at that, and so did I. The evil twins had disappeared, leaving me rolling around in bed with Marcia Brady and Laurie Partridge. It was goofy, silly, a little like being part of the Babysitters' Club, but it was fun anyway. We messed around a while longer and then we took showers, toweling each other's backs. We did each other's fingernails; this was serious business, they had to be short and their edges silken-smooth. A maid—part of the staff that came with the rented house—brought us lunch, little troughs of food and water. She was terrified, uncertainly putting the troughs down on the floor, as Steve must have told her to do, and skittering out the door.

The food was as wholesome and charmless as any food I'd gotten anywhere. Stephanie and Sylvie assured me that the food Kate gave them at home in California was a lot better, though they admitted that it was also pretty bland and healthy. They talked a lot about Kate—and home—beginning at least half of their sentences with, "Kate says...." They seemed to feel that living with Kate was their real home—their real life, and not some kind of fantastic intermission from it. Happy families, I thought. Wow—they're not alike at all.

"But, you know, even the others at home get to have sex with each other, sometimes, for treats," Sylvie was saying.

"The others?" I asked.

They pouted a little at my question. But then they patiently explained. It seemed that Kate owned the both of them and Randy outright—her name was on their papers. But the other six slaves at the place in Napa were owned by Kate's corporation.

"Well, she might fuck one of them, there's nothing stopping her. And we're all trained together in the mornings and disciplined together in the late afternoons. Steve takes care of a lot of the details, but it's really Kate that everybody tries to please. Still, it's different with us three, because we keep her satisfied on a daily basis. We bathe her, do her nails, and she takes us to bed with her. Mostly, they take care of clients. Which we do too, of course. But she's our mistress. I'd hate it if I didn't have one mistress, or a master, I guess, to please."

"Well, there's Marco," Sylvie said pensively. "Sometimes, I think that if Kate didn't own me, I'd want…"

"Marco?"

Sylvie explained. "He lives at Kate's. She boards him, trains him, has him worked and used along with the rest of us. And sometimes—sometimes quite suddenly—his mistress appears and he's all hers. I was there last week, serving tea, when she visited—she'd shown up without calling or anything—and they'd had to find Marco on one of the pony trails and unharness him, and wash him down quickly. And then they led him in, looking very pretty I must say, and he kissed her feet and presented, and she examined him very carefully—I love it when somebody looks me over that carefully—and then she complimented Kate on how improved he was. And you could see how happy he was. I mean, it must be wonderful, that moment, when you haven't even prepared or anything, and you know that they're pleased with how you're coming along. It must make the time you're separated...I don't know, romantic."

Stephanie shrugged, obviously less romantic in her tastes. "Well, anyway, we serve her directly. I'd hate it any other way."

"And when Jonathan comes to visit?" I asked.

"Oh, he gets everything he wants," she laughed, "us, her, anybody else. And lately, she's been trying out entertainments for him, things she's working up for important clients. We all try extra hard, too—even Steve, lately, have you noticed, Sylvie?—we're all extra sweet to him because Kate's in such a good mood when he's there.

"But a lot of what we do," she continued, "is help her with her scenes. I mean, she uses the others when she has to, like she's using you today, but mostly, the three of us have it sort of covered."

She added that I'd see what they were talking about soon enough.

I could feel my nervousness returning.

"So, uh, could you prepare me a little for what I'll have to do?" I asked.

But they said that they'd been forbidden to.

"And anyhow," Stephanie said, "it's getting late, and we have to get dressed. The best thing is probably for us to get dressed ourselves first. And then we'll dress you."

I watched them lace each other into black corsets, roll high black stockings over their legs, tromp around in six-inch spike-heeled shoes like they were wearing Keds. They dressed me exactly as they were dressed. And then we all sat down in front of mirrors, at the window, in the summer sunshine, and made up our faces.

The window looked out back across a smooth, emerald expanse of lawn, sloping down to the Hudson River. There was a path along the water's edge, and I watched Steve running powerfully along it, and then uphill, to the house. His white shorts and T-shirt were sweaty, sticking to the muscles in his hips and stomach.

"Poor Steve," Sylvie chuckled. "The one awful thing about this scene that's coming up is that he has to play butler, which he'd never do at home, and answer the door and serve drinks. It's a real indignity—he has quite enough work looking after us and supervising Kate's events. But the real butler in this place is hopeless. They really cheated Kate on the quality of the staff."

"Well, it'll be any minute now," Stephanie said, "so he'd better hurry and get dressed, even if he wants to wait until the very last instant to get into his uniform."

They told me that we could look out the other windows, the ones facing the front of the house, so that we could see the guests arriving.

"Don't worry," Sylvie kissed me lightly on the forehead. "It's just like playing pretend. You'll see."

And Stephanie stroked my breast as we peered out the front window. "You'll be fine," she whispered. "You just have to obey."

And there they were, our guests, driving up the semicircular driveway in front of the house. I was fascinated by the low, beautiful open car, its flawless dark green paint mirroring the house, the lawn, the sky and flower beds in elegant curved lines that receded to their own little vanishing points, its spoked wheels reflecting the sunlight in dizzying double spirals. I don't even know the names of cars like that. "Is it, uh, a Jaguar?" I asked hesitantly, which Sylvie and Stephanie found hysterically funny—quaint, almost.

Steve looked fantastic in his livery, too, dignified and utterly at ease. Except for his thick black hair being slightly damp from the shower, he looked as if he'd been doing nothing all day but, well, whatever it is butlers actually do all day. He opened the car door now, helping a young woman out, while the driver got out on his side and then handed him a small suitcase. They were pretty, these guests, and beautifully dressed. I liked his cream linen suit, her pink and white candy-striped summer dress, the widebrimmed straw hat she carried, with its pink grosgrain ribbon around the crown.

And they were young. Maybe three years or four older than I was, but babies. I looked at Stephanie, peering through her window pane, her moistened lips parted with anticipation and amusement. She smiled at me, gesturing with her long lashes at the couple who were now walking up the wide steps to the front door. "I was never that young," she whispered, and I nodded. I didn't know how old she was, but she seemed ageless, a beautiful toy created eons ago to entertain an emperor.

We could hear Kate greeting them now, her throaty voice tinged with amusement. "Mr. Putnam, it's very nice to see you again. How are you today?"

Embarrassed murmur. Perhaps he was asking her to call him by his first name.

"Andrew, then, yes. And this is the young lady who needs some help with her manners, I take it?"

Another embarrassed murmur, still from the young man. And then a tiny, terrified voice, but clear and piping, "Thank you for taking the time with me, Ms. Clarke."

Answered sternly by Kate, "Well, we'll just have to see now, won't we?"

Sylvie whispered, "They're terribly rich, those two. I read about them going to openings, things like that. And their wedding, fantastic, her wedding gown: the beading took weeks. I think this is her birthday present to him. But maybe not. Maybe his to her."

"What's happening now?" I asked. I'd heard them all go into a parlor, and the door shutting behind them.

"Oh, not much yet," Stephanie said. "Steve is serving drinks to Kate and the young gentleman, while the young lady is taking off her clothes and learning how to kneel at attention in the center of the room. Kate'll call us in a minute. Do you have everything, Sylvie?"

Sylvie nodded. Then they both turned to me, looking me over carefully. "You need fresh lipstick, Carrie," Stephanie said. "Quick, Sylvie'll put it on you."

Sylvie had just finished with me when we heard the sound of a little silver bell, and immediately we got up and floated down the stairs on our spike heels, silently and rapidly, in single file. Sylvie and Stephanie were carrying baskets of complicated clothing and hardware, but I didn't know any of the routines, so I was embarrassingly empty-handed.

In the parlor, the sunlight was diffused through heavy cotton lace curtains.

The young gentleman was sitting in an armchair, holding a drink in his hand and looking even younger than I'd expected, now that I could see him face to face. There were a few copper freckles across a short, sunburned nose, and, though he had a beautiful, expensive haircut, you expected to see cowlicks. He was big—you could see powerful thighs under the cream linen slacks. And he was pale and thrilled, staring at his wife, who stood in front of Kate, blushing, trembling, a few silent tears sliding down her flushed cheeks. She was dressed only in her ivory stockings, flat shoes, and a narrow garter belt that seemed to be nothing but little pink satin roses. She was all the colors of a rose, in fact—one of those little ivory ones you can buy inexpensively on the street, their petals edged in pink. The wispy tendrils of hair in front and behind her small ears were almost tow-colored, the hair above her cunt more like honey.

While Kate, curled up on an ottoman upholstered in Turkish kilim fabric, looked like a gorgeous moth, in a filmy pale green silk shirt and loose black slacks. Her sandals lay on the floor next to the ottoman. She was barefoot, her finger- and toenails a dark mauve color. She rested her chin in one of her hands thoughtfully, while the other one cruelly probed the young lady's cunt.

"You've never restrained or disciplined her?" she was asking the young gentleman. "Not even used her silk scarves to tie her to the bedpost?"

He shook his head.

"Good," she said. "She's like a pampered baby. It will be a great pleasure to teach her obedience." And then, moving

153

her hand between trembling thighs, she probed in the direction of the young lady's asshole. I heard a little intake of breath. "Don't hide from me, you little bitch," Kate said evenly. "I'll turn you inside out if I want to."

"But first," she said, turning back to the young gentleman, "let's get her properly outfitted." She nodded to Sylvie and Stephanie, who stepped forward with their baskets of shoes, clothing, and assorted hardware.

"And Carrie," she continued, smiling at him, "will amuse you while you watch."

There was no mistaking what that meant. I knelt in front of him, unbuttoning his pants, taking his engorged cock gently in my mouth. Although he sighed contentedly, I could tell that most of his attention was focused on his wife, being stripped and then dressed in the clothes from Sylvie and Stephanie's baskets—dressed and collared and cuffed.

I wished I could watch, but they were standing behind my back. I could hear little squeals every so often from the young lady, and I supposed they were lacing her into the tight black corset I'd seen in the basket—the same sort we were wearing.

"Little steps, little steps, that's it, sweetheart," Stephanie cooed softly to her, doubtless walking her around the room for the first time in her six-inch spikes.

And then, just before the young man grabbed my head and started breathing hard and probing for the back of my throat, I heard a little click, the unmistakable click of a spring lock in a collar. "Got it," Sylvie murmured, just as a small river of hot cum spurted into my mouth. He did have timing, our young gentleman.

He pushed me aside, sending me crashing onto the floor, and when I picked myself back up onto my knees I saw him sprawled in the armchair, a little smile on his face as he contemplated the tableau arranged in front of him: Sylvie and Stephanie with his terrified tow-headed wife between them, all of them arrayed identically in their black corsets, stockings, spike-heeled shoes, collars, and cuffs. Downcast eyes, gently heaving bare breasts. Three slaves, meekly awaiting his pleasure.

"Look at me, Jane," he said, and she slowly raised her eyes to him. A few tears slipped down her cheeks.

"But you're very rude," he continued. "You must always acknowledge me when I speak to you. Didn't I tell you that in the car?"

I wasn't surprised at how much of a struggle it was for her to get the words out. She had to try several times, until she was able to shape the words, and even then it came out as almost a whisper, "Yes, my lord."

His face shone with awe at hearing the words he'd only dreamed about coming out of her mouth. He wasn't sure of where to go next with it, though, and I saw him sneak a glance at Kate, for reassurance, and register her almost invisible stage prompt.

"I like to see you dressed like that," he continued. "In the future, at home, there will be one particular servant charged with dressing you as a slave when I wish it. But I'm afraid that she won't be as gentle with you as these young ladies have been."

And when she didn't answer he spoke more sharply. "No answer for your lord, Jane? Well, her other job will be to whip you, whenever you need it, like right now."

"Get down on your knees, you disobedient little slut," Kate said lazily, and Sylvie and Stephanie helped her down, as she wept out her apologies, promising always to remember to address him in the future when he spoke.

"I think, Andrew, that we should begin by introducing her to the riding crop," Kate continued, walking across the room to an umbrella stand and picking one out.

"What do you think of this one?" she asked him, but he smiled and shrugged his shoulders, shaking his head. His wife, he said, was a horsewoman and would know a good riding crop, though. Of course, he supposed that feeling it laid on her flesh would be quite a different thing from using one.

I could see her look of outrage as Kate passed it over her breasts, tapping them lightly. "Likes horses, does she?" she asked. "Perhaps later you'd like to try her in a bit and bridle, then. But not right now. Right now, I think we'll just bend her over a block and teach her how to count the blows when we hurt her, hmmm?"

He smiled again and nodded, and, at Kate's command, Sylvie and Stephanie pushed a large block of hardwood into the center of the room. It was about three feet on each slightly rounded edge, and it looked as though it had been worn smooth by having generations of penitents kneel over it. Maybe it had, for all I knew. The young lady knelt over it, Stephanie gently prodding her into place, until she was nicely, if precariously, balanced over it, Sylvie and Stephanie each holding one of her arms.

"Twelve," Kate announced, as though any fool could see that twelve strokes of the riding crop was exactly what was needed in this situation. And, tapping the young lady's thigh lightly with the crop, she told her that she should call out each blow by number, being sure to thank her master as well.

"Yes, Ms. Clarke," the young lady replied, and Kate handed the riding crop to the young man.

"Try it on your own hand first," she said, "and then on Carrie."

He had a strong arm. And he was also a quick study, learning to use his wrist to make the crop whistle through the air. Leaning over a little table in the corner, I tried not to cry out too loudly. No use frightening his sobbing wife more than she already was. But on the other hand, I thought, no use letting her think she was in for a walk in the park. And anyway, I knew that no sound I could make would be as frightening as the thin, high whistle the riding crop was making. I let myself whimper, and I was weeping softly by the time he'd finished. But I think I did okay, because as I turned and dropped to my knees to thank him, I saw Kate's approving nod.

He waved me away impatiently, though, turning back to his wife, who was waiting bent over the block in the center of the room. His broad back obscured most of my view of her, and all I could tell about what she was feeling was from the cries she made, and the sound of her voice, as she kept count of the blows.

Her first cry was more one of rage than of pain, astonishment almost, that he would really dare to hurt her. She managed a gasping, prideful dignity through a few of the next blows, but the cries and sobs finally broke through. And after he'd finished, and she'd sobbed out "twelve," Sylvie and Stephanie had a difficult time nudging her into an upright kneeling posture in front of him, where she could thank him for the beating, and promise to keep his rules better in the future.

She managed it, though, and then Stephanie snapped a leash to her collar, and led the couple, Jane crawling on hands and knees, up the back stairs, where I guessed that a room had been prepared for them. And I figured that Stephanie would be staying with them, to fetch and carry, to be an extra mouth or tongue if needed, and just (just!) to watch, to witness, to make it impossible for Andrew, and especially for Jane, to forget that this was not just a fantasy, this was happening in the real, all-too-physical world.

I didn't know whether or not I should be helping Sylvie tidy up the room, but Kate nodded to me to stay on my knees.

"You did well, Carrie," she said. And then she turned her attention to Sylvie, who had put everything away, and had dropped down to her knees as well, the neatly packed baskets lined up at her side.

"Come here, darling," she said, and Sylvie crawled over to the big red plush armchair where she was sitting and kissed her feet. "Good," Kate said softly. And then, "Present, darling. I haven't had time to look you over today."

It was a long presentation too, perhaps because Sylvie had collected quite a few bruises and welts, at the race yesterday and then at the party. I watched her serene face, her open mouth, as Kate bent over her, prodding her, lightly and sometimes not so lightly. What had she said earlier? *I love it when they look me over carefully.* She did, too, breathing deeply, sometimes gasping rapturously. And then she kneeled up and Kate smiled at her, kissing her gently on the mouth. "Very good," she said. "Steve said you took your whipping well last night, too, and you all did very well this afternoon."

"You'll serve dinner," she said, "you two and Carrie, at eight. I think we'll get little Jane to help, too—she'll probably find waiting table every bit as humiliating as anything I'll have her do while they're here."

She stood up then. Which must have been a signal, because Sylvie sprang into action. Gently, but quickly and deftly, she unzipped the silk pants, unbuttoned the blouse, expertly laying the clothes on the back of a chair so that they wouldn't wrinkle. It seemed that Kate hardly had to move, except to stretch, and then to settle back into her chair and pick up the drink she hadn't finished.

"Come here, Carrie," she said, and I crawled forward. It was hard to keep my eyes down, I wanted to look at her so badly. At her breasts, her skin—Renoir skin, I hadn't known it really existed—at the pink and brown and apricot at her cunt.

And to Sylvie, she said, "Beat her on the breasts."

"Yes, Kate."

I watched Sylvie go to the umbrella stand to get the proper whip. I knew they'd use the same small whip Annie used, and I steadied my breathing, propped my hands under my breasts, and arched my back to receive the strokes. "Not too hard," Kate cautioned Sylvie. "I'll want you to do it again tomorrow morning while Andrew watches."

And then she sighed contentedly, sipping her drink, her other hand creeping to her cunt. "And I'll just have to rough it and do myself while I watch," she smiled, "since the two of you will be occupied. We really need another mouth around here, don't we? Amazing how spoiled one gets."

Andrew asked about the marks on my breasts later that evening, at dinner, as he helped himself to potatoes from the platter I held at his elbow. "May I touch her?" he asked, as he laid the silver serving utensils back on the platter. Kate nodded, and he traced the painful red lines with a thick index finger. I kept still, breathing softly. "But they'll fade by tomorrow," Kate said. "So after breakfast, we'll give her some new ones."

"It's very provocative," he said.

"And I imagine it would hurt her quite a bit," he added, "if I slapped her, where she's marked, and uh, clamped, you know." He touched one of the little silver bells Steve had clipped to my nipples, making it ring softly and melodiously.

Kate laughed. "I imagine it would. She's not mine, you know, but she's had some good training…well, since the last time I saw her, anyway. So I don't think she'd cry out. And she certainly wouldn't spill those potatoes."

He moved his chair back, to get a better swing. And no, I didn't spill the potatoes. I held them carefully, even remembering to hold them away from me so that I wouldn't get any tears on the platter.

"Ah yes," Kate said, "training is everything. And those bells have a pretty sound, don't you think?

"But," turning to Andrew again, "it will be a good lesson for you—watching her being whipped tomorrow. It'll teach you a little precision." And then, throwing a stern look at Jane, who was holding a bowl of creamed peas and onions in trembling hands, "And if you drop those peas, Jane, we'll slap your breasts until you scream."

We four—Sylvie and Stephanie and Jane and I—had been fed earlier, from a communal trough of raw vegetables and whole grains, on the kitchen floor. Jane had knelt hesitantly when she saw the other three of us silently getting to our knees under Steve's stern look. Well, she'd seen more than the expression on his face—she'd also seen his hand moving to the little rubber truncheon that hung from his belt.

And after we'd eaten, and bathed, and made ourselves up again (Jane timidly copying the rest of us), he inspected each of us, straightening collars, moving stray tendrils of Stephanie's hair into place. We were barefoot, and completely naked, except for narrow wreaths of flowers around our heads, the leather restraints at our wrists and throats, and the bells that he'd produced at the last minute. The bells did have a lovely sound—so soft and subtle that they seemed to mingle with the flowers' perfume, wafting around the room on the warm breezes that floated in off the river, as the evening slowly darkened in the candlelit dining room.

As I crossed to the sideboard to put down my serving bowl and drop to my knees until I'd be needed again, I saw Andrew's eyes move from my breasts to Jane's. They were pretty, just a bit heavy for her slender frame, and I could see that he wanted them criss-crossed with painful red lines too. And I knew that she could see it, as well. Her face flushed and at first her eyes looked frightened, and then I could see a new knowledge gathering within them. I watched her back straighten, her breasts lift under his fascinated gaze. Happy birthday, Jane, I thought, and I wished suddenly that I were back on the island, Mr. Constant's eyes on me as I preened for Annie in the corral. I was envious, I realized. Of Jane, but really, of course, of Stephanie and Sylvie.

Especially Sylvie. Because Kate, you see, had not just "done herself," as she'd said she would that afternoon. I mean, she started that way, caressing herself while Sylvie skillfully laid those even marks on my breasts. But she was also watching carefully, too carefully to abandon herself to pleasure. She called out sharply when I'd had enough, and then, her voice clotted with desire, she called Sylvie to her, and pulled her head, by its honey-blond hair, down to her cunt. And only then did she let go, moaning delightedly under Sylvie's mouth while I watched helplessly, invisibly, still presenting for the beating that was over and done with. I remembered what Stephanie'd said up there in the nursery. She'd been right: You needed a master or mistress all your own. It was awful, being—what was that phrase Kate had used?—an extra girl.

So I was glad to concentrate on clearing away plates and dishes, and to help serve dessert and coffee. And anyway, things had begun to get a bit strained at the table, the conversation becoming rather halting as Andrew grew content simply to look at Jane, and to drift off into reveries. I thought Kate would just send them to bed—it appeared to me that the scene had been a big success—but she seemed surprisingly edgy.

"You would like to see her bridled, wouldn't you?" she asked sharply, and when he nodded absentmindedly, she called Steve over and whispered something to him, causing a hint of a scowl to appear at the corner of his well-behaved mouth, below the squared-off edge of his mustache. He disappeared, and soon after, Kate told the four of us to go out the back door to the garden shed, and let the regular house servants finish clearing away.

"We're just camping out here, after all," she smiled at Andrew. "There isn't a regular stable, but we've set up a kind of makeshift tackroom and there's a nice two-seater pony cart. I thought Sylvie and Carrie could take us for a little night ride while Jane learns a few of the basics."

He agreed politely, and the four of us filed out, Sylvie and Stephanie exchanging little shrugs as soon as they were outside Kate's purview. Sylvie raised her eyebrows and nodded in my direction, and Stephanie scowled back at her— Steve's scowl in graceful miniature. I followed Jane, surprised at how confident and serene her step had become, as we walked barefoot across the soft grass of the back lawn, to the gardening shed, which was down near the river, and where Steve was waiting to harness and bridle us.

He hadn't had time to take off his dark blue butler trousers, but he'd put on a fresh pale-yellow oxford cloth shirt. I thought of an actor in a repertory company, who has to double up on roles, making bits and pieces of costume do double duty during quick scene changes. The trousers were disconcertingly stodgy and butler-like, even with the leather suspenders dangling down his hips. But the shirt, the cuffs folded one impeccable turn up over his powerful forearms, was every bit as much a costume. I mean, he was clearly playing the role of Steve now, whose job it was to get us harnessed and bridled in no time flat.

I watched Jane, wondering how she'd respond to being harnessed up her first time. And she surprised me, bending and opening so eagerly and obediently that you couldn't miss how much she was enjoying Steve's hands on her. Oh dear, I thought, I don't think this was supposed to happen.

Steve led an eager Jane and a slightly grim Stephanie to a pole, attaching their collars to the long thin chains that hung from the top, in a kind of maypole arrangement. They'd circle the pole, Jane copying Stephanie, as Steve put them through all the elementary pony gaits—walk, trot, canter. It's how you begin pony training, you know, and it's not as easy as it looks. But it all seemed blurred, somehow, by the confusion in the air—confusion that I felt inexplicably guilty about, as though there were a way that I, and only I, could set things to rights.

Although what, realistically, could I possibly do, standing there in my boots and bridle and tail? Well, if you could use the word realistic to describe the scene at all. Maybe, I thought, I'd better just chill out and enjoy the ride.

It's not my problem, I thought, as Steve harnessed us to a two-seater pony cart on the path by the river. Hey, I told myself, as he pulled straps and buckles tight against me, I'm only a pony, and I'm not responsible for whatever strange emotional muddle these people have got themselves into. The tight harness held me upright when I almost blacked out for a few moments after the clips came off my nipples. And then I just enjoyed the breeze, and the moonlight on the river, and the feel of Sylvie—her warmth, her breath, her smell—strapped and harnessed next to me. Kate stepped into the cart, with Andrew after her, and snapped the whip over us; we trotted obediently, sharing our understanding of the reins' tugs at our mouths, the whip's sting at our asses. After you've raced, you know, a gentle night trot can seem like the height of polite civility. Although toward the end I began to wish that we could go faster, so that I could show off more. But maybe, I thought then, she didn't want us—me—to get too tired. Because maybe, later tonight, when she was finally finished with Jane and Andrew, maybe, I thought, Kate would…well, I was afraid even to think about it.

But she didn't. She kept Stephanie with her that night, and Steve put Sylvie and me to bed in the nursery, chaining us so that we couldn't touch ourselves or each other, and warning us not even to think of whispering. Silly of me to have imagined

164

anything else, I thought, willing myself to sleep, to forget the day's confusions and frustrations. And when I did sleep, my dreams were crowded with sitcom and fairy-tale characters in lascivious positions, eagerly sucking and eating each other, within overlapping dream narratives that gobbled each other like snakes swallowing each other's tails.

And after Sylvie had punished my breasts again the next morning, for Andrew's instruction and entertainment, I thought of those dreams again. And of the end of *Through the Looking Glass*, when Alice wonders who had dreamed all these adventures, she or the White King.

Well, Andrew'd paid for the scene after all, so I guessed that made him our young white king. The scene had been his dream, the rest of us symbolic actors within it. Only I wasn't so sure. I glanced at him in his armchair, Jane kneeling between his legs, her naked back against his groin. He leaned forward, forearms on his knees, eagerly drinking in Kate's hints and instructions, his big hands on Jane's bare breasts. Kate had positioned her that way, so that she could also watch me being beaten. And also, I suspected, so that Andrew wouldn't notice the slight disappointment that had started up in her eyes when breakfast had been served by the house's real butler, Steve being conspicuously absent.

The visit wound down quickly. There was a light buffet lunch with champagne and a birthday cake for Jane, decorated with lilies of the valley and candied violets. Jane looked chic and grown-up now, in a short black cotton knit dress, bare legs and sandals, and she chattered to Kate, in a brittle and determined voice, about the last Gaultier show, while Andrew watched her proudly and possessively. And then the butler—the real one, again—carried their bag out to their beautiful car and they got in and drove away. And soon after that, Kate and Steve brought me back to Mr. Constant, and they all watched Tony and Randy win the boys' pairs race.

"And she never made love to you?" Jonathan asked slowly.

"No," she answered, "and that made me very sad, you know, because I did want her very badly. And maybe I was kidding myself, but I thought she wanted me too. But I guess I was wrong.... Because, you know, I've thought about this over and over, and I'm sure of it...the whole time I was there, in that house, she never once touched me."

He made a small noise that she couldn't decipher. Amusement, amazement, and something else, she wasn't sure what. Happiness, she surprised herself by thinking. Yes. She'd never seen him so happy.

"Oh, she wanted you, all right," he said. "You weren't kidding yourself there. She wanted you so much that she lost control of her scene a little at the end. No wonder Steve got ticked off at her."

She shrugged in bewilderment.

"Oh, come on," he said. "I mean, you told me the story yourself. The story she wanted you to tell me. Well, she wouldn't have expected you to observe Jane and Andrew, not to mention Steve, in such detail, but..."

"But?"

" ...but she wanted you to tell me that she practically staged that whole scene around you...and she didn't touch you. Because she didn't think she had a right to."

"But Mr. Constant wouldn't have cared...."

He shook his head.

CARRIE

Okay, I guess I did understand. Typical, Carrie, I thought; you knock yourself out trying to understand what was really going on. Was it Andrew's story? Jane's? Maybe you even thought it was yours. And the answer's been there the whole time. Annie told you that morning in the stable. It's all about him—Jonathan. Or it finally became so, when you obligingly delivered Kate's message for her.

He sat down on the side of the bed and stroked my shoulders. "You're chilly," he said. "Come on under the covers, I'll warm you up."

I hadn't noticed how cold I felt. He lay on top of me, kissing me slowly, holding my hands.

"I can understand why you found it so confusing at her place—all the overlapping scenarios everybody's playing. It used to drive me bats. But she keeps it remarkably coherent—I mean, this was an unusual situation, her lusting after you and not letting herself have you—mostly she runs quite a tight ship. Anyway, one gets used to it. You'll see.

"Look," he said then, "I know we're not done with our storytelling. But can we take a break for a while?"

"Okay," I said sadly, "I guess."

"Things will get clearer, I promise. There's more story to go. Indulge me." He smiled as he said it—probably, I thought, a lot like how he would smile at Marilyn the receptionist.

He picked up the phone, to make dinner reservations. It would be the first time we'd be eating anywhere you'd need a reservation. Pretentious, snobby, I thought, absurdly.

"Well, we didn't have any lunch," he said briskly, as though I'd asked him for an explanation. And then, continuing to smile, "Why don't you wear your little black skirt, okay? and you've got a little short black T-shirt, right?...so there'll be this half-inch of skin above the top of the skirt...."

And, not too surprisingly, the food was great—incredible really, famous, he said—and dinner was fun. He'd been reading this article in a French architecture journal. Well, trying to read it—he needed help with some of the vocabulary. Not the technical terms, of course. He explained some of them to me, as they came up, and I remembered that he was a terrific explainer—he liked talking about buildings, and about what he actually did when he was running a CAD program, the ways it was better than the old ways of doing things, and the ways it wasn't. But the author of the article had used another kind of technical vocabulary as well, borrowed from literary criticism, which was what he needed help with. He nodded appreciatively as I ran through the basics.

"Well, there's something to that, I guess," he said. "Maybe I'll give it another shot."

And then we were both silent, sipping our coffee, looking at each other.

We were still silent when we got back to the hotel room. We were nervous, fumbling with buttons and zippers.

"Hold it," he said, going to the bed and sitting down on it. "Come over here, in front of me." He peeled off the little black T-shirt, pulled the skirt off over my head. He finished unbuttoning his shirt and opened his pants, pulling off the belt, taking off his shoes. He'd already helped me with my cowboy boots, thank goodness, and I knew he didn't want me to take off the black stockings and garter belt. I knelt in front of him, kissing his belly, the muscles, the fine black hair. His cock was stiffening between my breasts, and I'd begun nibbling slowly downward, when he stopped me, lifting my chin with the knuckle of a bent index finger.

"It's time," he said softly, "for you to come back to me, don't you think?"

Had he planned it to happen this way? I didn't think so. I knew he had more to tell me. And I had another story for him too. I stared dazedly at him, my chin still resting on his finger. He stroked my jaw with his thumb. He was still smiling, but there was something darker in his eyes, and at the corners of his mouth.

"That's right," he said, "take a little time to get used to it. There's plenty of time."

But what about the rules, the arrangements? I need to know more, I thought, I need to come to terms. But I didn't know how to ask. The lines of force between us had shifted, the iron filings lined up around the poles of the magnet. I leaned forward—I didn't know what was holding me up, the energy field or his finger under my chin. And I decided that I knew everything that I needed to know. He could tell me whatever he chose. Moment by moment. Or not at all.

I lowered my eyes, relaxed my jaw. I felt my back straighten, my body rearrange itself under his gaze. He traced my eyelids with his fingertips.

"Good, good," he said, in a soothing tone. "Oh, yes, that's my good girl. Now tell me what you are."

And I wasn't surprised by how matter-of-fact my voice sounded.

"I'm your slave, Jonathan," I said.

Bingo. Just like that. The jolt to the solar plexus. I wanted to come right then, between her tits. No. Not now.

"My belt's on the floor," I said, "next to your right knee. Get it for me."

She bent gracefully, picked it up with her mouth, and dropped it into my outstretched hand. It was a shame I didn't have anything better, I thought, but this would have to do for now. I stuffed one of my handkerchiefs into her mouth and tied it in place with another. A nice, gentlemanly, old-fashioned habit, using big cotton handkerchiefs. I'd learned it—and a lot of other stuff that has come in handy over the years—from my Uncle Harry.

"On the bed," I said, "hands and knees. You won't need to count the strokes. I'll beat you until you can't hold position any more."

I knew that she wouldn't cheat. And when she did finally collapse on the bed, sobbing behind the handkerchief gag, I could see that she was ashamed that she hadn't lasted it out any longer.

I took off the gag, and then I sat down in the armchair to wait while she cried a little more. But she was already scrambling to her knees on the floor at the side of the bed. She was sobbing silently, her breasts heaving, huge tears coursing down her face.

"Stand up," I said, "and go to the mirror. Let's see how I've marked you."

I had done quite a job—the flesh marbled under the darkening welts. We'd sit in a restaurant the next evening, I thought, and I'd explain what I'd planned for us, what she could expect. I'd let her look at me, so that I could look into her eyes. And as we spoke, I'd enjoy knowing how much it hurt her to sit down. But meanwhile, I liked watching her inspect the damage. I even liked her momentary little look of pride that she'd taken as much as she had. I knew I should discipline her for it, but what the hell. Look, I knew by now that I was too lazy and self-indulgent to be doing this job alone. I was glad I'd have help this time around.

"Thank you, Jonathan," she said, turning around to face me.

"Yes," I said, "you look very nice that way."

She dropped to her knees, crawled back to me, and looked shyly at the belt, which was still in my hand. I let her kiss it and then to bend from the waist and kiss my feet. I leaned over and raised her chin in my hand again.

"Or rather," I continued, "you would look very nice, with a collar and cuffs. You look a little silly without them, don't you think? Well, tomorrow we'll go to Paris to start outfitting you. I'm very happy to have you back, you know. Now bring me my cigarettes and an ashtray."

The Fourth Day

CARRIE

And so, the next afternoon, I found myself in front of a three-part mirror, modeling collars and cuffs, leashes and bridles and harnesses. We'd taken the train to Paris that morning and headed directly to the shop. It was small. You got to it through the cobbled courtyard of a shabby building near the Place de la Bastille. Of course there was no dressing room, and anybody could have walked in on us while I tried on the fetishes, sturdy leather and cold metal buckled tight against my naked skin. The proprietor (Jonathan had told me he was a saddle maker—with sidelines) was old, small and wizened, courtly and loquacious with Jonathan, and terse and direct with me, communicating in short commands— kneel, turn, bend, open.

They were fitting me with full pony equipment—harness, boots, and bridle. And tails, of course—several different ones, actually, more than I'd really need as a pony. Jonathan hastened to repeat that, after all, I'd won the big pony race in New York, and that he'd certainly be racing and showing me some more. Which surprised me, because he'd never shown any interest in that sort of thing before. Still, he was buying all this custom-made gear. The saddle maker said that it would take a week or so to finish it and pack it up to send back to California. Jonathan nodded thoughtfully. "But," he said, "I must have a whip today."

"*Bien sûr, Monsieur,*" the saddle maker agreed, heading toward his stockroom. He came back into the fitting room with several of them, and together he and Jonathan agreed on the most evil and beautiful riding crop I'd ever seen. The piece of cane, encased in buttery russet leather, was so supple that you could touch its ends together, make a circle of it. There were thin gold bands on the handle.

"She is made for a whip like this, Monsieur," the old man said, tracing the furrow of my ass with it. He'd removed my harness and bridle, but I was still wearing a collar and cuffs, high boots and tail. I stood sideways in front of the mirror, my back deeply arched, my ass sticking way out, my head very high. It was a classic dressage posture, and I'd won a contest with it once. I could see that the saddle maker understood the pose, the slope of my neck, the tense line of my belly. My muscles strained to hold position, and I could feel my cunt becoming visibly wet and shiny along its slit in front. Well, that's why they'd shaved me, after all, so that you could see. I felt the old man's critical eyes on me.

"She is very nicely trained," he complimented Jonathan, who smiled proudly, "and very sensitive." He flicked the whip at me—underhand, lightly hitting the underside of my breasts and just skimming my nipples. The air whistled, and I winced at the sting. And then—quickly, while I was still steadying myself—he rotated his wrist sharply, and swung squarely at my ass, across the welts Jonathan had raised the night before. He did it so casually that you couldn't see how much force he was putting behind the blow, and I really had to work to keep my balance when it hit me. I shuddered, shook the tears from my eyes, and murmured my thanks as formally as I could. *"Je vous remercie, maître."*

"Oh, yes," Jonathan said, "this will do very well."

The old man told me I could get dressed then, that we were finished. He unbelted the tail from me and pulled it out brusquely. I unlaced the boots and handed them back to him. Of course there was no question of my taking off the collar and cuffs. While I was dressing he wrapped the riding crop carefully in brown paper. And when we were ready to leave, he gave it to me to carry. I knelt to take it, and to kiss his gnarled, age-spotted hand.

"And if you ever race her near Paris, Monsieur," he said, as he escorted us to the door, "please let me know. I'll come and I'll bet a thousand francs on her." Jonathan laughed and assured him he would.

The lingerie store was in a much classier part of the city—in Passy, where the great courtesans in Colette's stories used to live. Of course there was a dressing room here, quite a roomy, comfortable one, its chairs upholstered in warm peach velvet. Otherwise, though, the experience was fairly similar to the one at the saddle maker's—well, nastier, actually, in ways.

Not that I didn't love parts of it—like feeling the sales-girl's little hands rolling the fine, black, seamed silk stockings up my legs, and attaching them tightly to the garters hanging down from my waist. And I loved the feel of the corsets themselves. I imagined them being handsewn in convents, by wistful novices who'd never get to wear them, but who'd dream about it sometimes, in shadowy, troubling images, very late at night. They were so expensive, these productions of silk and lace and cruel steel ribbing, that Jonathan was getting the royal treatment from the sales staff. The pretty shopgirl, with a cute, retro smock over her sweater and short skirt, flirted with him while she fetched and carried items for me to try on. And the severe-looking store manager in her credible knockoff of a couturier suit pointed out the fineness and subtlety of the stitching. Of course, Jonathan might have gotten that kind of attention even if he'd been spending less. But I could see from the glances the women exchanged that they were genuinely impressed by the money he was laying out.

And I could also see that they were annoyed at me, for watching them. There wasn't enough time to lace me really tightly, since we were trying lots of garments. But they did pull the laces as sharply, as spitefully, as they could, every chance they got. They'd pretend to explain something to Jonathan—you see the curved panels here, Monsieur, and the double seams at the back—but the real point would be my gasp as the corset's ribs suddenly dug into me. They shoved me here and there, staring insolently at my collar and cuffs and at the stripes and bruises on my ass. I knew their contempt was salted with envy, but it was powerful for all that and I lowered my eyes under its force.

Which didn't stop them. They kept at it until they finally realized how much Monsieur was enjoying the show they were putting on for him. It was one of his nastier modes, his sneaky way of politely and innocently inviting other women to torment me. And by the time they'd figured out what he was up to, it was time to wrap up the *prêts à porter* and tally the custom orders, to be sent to him later, in California. They were a bit stiff and sullen with him then, but he thanked them politely, with that infuriatingly modest smile of his, for all their sage counsel and charming assistance.

Oh, and we did another errand in between. One that was more unambiguous fun—well, for me, anyway. After the scruffy Bastille neighborhood and before the snooty sixteenth *arondissement,* we stopped at the street called Gaité, with its all-day sex shows, sex toy emporia, and peephole theaters, to get me some shoes. Nothing made to order here, just your basic trashy sex shoes, with six-inch spike heels, pointy toes, and ankle straps that locked with little keys Jonathan put in his pocket. The skinny, unshaven proprietor, wearing tight red and black striped pants and a Fabulous Freak Brothers T-shirt, *tutoyer*ed both of us as comrade sexual outlaws, gesturing expansively with cigarette-stained hands as he delivered a rambling lecture on the theme *liberté, égalité, fraternité.* His interpretation would have surprised Robespierre, I thought, but it would have made total sense to the Marquis de Sade.

I loved the nutty speed-freaky theorizing. Although when the peroration got to identity politics, both Jonathan and I almost lost it—him in fidgets, and me in suppressed giggles, watching him contain himself. He hates situations like this, I thought, times when the lower orders—artisans, salespeople, receptionists—forget that they're only bit players in his movie. He needs them to fuss over him, he floats through life on their ministrations (in an earlier century, he probably would have called them "tradespeople"). And he thinks they should keep to their places; he almost shudders when they intrude their own agendas. Fancy bastard. In an earlier century, I grinned to myself, tradespeople might have sent him rolling off to the guillotine. But, I chided myself, I probably wasn't allowed to have thoughts like this any more.

And, in all fairness, the speech *had* thrown us off schedule. Jonathan had also wanted to buy me a dress to wear that evening. But Freaky François had taken up so much time that when we'd finished at the corsetière, it was too late to do anything but head back to our hotel. I had a dress in my backpack that would have to do, though—just a dark red pullover sweater that came down to the middle of my thighs, but it was cashmere, with a big cowl neck. I had rolled it up carefully, so that it wouldn't wrinkle, and I spread it out now, on a chair next to the large three-part mirror in our hotel room.

Of course, I would have preferred wearing something Jonathan had chosen for me. But it didn't really matter. The essentials were in place. I'd been outfitted. Fitted out. Pressed into service. Rigged and appointed for use.

I gazed at my reflection, the new collar and cuffs, the black corset buckled tightly around my waist. Fetishism, I thought—fetishism is commodities talking dirty. Inanimate objects calling the shots, brute matter laying down the law. Jonathan had been right the night before. I'd looked silly without restraints—sloppy, dreamy, forgetful. I needed to be put in my place. To be called to account by leather pressing against my throat and steel nipping at my waist. To be thrown off my natural, accustomed balance by spike heels that tilted my pelvis way back and flaunted my ass. I couldn't speak without permission, but the fetishes were loud and insistent—a chorus, a carapace, of ritual and regulation. Of rank and authority, hierarchy and order, my mute bruised body a perpetual novice in orders.

"Fix your makeup," Jonathan had said a few minutes earlier, when I'd lifted my head from his cock. He'd reached into his pocket and handed me a new lipstick, in a dark plum color, almost black. It would need to be precisely applied. Going outside the lipline would make me look clownish.

"It's time to go to dinner," he called now, as I carefully blotted my lips. (He'd taken my watch from me that morning when I'd reached to put it on.) He was still lying on the bed, in bluish early evening shadow. We hadn't turned on any lights except the bright one I was using for my makeup. I could see his legs, reflected in the mirror, his long, narrow feet. My makeup looked okay, I thought.

"Put on your dress and let me look at you," he added. I pulled it down over my head, smoothed the skirt around my hips, and moved the cowl neck downward, slightly, in front, so that—if you wanted to—you could see an inch or so of leather at my throat. I turned toward him, eyes lowered and dark mouth slightly open.

And he didn't give me permission to raise my eyes until dinner. To his silky gray shirtfront, bisected by a paler gray tie. And his shoulders, his dark jacket, silhouetted against a planter filled with gaudy parrot tulips. And his eyes flickering like candlelight. He leaned forward on his elbows, and smiled lazily.

"It's been a nice day, hasn't it?" he asked. I agreed that it had, Jonathan.

"And all in all, you've been very well behaved," he continued. I thanked him, but I wasn't sure I liked that *all in all.*

178

"Of course," his tone sharpened, "you had rather too good a time at the shop on Gaité. I'll have to punish you for that." I thanked him again, for catching that.

"But even if you hadn't betrayed that little slice of attitude, I'd be planning to beat you tonight, you know, just to try out the new whip." His smile became savage.

"Tell me, Carrie, do you prefer being whipped as a punishment or to give your master pleasure?"

Actually, I'd given some thought to that conundrum. I mean, I never exactly *prefer* being whipped—but, well...I took a breath, choosing my words carefully.

"Well, Jonathan, being punished is more, uh, *necessary*. I mean, it's sort of like keeping accounts straight. But being whipped purely for a master's pleasure, well, it's more profound. And a whole lot more difficult to bear." I heard my voice tremble at the end—I was remembering the saddle maker touching the ends of the new whip together. I arched my back, feeling the sting at my nipples. Jonathan watched, nodding appreciatively.

"Good," he said, "that's clearly put. Well, the first five I'll give you will be for Gaité. And then the rest—I don't know how many it'll be—will be for my own pleasure. It'll be nice knowing that you understand."

He took my hand and kissed it.

"It's nice, isn't it," he continued, "being out in the world like this, I mean. We'll take more trips like this. There are other interesting venues for this sort of thing. Some of the Eastern European cities, I'm told. Tokyo. Hong Kong, too."

"Yes, Jonathan," I said, "it's very nice. And will you be entering me in many pony races?"

He looked down at his plate for a moment. "Well, sort of," he said, looking unsure of how to continue. And then he took a deep breath. "Look," he said, "You want to know the terms of our arrangement. And you're right, you've been very patient and good, but you've got every right to know. But I need to tell you one more story, before you'll really understand...."

ONE MORE STORY FROM JONATHAN

I would have thought that being censured by the association and disciplined by Brewer would have wiped out the stain of my little transgression. But it wasn't that easy. Because Kate was still furious at me. I called her—dozens of times—but she wouldn't answer or return my phone calls. They even turned me away at the gate when I drove up to her place in Napa. Finally, desperate, I hit on a plan.

I phoned again, but not her personal number. This time, I phoned her appointment secretary. I'd never actually used the number, though I'd given it out once or twice. It had gotten lost from my Rolodex, and I'd had to call Uncle Harry to get it. I explained what I wanted to do—I wasn't surprised that he already knew why she wasn't talking to me.

"You can use me as a reference," he assured me.

"Thanks," I said, "I intend to." I'd lined up a pretty high-powered list of references already. The phone calls hadn't been pleasant, but everybody had finally been willing to help me. And vastly amused, it seemed, that I'd gotten myself into this mess.

The appointment secretary was new, and hadn't heard of me. I was lucky there, since the old secretary might well have hung up on me. But all this new young woman seemed to know was that I wasn't in the computer system. Well, I'd never been a client, after all.

"But I am a longtime membership of the association," I said. I could hear her computer keys clicking as she pulled up that database. "And I've got some good references." Which was what she really cared about. Mr. Brewer, Madame Roget…her polite, businesslike voice notched up a bit on the receptivity scale.

"I'm faxing you an application right now, Mr. Keller," she said. "And if you're accepted, Ms. Clarke will want to schedule an introductory interview."

The fax was coming through my machine as we spoke. Kate's obsessive about keeping her technology up-to-date. I scanned the pages quickly. Good—they'd included a nicely done-up brochure, listing all the services she provided. The application form had lots of questions (long answer, short answer, multiple choice), and a blank page for a personal essay. The overachiever in me found it very reassuring. Getting into Kate's, I promised myself, wouldn't be all that different from getting into Yale. There was no return address on the application, just the fax number.

"Thanks," I said warmly, smiling as I said it and hoping she could hear me smile through the phone lines. "Yeah, I think I've got everything. Thanks for all your help, Ms. Green. You'll be hearing from me very soon."

Kate charged by the hour, by the afternoon, by the day, the evening, and the weekend. She didn't preside at every encounter—but the brochure I pored over made it clear that she had to know you pretty well before she'd leave you alone with Sylvie, Stephanie, or Randy, or any of the others. Well, she'd probably know you by the time she'd read your application. It was logically constructed, and the instructions were clear and to the point. I was impressed, and then surprised that I was impressed. What did I think she did all day, anyway, when she wasn't with me? Of course, the unpleasant truth is that I'd never thought about it one way or another—she'd always treated me like a pasha when I'd visited, and that had been good enough for me.

I breezed through the short-answer questions. But here were some paragraph-long items that would take some thought. I sharpened a pencil. I needed to work these out on scratch paper first.

First sexual encounter?

You know, Kate. You and your family had gotten home from South America two days before. We'd hardly spoken to each other at the welcome-home party—we'd been too busy assessing all the ways each other's adolescent bodies had changed during the year you'd been away. I skipped school the next day, to meet you in the garden shed. I don't think we planned it. I just knew you'd be there.

But was that the *first*, really? How about all the years of peeking and grabbing before that? Places we'd begun to put our fingers and our tongues. I don't remember a *first* first. Not really. Do you?

Other important early sexual events?

The first time we slept together, all night long. I'd bribed your brother not to rat on me—not to tell anybody that I wasn't in his room, in the top bunk. I got all tangled up in your long, fine, straight hair—I woke up with it around my neck and in my mouth. We'd had to squeeze together in your bed (it was still a little girl's bed, shaped like a sleigh), but we liked that. We couldn't understand why grown-up couples, who were allowed to sleep together, would want those enormous beds they always seemed to have. Wasn't the idea to be touching each other every place you possibly could be touching, tangled in each other's hair, mingling your breath? Flowing into all the nooks and crannies of each other's bodies, intertwined?

First experience of fetishism?
Summer. That summer we'd ridden our bikes down a different road, and had peeked through the fence at Sir Harold's Custom Ponies. We'd stood there staring for hours, fascinated. And had been caught, with our hands in each other's jeans. Well, maybe we'd wanted to get caught.

First sexual disappointment?
When you told me that you didn't want to be with me— *exclusively* with me, I mean—forever.

Well, that was some of the first draft, anyway. I'd have to tone it down and polish it up before I sent it in. Moving right along to the SERVICES DESIRED section....

I put a big check mark in the box next to WEEKEND SCENE. For thirty thousand dollars, you can be Kate's slave for an entire weekend. Funny, isn't it, Carrie, that you got almost that much for free?

And then, in small block letters, almost as evenly spaced as the print, I added (WITH VARIATIONS; SEE ESSAY).

183

Because I wanted a weekend, all right, but not the one she was offering. I didn't doubt that it was a hell of a package—custom designed, with costumes and staging and equipment and the three little cherubs in attendance. Paced slowly, like a nineteenth century novel—just the thing for somebody kicking back after a week of hostile takeovers or big movie deals. Maybe later, when I'd earned it. But right now....

I turned to the essay question, where I explained that I wanted to design a weekend scene where I'd be the master, and Ms. Clarke the slave. Of course I knew that she wasn't in that kind of business. And I would have bet that, over the years, she'd gotten so good at what she did do that she could hardly remember the last time somebody had forced her to her knees.

He frowned slightly, in response to Carrie's almost imperceptible change of expression.

"Well, we're both awfully busy with our lives," he said, as though she'd asked for a fuller accounting. "I mean, we fuck a lot whenever we see each other, but playing like that...well, especially with her doing it big-time, for a living...well, she, I...."

She dropped her eyes slightly. You don't have to explain it to me, Jonathan. You don't have to explain anything to me, remember?

The application would get her attention, anyway. It was an audacious shot, but I'd told the truth about us, in a lot of ways, and I wasn't sorry. And as for how she'd respond—well, I'd just have to wait and see.

She let me sweat it out for two weeks. Finally, I got a call from a slightly addled-sounding Ms. Green, telling me that Ms. Clarke agreed to the weekend. For *forty* K.

"You got it," I said jubilantly. As though I could actually afford it. As though I could have afforded the thirty, for God's sake. But I'd worry about all that later. Right at that moment I didn't care about anything, the expense, the planning. I was going to get to see Kate, that was the important thing. I hadn't realized just how much I'd depended on seeing her when I wanted, even if sometimes (well, when you were with me), I'd let months go by between visits.

Ms. Green set up a planning session with Steve, he'd drive down to my house to discuss the arrangements. Kate wouldn't know the nature of the scenario ahead of time, so he'd be in charge of all the details and the staging. And the menu—Saturday night dinner, for me and a guest.

He was polite, took copious notes, and made it abundantly clear that if it were up to him I'd never darken their doorstep again. He drank a lot of my liquor, too, though he didn't show any effects. I felt uncomfortable—Bertie Wooster to his Jeeves—flaky, irresponsible, Kate's regrettable weakness. And then I got pissed. All those veiled scowls, and the little grimaces under his mustache. Oh, fuck you, I thought. I knew he was imagining whaling hell out of me with that little rubber plug of his. It made me want to flirt with him, to camp it up a little, just to annoy him back.

Is he jealous? I wondered. But I knew he wasn't, not really. He was devoted to Kate, but he had his own life, his own haunts and habits. No, what he was really trying to do was protect her. Not physically—he just didn't trust me not to take emotional advantage of her. Which wasn't flattering for me to contemplate, but I could see why he might put that kind of construction on things.

I took a deep breath. We needed to shift gears, if we were going to make this thing work.

"Uh, Steve," I said hesitantly. "Look. I'd, uh, like it if Kate really enjoyed this weekend. So, I mean, could you help me? Please?"

And he did, too. I owe him.

Well, I thought contentedly, relaxing in the Jacuzzi on a sunny Saturday morning three weeks later, they do take good care of you here, at her place. Not that I was surprised, but it was fun to see it as a client, rather than whatever I'd been all those years. I'd begun with breakfast out here on the deck a couple of hours earlier—hot rolls wrapped in a linen napkin, silver coffee pot, a bunch of violets in a bright little china pitcher. And my four slaves—Sylvie, Stephanie, Randy, and Kate—kneeling at attention, their heads bowed. Nice. Randy poured me juice and coffee, and brought me the papers and a dog whip. And after I finished eating, while I was drinking my second cup of coffee and he was lighting my cigarette, I'd had the three women stand up and show themselves to me.

Sort of the standard presentation, of course—more or less like the one she staged for Andrew. Only this time it wasn't a frightened client standing between Sylvie and Stephanie, but Kate herself. In cuffs and collar, corset, heels, stockings. Lowered eyes and darkly painted slightly open mouth. And her breasts evenly rising and falling below my gaze. I was very moved, but I forced myself to stick to the script Steve and I had outlined.

"Damn it, she's too small, this one," I murmured, lightly flicking a bit of cigarette ash over her breast. "She's pretty enough, but she's really too little." She *is* a good four inches shorter than Sylvie and Stephanie, she's always wished she were taller. "Too small to be a good slave," I repeated, but then, brightening up, always the good sport, "but, hey, I bet she'd make a cute puppy."

She played her part meticulously, remaining passive and docile while a frightened Sylvie undressed her. I smacked her belly lightly with the whip. "Ass," I said, and she turned, bending and opening so that I could insert a dildo and belt it into place. The tail attached to it was short, grotesque, a stubby little thing with wiry hair on it, like a terrier's.

"Sit," I said sternly.

And then, "Wag your tail, Kate." She became silly, adoring, obsequious, licking my fingers clumsily and eagerly, without any grace or dignity at all. And when I disciplined her with the whip, she whimpered and howled.

"Naughty puppy," I said, smacking her nose with my rolled-up newspaper. And then I snapped my fingers for Sylvie to bring a large white china bowl of water, a tureen almost. "Drink it all," I said to Kate, pushing her neck down with my foot. She wasn't quite fast enough, though, so after she finished I punished her by muzzling her, and attaching her leash to a post in the deck's railing. The wood of the deck would be hot under her knees, I thought, sliding into the Jacuzzi. I closed my eyes, luxuriating in the quiet, the sound of birds in the trees, and the distant jingle and rattle of a pony cart on the path. As I said, they take good care of you there. I might have dozed off, had I not felt Stephanie's fingertips in the spaces between the muscles in my shoulders, smoothing out the tightness.

Was that a whimper? Too faint, too shy, I thought. No need to move so soon. I bent my head a little to kiss the fingers of Stephanie's right hand. No need, certainly, to open my eyes yet. And again, the whimper—plaintive, a whine almost. "Damn," I said, stretching.

I opened my eyes, turned my neck to look at her. A little flushed from the bright sun, and still up on her knees at attention. And she had to pee. She tried not to move, but I could see the tension in her thighs, the tightness in her belly. She whimpered again, through her muzzle, humbly pleading with huge, sad eyes. I sat up straighter in the water and motioned for Sylvie to light another cigarette for me. And I watched Kate watch me smoke it slowly.

But now we were finally out for a walk, Kate crawling behind me in heavy little boots, kneepads, and gloves. My deck had some back steps down to the garden, but I hadn't used them. I'd led her out to the hallway, and she'd followed me, carefully descending the big, curved, graceful main staircase on her hands and knees, past the maid rubbing the newel post with lemon oil, through the entry hall, and out the front door.

I wondered if she'd be feeling the pebbles through her kneepads, as we ambled slowly down the path. "Heel," I said sharply, bending to sniff the lilac hedge. The flowers were doing nicely—the phlox, the impatiens, delphiniums and poppies and beds of lavender. We'd pored over the seed catalogs together when she'd redesigned this path. Of course, she couldn't pee here.

"Come on," I said, tugging at her leash. "Good girl." The words had slipped out. But damn it, she *was* being too good. Well, I'd known I'd have to work against her fearsome self-discipline.

We crossed to a pretty meadow between the lawn behind her house and the stables, the dressage ring, and the bridle paths that led into the hills. I headed toward a stand of eucalyptus, and yes, good—here were two of her clients, a young woman, dressed only in thigh-high red patent leather boots and torn, faded jeans, and a naked young man kneeling at her feet. There were fresh stripes across his chest and back. And now, I thought, he was in for a more unusual treat.

I led Kate in the couple's direction, feeling her leash grow taut in my hand as she hesitated. She knew what I had in mind. "I felt that," I said mildly. She whimpered, her eyes pleading and puppylike. Please Jon, she was telegraphing to me, please, not in front of my guests. "You're a naughty puppy," I said, jerking her leash, "getting me out of my comfortable tub when you didn't really have to pee. Well," I turned sharply, "let's go back to the house. Perhaps you need another bowl of water."

She bowed her head resignedly, and I turned again, back to the couple in the meadow—he was standing now, his legs spread wide, and she was probing his balls with a shiny little metal device. But they both turned to look at us.

"Sorry," I called, "I didn't mean to disturb you. I'll be on my way as soon as the puppy does her business."

And that was fun, their dumbstruck looks. They dropped roles and stared at each other in astonishment. Can that really be *her?* I could read in the young woman's expression. And oh yes, here was his urgent nod back. Absolutely. Oh, my god, it *is* her, Liz, I know it, I can tell—she was unforgettable, that first weekend when she showed you how to whip me. I'd recognize her anywhere.

She was peeing now. You could hear it, hissing as it hit the dusty ground. A weak little stream, her muscles were probably too cramped to let it out any more quickly. Good.

It would last longer. She was squatting, her hands behind her back, her eyes—in her muzzled face—open to my gaze. Helpless, needy, open, exposed, and (finally) humiliated. It didn't last nearly long enough. The couple by the trees were transfixed, watching her shake herself now, to get rid of the last drops.

(It had been Steve's idea. "But," I'd asked hesitantly, "is that okay? I mean, don't her clients depend on her, for a certain image, you know?"

He'd nodded solemnly.

"Most of them," he'd said. "But there are a few who'd be...honored."

And somehow, he'd seen to it that they'd been in attendance that weekend.)

"Roll over," I said. And I laughed to watch her get all tangled up in her leash. I hunkered down to scratch her belly and she gave a low growl of pleasure, rolling around at my feet, sniffing at the inseam of my jeans, and then back up on her knees, licking my face rapturously after I unhooked the tangled leash and took off her muzzle. And when I picked up a stick and tossed it into the meadow, she scrambled off as fast as she could go. We zigzagged across the meadow that way, me throwing, her fetching. Just a boy and his dog—Timmy and Lassie—sweaty and carefree on a sunny spring morning.

All the way to the paddock, where Randy had been harnessed to a cart. He looked quite beautiful in his tail and harness, and he'd attracted some admirers. Interesting-looking people he was posturing for—the small, dapper man with beautifully cut short white hair, the skinny, striking, neurasthenic-looking girl. I smiled cordially at them. Time for some grown-up games.

"Pretty pony, isn't he?" I asked, stroking his head under his bridle. "I've reserved him."

The man smiled, and the girl nodded her head slowly. "He's beautiful," she said, in a low, tuneless voice, almost so quietly that I couldn't hear her.

The man put out his hand. "Arthur Geist," he said. "And this is Ariel."

His name was distantly familiar. He'd written books, I thought—semiotics, that sort of thing. I introduced myself, exchanging some urbane guy noises with him, while Ariel stared politely into the middle distance. She looked so bored with the two of us that I wondered if perhaps she was his daughter. Or a student he was going to have to fail.

"Nice dog, too," Arthur was saying, crouching down to stroke Kate behind the ears. She was still panting a bit, but she wagged her tail and licked his hand politely.

Ariel nodded absentmindedly, and then turned back to Randy. "May I?" she asked me. Her skin was very pale, bluish in the shadows of her cheekbones. And her dark blue eyes, under long black bangs, were just the slightest bit too close together.

I nodded, and she ran her hand slowly over his belly. She cradled his balls, and I saw her little pink tongue dart out and wet her lips. She stroked his cock a little with her thumb, lightly grazing it with a dark-purplish fingernail. Using her other hand, she pinched one of his nipples and then slapped his face with a sudden, percussive motion. Randy continued to breathe evenly behind the bit distending his mouth, but he widened his eyes.

"You use a whip when you drive him?" she asked me. There was a hint of Valley Girl syncopation underneath the flat rhythms of her speech.

"Of course," I smiled, showing her the whip, which was on the front seat of the cart.

She drew in her breath. "Oh," she said, "it's lovely." She looked about nineteen, but I didn't think she was. She could, I thought, just as easily be twenty-nine. I liked that indeterminacy about her—doubtless a function of a very skewed personality development. I was beginning to enjoy this. Especially with Kate sitting at my feet and watching me warily.

"Have you ever driven a pony?" I asked Ariel.

"God, I *wish*," she said. "But I have used a whip." She took it from me, inspecting it thoughtfully, weighing it in her hand. Arthur watched carefully, giving a small, delighted shudder.

Dope, I said to myself. She's his mistress, of course. His domme. Amazing—he's so smugly self-confident that I didn't realize he's the bottom. But now that I'd gotten it straight, I could see it clear as day. He drives over to her place south of Market, I thought, in his little BMW. She rings him in, he rides the industrial elevator up to her loft. Maybe she's chewing gum while she lets him through the industrial-strength security system. She knocks back a beer while he takes off his clothes—the camel hair coat, the very neat little Italian loafers. And she doesn't smile until she's beat him to a pulp.

"You'd be a good driver, I bet," I said to her. "There's room for two in the cart, if you'd like to join me." I could see a shadow of concern for Randy pass over Kate's face.

Laudable, but a little inappropriate in a puppy. "Watch it," I muttered.

Ariel climbed into the seat. "Wait here, Arthur," she said.

"Of course," he said. And to me, "Should I watch your puppy for you?"

"Thanks," I said, pulling Kate to her feet sharply, by the ring in her collar, "but she'll enjoy running alongside the cart." I climbed in after Ariel.

I showed her how to signal Randy what direction to go in, and how fast. "I'll work the brake," I said. "You just concentrate on driving." I didn't bother saying anything about the whip, just handed it over to her, admiring the strength and elegance with which she snapped it.

"I want him to gallop," she said in her determined monotone, as she drove him on. He was galloping a lot faster, actually, than I'd been planning on, especially with the extra weight in the cart and Kate running alongside. I sneaked a look at her—dancing and capering, snapping at shadows and butterflies. She was breathing hard, but she wasn't winded, so I let Ariel do what she wanted for a while. But I was still uneasy. Not that I could tell Ariel. I wanted her to like me—and to think I was as tough as she was.

"If you go slower," I said, as we reached a sunny straightaway, "Randy will show off his form for you. Correct him if you think he needs it." I felt like a child psychologist, trying to cajole her to behave.

She did enjoy putting him through his walk-trot-canter routines, and he didn't disappoint her. He performed for her, preening and prancing his exhibitionist little butt off. A more experienced driver might have disciplined him for what was in fact a disgustingly self-indulgent performance, but hey. She loved it, and that was what I cared about right then. That and keeping her under control. Anyhow, she seemed to have decided that we were friends, because, as we headed back to the corral, Randy in a graceful, leisurely trot, she turned to me. "Do you ever go out and get yourself whipped?" she asked pleasantly, not exactly smiling, but showing her small sharp white teeth, with very pointed canines.

"On occasion," I said.

"I mean," she said impatiently, "by anybody besides *her?*" She jerked her head in Kate's direction.

I had to laugh. Smart girl.

"Yes," I said, thinking of my recent session with Brewer. "Well, on rare occasions," I added.

"Take my card, then," she said. She didn't give it to just anybody, was the implication.

I'd expected the card to have heavy metal motifs emblazoned on it. But it just said ARIEL, in twelve-point Garamond, with a phone number. Nice expensive stock, no design or slogan at all. I put it in my wallet.

"It's a pretty name," I said.

"It's not my real name," she confided, as though I'd find that difficult to believe.

"No, I guess not," I answered.

"But my real name would be like the worst, *the world's* worst name for somebody who does what I do."

I'm not good at guessing games. "Lucretia?" I asked. "Pollyanna?"

"Dominique," she said tragically. "My geeky parents named me after Patricia Neal in *The Fountainhead.* Can you believe that?"

Poor baby. On impulse, I leaned over and kissed her mouth. She let me, though you could hardly say she kissed me back. I wondered what exactly she did for sex. Well, for recreation, you know.

"Come to dinner tonight," I said. "Bring Arthur."

She didn't respond to that. We were approaching the pony ring now, concentrating on using the reins and brakes together to come to a graceful stop. We did pretty well, too. A stablehand came running out to meet us, to unharness Randy and start to rub him down. Ariel turned to me and reluctantly handed me the whip. "Thanks," she said, "that was fun."

And then she stepped out of the cart, putting her high-heeled boot squarely into Arthur Geist's waiting, cupped hands.

I got a rag from the stablehand, to rub Kate down. Didn't want the sweaty puppy catching cold. She was exhausted. And filthy. It was a hot, dry day, and she'd been running in the cloud of dust that the cart's wheels had raised. Her hair was matted, and sweat was making filthy rivulets down her body. Her eyes were red and teary, too. I rubbed her gently, thoroughly. She kept her eyes down, shivering a little. The stablehand led Randy away to be hosed down, and another stablehand came and wheeled the cart away.

Ariel turned to me. "So," she said, "what time should we come to dinner?"

Kate looked up sharply.

"Eight," I said, "I'm in the big guest suite in the big house."

And there it was, finally, the outrage I hadn't managed to create any other way, writ huge across her face. Mess up my cook's dinner preparations, Jon? You wouldn't dare, not even you! Her chin lifted. Her eyes flashed, green electrical storms.

I slapped her, sending her sprawling.

"That's three," I said coldly, while warmth flooded my groin.

I'd brought the blunt little dog whip along with me, tucked in my belt. I pulled it out now and raised my arm to flog her. But wait a minute.

"Hey, Ariel," I said, "could you help me out here?"

She took the whip from me. "Cool," she said.

"But," I frowned, "I wish I could sit down." I was undoing my pants.

She shrugged. "Use Arthur."

He made a good bench, down on all fours.

I didn't have to tell Ariel what I wanted. Well, we all understood what I wanted, especially Kate, on her hands and knees in front of me, her mouth full of me, milking me with her lips and playing with me with her busy puppy tongue. Give it up, Kate—no responsibilities toward cook or clients today. Just to me. She winced, shuddering from time to time, when Ariel pulled off a particularly nasty snap of the whip, and she began to cry about halfway through, her tears silently streaking down her dusty cheeks. But she never broke rhythm, never lost her focus. She drained me, and then, staying in puppy role, dribbled some cum down her chin and onto the ground in front of her.

I almost lost it there, I was so charmed. Just as she knew I'd be—Kate probably hadn't given sloppy head since we'd been teenagers. "Bad puppy," I said severely, catching my breath and somehow managing to maintain the rhythm of the script. "Lick it up."

I stood up and hugged Ariel's skinny shoulders. "Lady," I said, "you got some wrist. Thanks."

She had her eyes on Kate, though, delicately lapping at the little spot she'd made in the dust. "She was good," she said in a distant voice.

"Yeah," I said briefly, "I know. See you at eight. Heel, Kate."

When we got back to my rooms, Steve was waiting on the deck.

"Get her cleaned up," I said, "and fix her up for this evening. Bring her back after she's gotten some food and rest." I hadn't really wanted him there—too much like he was checking up on me—but I wouldn't have trusted anybody else to treat Kate as a puppy while I wasn't watching. Sylvie and Stephanie would have just brought her back to her own huge, claw-footed bathtub, dumped in a whole bottle of healing rosemary bath oil, and, after they'd gently rubbed her dry with warmed towels, knocked themselves out giving her a massage and a pedicure. No, it was only Steve who'd wash her off in a big galvanized tub outside the stables with an ordinary scrub brush, feed her some water and dog food before giving her a nap in the straw, and then fix her up according to plan and bring her back to me.

He probably was checking up on me, too, but Kate looked so calm (even if exhausted) that he couldn't find any cause for complaint. Well, not until I told him that I'd invited Ariel and Arthur to dinner and would he please take care of the arrangements. He grimaced at that, before he led Kate off, leaving Sylvie and Stephanie to take care of me.

A bath. Sylvie got into the big sunken tub along with me, scrubbing me gently, shaving my face expertly with a straight razor, and then handing me over to Stephanie for a massage. And while I rested for a few minutes on the massage table, I heard the two of them fussing with the chairs and umbrellas out on the deck, making sure I had a nice shady spot for lunch. Berries for dessert, served on a silver tray that Stephanie hugged to her front—the strawberries and raspberries and blueberries were heaped around her breasts.

"Clean off the berry stains," I told Sylvie, and she licked away all the reds and purples, while I sipped minted iced tea. And then finally a nap, inside, with just a little bright afternoon sun slanting through the blinds, the two of them curled up on either side of me, each sighing contentedly whenever I chose to stroke her.

My friend Tom arrived soon after that, for a pre-dinner game of racquetball. He'd get to stay the night, too—the suite included a guest room.

"Oh, and I forgot to tell you," I said afterward, in the Jacuzzi, "we've got a dinner guest. Arthur Geist."

Tom whistled. "*The* Arthur Geist?" he asked. "The guy who wrote *Semes, Memes, Genes: Sites of Limnal Alterity*?"

I glanced over at Kate, half hoping to see her sneer at that monstrous title. But she was calmly retrieving the ball Tom had tossed her, as though she didn't understand a word we'd said. Well, what would a puppy care about semes or memes? Especially the gussied-up show dog we'd found waiting for us when we'd gotten back from our game.

Incredible job Steve had done on her—I doubted that she'd gotten any rest at all while we'd been out playing. She had a poodle tail now, with a curly, silvery little ball of hair at its end, tied in a little pink bow. Her hair was curled into humiliating Shirley Temple ringlets, the ones at the sides flopping over like puppy ears, the one at the top tied in a bow to match her tail. My poodle, with her lips and toenails lacquered a bright, tasteless pink. Her nipples, too. And her pubis was shaved, to show that its lips were also outlined in that awful pink.

We fucked her a little, with the handles of our rackets, and now we were tossing her the ball, which she'd fetch in her mouth, sitting very straight at the edge of the Jacuzzi. She wasn't as quick as she'd been in the morning though, because they'd tied her hands into little mitten-like booties, and doubled her legs back, strapping them into place. So it really was like she was getting around on four paws, on her balled-up hands and bent-back knees, her back arched, tail held high. But she still managed to retrieve the ball each time. I wondered, idly, what I'd do to her if she missed one of my tosses, if I threw it a little too hard and it bounced a little too high, over the deck's railing and out into the yard.

"Arthur Geist," Tom was shaking his head. He's better read than I am, and he was extravagantly impressed. "Wow. If I'd known, I would have spent the week cramming."

"He may not say anything at all," I answered, and told him about Ariel.

Which just shows how little I'd scoped out Arthur, who's one of those people who lives for the sound of his own voice. And—which is much more rare—one of the very few who gets away with it, because he's that good and interesting a talker. Except, I suppose, when he's alone with Ariel, and she makes it abundantly clear how little he has to say about anything that really matters. It probably clears his head, like wasabi.

You would have enjoyed hearing him, Carrie, rolling out his elegantly formed sentences, while he knelt at the table on a padded footstool he'd brought along with him. He couldn't sit, evidently. I mean, it seems that while Tom and I'd been whacking a ball around the racquetball court, Ariel had been doing similar things to his ass and back. So he'd come to dinner in a loose, elegant silk robe, carrying his stool, and slowly lowering himself down onto it, settling into a comfortable position from which to hold forth on semes and memes. Well, for openers, that is, before he segued into the genetics of the trans-human body, after briefly checking in on the Renaissance, particle physics, and a shortcut he was working on for mastering the two thousand Japanese *kanji*. He had me and Tom enthralled, as we all tucked into Kate's cook's expertly prepared monkfish, served by Sylvie and Stephanie and Randy—wearing nothing but their collars, gold sandals, and slender gold chains around their waists.

Ariel was wearing a little leather skirt, thigh-high boots, and a transparent black blouse. Her breasts were tiny, almost nonexistent, and she'd painted her nipples the same pale silvery blue as her lips. She ignored Arthur, pushed her food around her plate, and tried to pretend she wasn't obsessed with Kate— who was under the table nuzzling our feet, accepting our pokes and caresses and kicks and the occasional scrap of food.

"Is it okay with everybody," I asked, as Randy started clearing our plates from the table, "if we have dessert and coffee by the fire in the other room?"

Because the other room was nicely set up for it, with comfortable armchairs arranged around a large glass coffee table that held a low silver bowl of round, old-fashioned roses, big crystal ashtrays, plates of cake and fruit, and a delicate black and silver coffee service. The heavy glass was nicely balanced on the backs of Sylvie and Stephanie, who had little rubber suction cups attached to their shoulders and the cheeks of their asses, and who knelt so motionlessly that you wondered if they were breathing. Randy set out the coffee and brandy, and stood by to pour and serve. Arthur brought his stool, and Kate sat up at my feet.

But conversation was waning, our eyes all falling on Kate. Even Arthur seemed to be winding down. It was a comfortable silence, though, laced with coffee and brandy, the warmth of the fire and our mutual and separate anticipations of how the evening might proceed. Tom did us the service of moving things along.

"Great meal, Jonathan," he said, "and great conversation," he nodded cordially at Arthur. "But," turning back to me, "shouldn't you be feeding that puppy?"

"I suppose you're right," I smiled, "unless you'd prefer to do it."

I handed him the leash. He looped it around his wrist while he undid his pants.

"In fact," he murmured, pulling Kate to him, and decisively clamping her head down over himself, "if the food and conversation had been any less great, it would have been utterly unbearable...."

And then there was just the sound of his moans, and our clicking coffee cups and saucers.

He finished quickly, and handed Kate back to me, nodding to Randy to button his pants and straighten his clothes.

"But you know," I said thoughtfully, "I think the puppy's still hungry. Well, she did have that long run out on the trail this afternoon. Arthur?"

He looked eager, but unsure, glancing at Ariel for instructions.

She was frowning. Good. I'd hoped to engineer a little confusion for her.

"Sure, Arthur," she said flatly, "knock yourself out."

He did, too, though Kate had to work a little harder at him than she had at Tom. Still, he smiled delightedly afterward, handing the leash back to me.

Okay.

"Ariel?" I said politely.

She nodded and took the leash, shooting me a tiny, furious look.

She tugged Kate toward her, between her slender legs in their big suede boots. And the room was dead silent while we all watched. I was glad she'd chosen the armchair she was sitting in, angled so that Sylvie and Stephanie could both turn their heads and see.

It would be slow, I knew. She wouldn't be able to take a lot of sensation at once. And I knew that Kate knew that too, that she'd build up as absolutely slowly as Ariel's tightly wound sensorium needed. We watched Ariel's blue eyes lose their focus, her face relax, her jaw loosen. And then the first sigh—I think I sighed along with her, and I heard a tinkle of crystal, as the tabletop trembled slightly.

She started to moan. "Oh, oh shit," she said once, and her hips began to buck. And her hands began to clench and unclench and then she dropped the leash. She looked sweaty. And she moaned and screamed. And kicked. Arthur looked troubled, disoriented, at first—I was afraid that I'd messed up his game for him—but, like Liz and her boyfriend that morning, he pulled himself together, looking, well…honored, I guess you'd have to say.

Her movements were almost convulsive—one more scream—well, not a scream, kind of a hoarse bellow, from very deep in her belly, and she collapsed in the chair, her blue lipstick bitten off, and her hair matted with sweat.

She closed her eyes for a minute. And when she opened them, it seemed as though she'd lost all her guile, and that she really was just nineteen years old. Or maybe ten, or five— she looked like a refugee child who'd just tasted her first ice cream cone.

She groaned a little, smiling ruefully, peering down at Kate, who was calmly wagging her tail. "*Oh* shit," she murmured softly to herself, in a kind of exaggerated, sitcom tone. And then she picked up her glass from the coffee table.

"Uh, more brandy. Randy," she called. And she giggled at how silly that sounded. We all laughed, and Tom raised his glass to her.

He's a talented guy, Tom. I mean he can size up the way things are going and move them in the right direction. So he began making gentle, joking conversation with Ariel. He didn't seem to need to outhip her, like I probably would have. He just said a lot of trivial, amusing, comforting things to her, giving her time to regain her equilibrium.

I turned to Arthur, picking up the thread of an earlier conversation. The splendid Pazzi Chapel in Florence, designed by Brunelleschi. Or maybe not by Brunelleschi after all, Arthur said. He'd heard there was some new research.... Ridiculous, I answered, tugging at Kate's leash for emphasis. But we agreed that it was a wonderful building, and we thought we might go look at it together, some weekend, in off season.

I stroked Kate's hair roughly, pinched her breasts, squeezed her between my knees, and let her rest her chin in my lap while I talked to Arthur. Her face was wan and exhausted, her eyes serene and accepting. "Water," I called to Randy, and he poured some into a little black saucer, putting it at my feet for her to lick. We all knew the evening was drawing to a close, conversation becoming fragmentary, the fire burning down.

I nodded to Randy to begin clearing the coffee table. And Tom took his cue, yawning ostentatiously, while Arthur started his slow progress off his knees and onto his feet.

"I'm as tired as Tom is," he said. "And at my age, that's saying a great deal. I think we'd better go, Ariel." In a mild voice that allowed no room for discussion.

And she'd regained enough of her cool by then to mutter something as she also got to her feet.

I was grateful to all of them.

"Take the girls, Tom," I said, as Randy lifted the tabletop off them. They kneeled up, presenting themselves in Tom's direction, eyes lowered as usual, and only the subtlest of signals—an unwonted pinkness on Stephanie's breasts, and on Sylvie's cheeks below her freckles—to show how much they'd enjoyed the evening. And Tom would enjoy them, I thought. He deserved to.

"And tell Steve to have you harnessed tomorrow morning," I said to Randy, "so this lady"— I nodded to Ariel—"can practice her driving. She's quite ready to take you out by herself, I think." Ariel shrugged, implying that it was all the same to her, and I knew I'd scored a hit. And Arthur probably wouldn't mind sleeping in.

Another round of thanks and compliments at the door. And they were finally gone, and I picked her up and carried her to bed, wordlessly removing her cruel little mittens and kissing her fingers, unstrapping her legs, massaging the stiffness from her knees so that she could get some sleep. So that that we both could sleep, that forty-thousand-dollar Saturday night, in the middle of an enormous bed, our bodies and breaths as commingled and intertwined as they'd been in that little sleigh-shaped one, a million years ago.

CARRIE

I wouldn't cry, I told myself. Not, I supposed, that it would have mattered, since he wasn't really looking at me across the small restaurant table. He was looking past me, or through me, back to that Saturday night, or even further back.

He blinked, focused, smiled at me apologetically.

"Well," he said, "I hadn't really meant to lay that last little bit of middle-aged sentimentality on you. Let's just say that the weekend continued hot, and, and, well, meaningful, to us...."

JONATHAN'S STORY CONCLUDED

And late Sunday afternoon, I handed her a check for forty thousand dollars—it might have been a sentimental journey, but there was no question of not paying up.

But the money part worked out okay, too—having less income of my own to live on gave me more impetus to get my business going again. I put in some seventy-hour weeks, but I enjoyed it—it was a relief to find out I still liked being an architect. And Kate had meetings in the city that summer and fall—she and Brewer were overseeing the design of the new computer system the association was building. So we'd meet, lunch hours, which helped, because I was too busy to drive up to Napa every weekend. But we both learned to juggle our schedules, and we played more than we had in years, sometimes just the two of us, and sometimes she and I and all of them. Even Steve. Things went well. I stopped smoking.

And early last December, we celebrated my thirty-seventh birthday together. Lavishly. And exhaustingly. Well, not just my birthday. A design of mine, something I'd been fooling around with for a long time and finally figured out how to complete, had won a prize. Just a commendation, really, but Kate made a big fuss about it.

Anyhow, she'd finally sent Sylvie and Stephanie and Randy to bed, but she and I were too tired to pick ourselves up off the rug in front of the fireplace in her bedroom. It was a nice warm fire, which was good, because we couldn't seem to make it across the room to where our bathrobes were. It was about all we could do to sip Armagnac and touch and smile and sort of giggle stupidly from time to time. She began inspecting the bruises I'd acquired earlier that day—no, not what you think; she'd bought me roller blades, and, well, there's a knack to it, I'd discovered, the hard way—at least to stopping, on some of those slopes, in the hills of her place.

I picked up her hand, which had been tracing the edge of a quickly gathering black and blue mark on my thigh. I kissed her fingers. And then I moved closer to her, pulling her toward me.

"Stop," she murmured. "I want to give you your birthday present."

I laughed. "You mean those skates weren't present enough? Don't tell me you've got Ariel hidden behind a curtain, ready to beat me." Ariel worked for Kate now, though she'd insisted on maintaining a separate arrangement with Arthur.

Kate laughed too. "We're saving that for when you turn thirty-nine, sweetie," she said. "And don't even try to imagine what I've got planned for your fortieth."

I rolled over on her, pinning her down, my cock stiffening between her thighs. I kissed her slowly, cupping the cheeks of her ass in my hands. She kissed me back, running her hands lightly over my back. And then not so lightly. And then I guess we both decided that the present could wait a little longer.

"It's nice," I said afterward, "being the boss lady's boyfriend, I mean. I think I've finally adjusted to it after all these years."

She nodded, just a little grimly. Well, it's *taken* you long enough, the expression on her face said, and it took me some effort to completely kiss away the little line between her eyebrows. She pulled herself to her feet. "Your present," she said. "I almost forgot."

I rolled over on my belly, watching her ass sway as she walked across the room to her desk. That ass was present enough, I thought. I couldn't imagine what she could give me that could make me feel any better than I was feeling right then.

So I took my time, untying the curly rainbow-colored ribbons and undoing the silver paper wrapped around the flat, rectangular package, while she sat a little distance away, hugging her knees.

"Come on," she hissed anxiously, "tear the damn paper for once."

"I don't like to," I said. "You know that."

I finally did get the thing unwrapped. Legal papers. And I knew exactly what they said—what they had to say—before

I began to read them. I went hot. Then cold. Honestly, I started to shiver, though I knew that the air in the room was perfectly warm, from the fire.

"Do you like it?" she asked me nervously. "Is it a good present?"

The papers were meticulously drawn up, written in that half-pornographic, half-legalistic style that Brewer and his troops could do so well. *The slave called Carrie...to be purchased by Ms. Clarke and certifiably owned by Mr. Keller...under the direction and tutelage of Ms. Clarke's corporate agents....*

"You'd do that for me?" I breathed.

She nodded, averting her eyes, looking small and defenseless, behind her knees.

"Hey," I said, "come here. Look, it's okay. You don't...we don't...*have* to do this."

She lifted her chin. "You do still want her, don't you?"

I was ashamed to admit how much. Even though life had been so full those past few months, I'd still feel the yearnings from time to time. I'd find myself thinking of you, wondering how you were doing, and wanting to hear you tell me about it. Well, wanting a great deal more than that, really. Most of the time, I was able to ignore these feelings, but not always, not completely.

"I do," I said sadly, "but...."

"Just what were you planning to do about it, then, come next March 15th?"

I'd avoided thinking about it. Go to Avignon and wing it, I supposed.

She supposed so too.

She stood up, opened the French doors that led to the

deck, and walked out into the chilly night. I heard a sudden rush of wings. An owl, perhaps swooping down on a mouse or a hare. It was a wrenching sound, and a slightly arousing one. I followed her outside, pressing myself against her back, feeling her rotate her ass upward just a little bit toward my cock. That rotation was second nature, a way of adjusting for the difference in our heights. I took her breasts in my hands. Her naked skin was icy, the flesh below still warm.

"What do you want?" I asked. It sounded adolescent, the way I said it—a silly, portentous, metaphysical question about absolutes and the meaning of life.

And she answered me back like another adolescent.

"Everything," she said.

I tried not to laugh, but I couldn't help it. "Everything?"

"Everything," she repeated.

I remembered the last time we'd spoken like this—when she'd broken up with me, when we were teenagers. It had made no sense at all to me then. Well, she hadn't been very articulate, and I'd been stunned and enraged by loss.

"Everything," she said now, turning around and pressing her front to me. "As many pleasures as one has the will, and the energy, and the desire for—and the patience and talent to arrange."

And this time it seemed quite reasonable, out there on her deck, in the midst of the little empire that she'd built. I didn't need to feel guilty and dismayed by my desires for you. With enough patience and talent—and money—it could all be arranged.

"I'm having a very happy birthday," I whispered, my voice a little unsteady. We were holding each other tightly. "Thanks again."

We talked more the next morning, as we finished breakfast.

"You'll have to go to Avignon and get her to come back with you," she said. "She has to want to do this, and she has to understand—fully—what the terms of the deal are, and what she can expect. I'll keep her as exercised and disciplined as she needs to be, on a daily basis. I mean, you can't just stash her away like a princess in a tower, times when you're not using her."

"I've seen her," she added. And I guess she'd have told me the whole story, if I'd insisted on it, right then. But I let the moment pass, and she smiled, and continued.

"She's had an excellent trainer and she's quite acceptable now. Not quite on the level of my particular three, but she'll be able to hold her own, more or less, among the other six.

"She's become a pony, you know," she said then. She knew that I didn't know that. "She's had a good season, winning a few prizes I thought Sylvie would take easily. They've been sharing most of the big purses between them this summer and fall."

So that's what you'd been doing. I remembered the first time I'd seen you bridled, the thick bit distending your mouth, the fear and humiliation widening your eyes. I've never been much for the racing circuit—I know how cruel it is. So they'd been as cruel as that to you...interesting to think about. Breathtaking, actually.

And, even more interesting, the rapt look in Kate's eye.

"She's really," and she paused for a moment, "an *unusually* charming pony."

I thought at first that she was teasing me, flaunting the fact that she'd seen you—perhaps used you—sometime during the racing season, and that I hadn't. And then I realized that she wasn't thinking about me at all, she was treating herself to a hot memory of...something, I didn't know what. And the rush of jealousy almost knocked me over. Well, I guess I'd be jealous of anybody who made Kate lick her chops like that. But envying *you* that way, Carrie—well, it took me by surprise. It was a new sensation, a strange taste in my mouth, like tobacco or vodka or *foie gras,* one's first time. A dangerous taste. Rich and poisonous and strange and addictive.

Kate and I looked at each other, evenly, for a minute. *I know that you know.* And *same here, love.* And then we looked down at the table. I poured us a little more coffee.

"Of course," she offered, "she still has some untapped potential—she could be polished to a much higher gloss."

I nodded. "If you paid her a little personal attention, you mean."

"I don't know where I'd find the time." Now she *was* teasing me. And herself. "But there are a few things I could do that would, um, make all the difference."

"Oh, well, please," I said. "I mean, if you could find the time."

"And you'll let me race her, won't you?" she asked. "She'll be a good project for Ariel."

I nodded.

"And come with me to watch her run?"

You bet I'll come watch you run. I'll wear my gold-buttoned blazer, with Kate next to me in the stands, wearing a pale peach linen dress and a slightly silly hat that I love. We'll hold hands and pass the binoculars back and forth. We'll scream along with the rest of the crowd, and we'll bet big money on you. And you'll win for us. Well, especially with Ariel driving you.

I nodded again. Yeah, definitely the pony races.

"And sometimes," I asked, "you know, once in a while, I mean, you and I could use her together, maybe. Share her, you know?"

She smiled at me over the rim of her coffee cup, "Thanks, sweetheart," she said, "I'd like that."

CARRIE

I could handle the birthday present part, I thought. Well, it beat jumping out of a cake, anyway. And it made an odd kind of sense, her wanting him to have me—at her place, where she could keep an eye on things. *He makes her happy.* And she wants him to be happy, too. Although (I couldn't help taking a little pleasure in the thought) she must have had some not-so-happy moments while she waited for him to come around. But he *had* come around. As we all would, in a complicated protocol that was obviously delighting him, and which I was having some difficulty grasping at the moment.

Still, I didn't really have to understand it all at once, did I? I supposed that all I really had to understand was that everything could be arranged. I thought again of Kate's foot parting my thighs, her fingers tugging at the straps of my bridle, her careful attention while Sylvie punished my breasts with the little whip.

And I thought how, when O first comes to Roissy, one of the girls asks if it was her lover who brought her. Yes, O says, and the girl tells her that she's lucky, because they'll be much harder on her that way. And if it was the boss lady's lover who brought you, how hard do you think they—how hard do you think *she*—will be on you?

I decided I'd better ask a question. Keep it technical.

"Well, but, Jonathan, how are these things managed? I mean, the contract, and my, uh, price? I mean, well, if the sale doesn't happen at an auction, you know?"

He laughed. "You don't have to worry about your price."

"It'll be substantial," he added. "Annie's very highly regarded, and after all you've done so well in those races and competitions."

But the decisive thing, really, was that Kate was buying me for him. Because slaves exchanged between lovers were considered extremely valuable.

"You'll get to read the papers that Brewer drew up. Of course, we still need to dot the i's and cross the t's. And get you entered into the system."

He meant the association's new online information system. It was up and running now, he said, and I'd be measured, examined, filmed, and photographed, so that I could be accurately classified and represented on the databases, the Web pages.

Yeah, I thought, whatever. And then I felt my eyes widen, as an idea began to take shape far back in my brain.

He nodded, pleased that I seemed interested. "It's very impressive. Holds an astonishing density of information. Numerical, of course, about the, uh, population. But there are also graphical representations, film-clips. Well, you must have been on there at some point, now that I think of it. Didn't you tell me Kate said they'd filmed you winning that first race? Graphics take a lot of computing power, of course—a picture's worth considerably more than a thousand words online. But the hard part, it turned out, was building the security system. And we were lucky there, in a sense, because a hacker got in late last summer and showed us the weak points of the version we were running. He found a very subtle bug, and it took a long time to fix it."

Hmmm, I thought.

"Well, we probably shouldn't have put all that live auction and competition data up there quite yet," he said. "The hacker was on for about an hour, just looking around, it seems. Jerking off, I guess. No clue as to who he was. People who understand these things were very impressed with how cleverly he got in and out. They speculate that he could have covered his tracks completely, but didn't want to. Wanted to let somebody know he'd been there. Sorry—*he* or *she,* I guess I should have said."

I had to smile a little at that fastidious, PC touch. But it *was* a he, I thought. Because I know…. And I thought that maybe I should tell…. But surely, I thought, Jonathan can read it in my face, and will demand to know what I'm not telling him.

But he was drifting somewhere, still far away in the land of his story. He caught himself now, apologetically, willing himself back into the here and now.

"It was interesting," he shrugged, "to see how they put together something like that. Kate and I had fun learning a little about the technical stuff. But it's probably a lot less interesting to hear me tell about it."

"Oh," he smiled now, "and we'll make sure you get real books to read this time. We'll get that into the agreement as well."

I blushed as I thanked him. I was pleased that he'd thought of it.

"Which reminds me," he continued, "that book you were reading before the auction—and it was a cyberpunk book, too, wasn't it?, how appropriate—anyhow, which of the stories did you like?"

Well, why not talk about books? After all, we'd gotten all our business affairs out of the way. And maybe, I thought then, I didn't really have anything to tell him after all. Turned out we'd enjoyed the same stories in *Mirrorshades,* too.

He continued, "We could go to the movies, tonight, if you'd like to. We can probably find some interesting American film that won't open in the States for another month or two."

"Sure," I said eagerly, "uh…Jonathan." He nodded, enjoying the way I'd said it, the two rhythms superimposed. The casual chatty rhythm of a man and a woman planning an evening out—and underneath it, the fetishes speaking in their own measured cadences. He smiled at the angle of my shoulders, the little arch in my back that kept my breasts displayed to him, the stiff nipples outlined by the dress's soft red wool.

"They were right," he said, contentedly. "Kate and all those professional types. I didn't know how to train you, didn't know at all what I had. But I did find you, after all, which ought to count for something. And I've got you back now, that's the important thing."

We checked the movie listings. Easy to agree on one—the one with Isabelle Huppert as a sentimental pornographer. Not bad, either. Hip and knowing, if not quite coherent, we agreed, walking out of the theater into misty, light rain. And we do like the same movies (same books, too), I thought briefly, though I didn't suppose it really mattered any more. The sidewalks were slick, and I had to walk very carefully in the fetish shoes. We went to a nightclub, to slow-dance for a while. The shoes made me as tall as he was; my head was on his shoulder, one of his hands on my ass. I could feel his cock hardening.

"Enough," he finally whispered. "Let's get out of here."

And in the little gilded elevator, riding up the six flights to our hotel room, he said softly, "Play with yourself, make yourself come."

Obediently, I put my hand up my dress. I moved my finger slowly. I finished in the hotel room, standing up, teetering on the heels, while he watched intently.

"Take off your dress and hang it up," he said, after I'd gotten my breath back. "Leave on the shoes and stockings." And when I turned back to him, he was balancing the new riding crop in his palm, frowning in perfectionist concentration.

He took off his jacket, loosened his tie, and fixed a gag very tightly to my mouth. It was the kind with a rubber ball in it; he'd bought it at the store where we'd gotten my shoes. It would work well. It even stifled the sound of my gagging.

The room had a little alcove, in front of the window. He nodded for me to stand there. I could see the lights of Montmartre over the rooftops, through the thin curtains and the mist.

"Hands over your head," he said, climbing onto a chair to slip a chain through the hook that was mounted in the ceiling. He didn't have to tell me to arch my back, to spread my legs—so that I could balance better, be more open. I knew all those things, I did them without thinking.

I heard a clock strike somewhere. I think it was three in the morning. I remember the first blow, my stifled scream behind the nauseating gag. And then he whipped me until I fainted.

At least, that's what he told me afterward. He'd used smelling salts, he said, to bring me around, after he'd unfastened the hooks of the corset. I couldn't remember much, but I didn't think that I'd fainted from the pain. It had been the dizzying effort to understand what was happening to me.

Jonathan *and* Kate, I thought, rotating their names around in my mind. My goodness. It would be like having McCabe *and* Mrs. Miller. Well, if you could call it having them. I mean, they'd be the ones doing the having, wouldn't they? Slaves exchanged between lovers. Always the most valuable. I thought I might swoon again if I thought about it too hard.

He'd been disconcerted by my fainting. I'd never done that before, and he wasn't sure what to make of it. And I couldn't help him, though part of me wanted to. But my vertigo and confusion, and the detachment that they seemed to produce, were making it hard for me to know what I was feeling just then.

He rubbed salve gently on my ass, after using a wet towel to wipe away the little bit of blood he'd drawn. I could see that the blood had freaked him. Drawing blood was against the rules of the association, and Jonathan believed in rules. Especially after his run-in with Mr. Brewer. In any case, if the terms he'd outlined to me were a little much for my imagination, the blood and fainting were all a little much for the control freak in him.

He brought me brandy, stroked my face, gave me drags of his cigarettes. I lay on my stomach, facing the window. The clouds were clearing, and the sky behind Montmartre was turning to that inky predawn blue that makes you realize how soon it will be morning. He took off my shoes and stockings. He even loosened my collar a notch.

He told me things, stray marginalia from his stories, odd, confessional fragments of meta-narrative. "I didn't want to tell you about Kate, you know, until after you'd agreed to come back to me. I wanted you to come back to *me*, not to her and me. And I'm still a little afraid that you'll become more devoted to her than you are to me."

"I do care about you, you know," he concluded, sadly, but a little aggressively, a little self-importantly, as well. Yes, I thought, and as I reviewed all the stories we'd told each other these last days, I'd be able to figure out exactly how much. It might be a complex pattern, but it was a finite one, a closed system. I closed my eyes, seeing things I'd seen and things I'd just heard about—Kate a riot of Renoir flesh in a red armchair, Jonathan kissing Ariel in the pony cart. Everything not just itself, but a sign of power or passion or need. I'd be a cipher in this system, a tremulous ground for communication and fantasy. They'd use whips to write each other love letters on my skin. And they'd tease and torment each other—by how he indulged me, or she fine-tuned my discipline.

I felt dizzy again. Alice falling down the rabbit hole, flying past cupboards and bookshelves, maps and pictures on her way down to the center of the earth. Free fall through a closed system. But it wasn't really a closed system, I reminded myself. Not quite. It had a leak—somebody had sneaked in uninvited, an outsider had imposed his own point of view. I found myself concentrating on that rogue viewpoint, that intruder's eye pressed to the keyhole. When you're losing your balance you can steady yourself, you know, if you concentrate your vision on a still point somewhere in the distance.

Jonathan stroked my head, and put a sheet and a comforter over me. They were light and warm and silky, and didn't hurt my welts and bruises too much. I thought I'd be able to sleep.

I remember that the sky was grayish when I drifted off. And I don't remember him coming to bed. I think he was still sitting up, smoking and drinking brandy and watching me.

The Fifth Day

CARRIE

I didn't see him when I woke up late the next morning either. There were croissants and *pain au chocolat* and coffee in a thermos pot for me, and I was almost indecently hungry. My muscles were stiff, and my ass hurt, but really, it was nothing I wasn't used to. And as for last night's sadness and confusion—well, it's funny, isn't it, how you can fall asleep entirely confused and wake up clear-eyed and confident about what comes next. I got out of bed, stretching my body in the daylight that was streaming through the big windows. It was almost noon—a beautiful, unseasonably warm, gloriously sunny day. I did some yoga and lots more stretches, and took a shower. And then I ate the food and drank the coffee, made up my face, and got down on my knees in the pool of bright sunlight in the middle of the floor to wait for him.

He looked surprised to find me that way when he came in, carrying a few packages. He looked pleased, delighted really.

"Well," he said, as I bent to kiss his shoes. And when I knelt back up, he stroked my head. Then he reached behind my neck to tighten the collar.

"Well," he said again, "let's go for a walk, shall we? We can have lunch, too."

He handed me the packages. "Put these on."

I was surprised by the pretty, high-necked white dress, though less so by the elegant, mid-calf high-heeled laceup boots. "It's such a summery day," he said, halfway apologetically.

"I'll bet there's forsythia blossoming in the Bois de Boulogne," he added. "Perhaps even jonquils."

It's not as nice a park, actually, as Golden Gate Park in San Francisco, but it's sort of the same idea. And people dress a whole lot better there. I was glad he'd bought me the dress. And the boots, too—they were lovely and much easier to walk in than the shoes I'd had on the night before. Still, the heels were quite high, so I had to walk carefully. I was very conscious of my sore ass and stiff muscles, about keeping my back very straight despite all that, and my eyes lowered, as well.

Just like that boy over there, I thought suddenly. Odd to see somebody else who'd so evidently been whipped recently, as I had. A lady in a pale pink suit and hat was sitting on a bench, while he stood beside her, his eyes lowered. He was slender, very blond, very delicious-looking in a vanilla-colored shirt and white slacks, boat shoes, and no socks.

Two other ladies came by then, one a bit older than the other. The older one spoke to the lady in pink, and smiled at the boy, and then all three women laughed. And the boy knelt, for just a moment, to kiss the older woman's hand, much as I'd knelt for the old saddle maker.

221

I blinked. Was I imagining it, or were there other masters and slaves strolling among the forsythia that the false spring had forced into bloom? I couldn't tell for sure, but there seemed to be odd energy freighting the scene. I looked around. Yes, definitely. I mean, it was clearly a public thoroughfare, with all sorts of people on it, but there was also a pattern subtly woven through the random population, if you had eyes to see. Not everybody was participating in it, but for people who knew the code, it was a kind of parade, a ritual of display. My eyes were lowered, so I could feel, more than see, the appraising glances directed at me. I could feel eyes tracing the outlines of my nipples, marking the shape of my ass and my black-stockinged thighs under the thin white linen dress. And noting approvingly, from the care and slight stiffness with which I was walking, that I'd received a good whipping the night before. Of course they couldn't see my collar—the high neck of the dress hid it. But they didn't need to. Well, anybody who'd need to see it wouldn't have understood any of the gazes and postures, calculating frowns, and complacent smiles that were being exchanged on those sunny paths that day.

Jonathan took my hand. Once again, I could tell he was pleased that I was performing so well. Strange—my whole year with Mr. Constant, I'd felt as clumsy and eager as I had the first day. But today I could tell that I really wasn't a beginner anymore. I knew that I could hold my own at Kate's.

"Are you hungry?" he asked.

"Yes, Jonathan."

He led me along the path to the edge of the park, to a tea room, set in a garden surrounded by a high, ornate fence of old, and slightly rusted, iron.

The room had high ceilings, gilded moldings, friezes of nymphs and cherubs. I sat very straight at our table, like a child being taken for a special birthday lunch, and ate the fancy little sandwiches, cucumber and smoked salmon and rabbit terrine. We drank champagne and Earl Grey tea, and Jonathan had ordered *poires belle Hélène* for dessert.

A man in a green sport jacket came over to our table. He had a dark, weaselly face.

"Is it the American pony?" he asked Jonathan, stroking my head. "The one who surprised us all at the Hudson River Rainbow Races?"

I could see that Jonathan was startled to realize that I had a public, in a manner of speaking. And that he wasn't sure how he felt about that. Still, he smiled and nodded.

The man grimaced. "I lost seventy-five thousand francs on that race." He fondled my ear. "And I could not attend the party afterwards, unfortunately...." He paused, looking expectant and a little pushy.

"Uh, well, would you care to try her now?" Jonathan said. And at the murmur of thanks, he said, "Go with the gentleman, Carrie." Across the floor of the tea room, I could see our waiter turn on his heel, taking our dessert back to the kitchen.

Weasel-face led me to a door at the back of the room. The waiter standing by it nodded, and we entered what looked like one of those male smoking clubs you see in movies—big leather armchairs studded with brass tacks, oriental rugs. But it was co-ed. I mean, the people in the armchairs, getting serviced in one way or another, were both men and women. And there was a punishment corner as well, flanked with umbrella stands full of whips and canes. A waiter was caning a red-haired girl who was weeping behind her tight gag. I wondered if her master or mistress had specified that they use a cane, rather than a whip or a strap or a flogger. Perhaps all the available implements were listed on a special punishment menu they would bring to your table. Or perhaps the cane was the specialty of the day.

Meanwhile, my guy led me to a chair and ottoman in a dim corner. I knelt to undo his pants, and then he lifted the skirt of my pretty white dress and slapped my ass sharply. I turned and bent over the ottoman, my face against the leather, my skirt spread over me like an umbrella blown open in a storm. He took his time then, surveying the stripes and bruises that Jonathan had put on me. *"Mortel,"* he murmured, before he plunged in. It was the only thing he said the whole time, dismissing me with a nod afterward when I knelt at his feet to thank him.

The red-haired girl, I noticed, was kneeling at a little makeup table now, bathing her swollen eyes and carefully lining up the paints and brushes she'd need for repairing her face. She did a good job, too, looking quite lovely when her waiter led her back to her table a few minutes after I'd returned to Jonathan. She and her master weren't sitting too far from us—close enough that I could see that the chair the waiter pulled out for her had no seat. There was just an empty circle where the seat would be, like a heavily padded toilet seat. I wished I had one like it.

Weasel-face came back to our table later, to thank Jonathan, and to commend him on what a killer disciplinarian he was. I kept my eyes down, nibbling at my dessert, the pears and ice cream, chocolate sauce and *crème Chantilly* that the waiter had promptly brought when I'd returned. They'd probably had to remake it, I thought, toss out the one that had been on its way when Weasel-face had asked for me. The *crème* had probably gotten all runny while he'd been buggering me. Probably that was why the prices on the menu were so astronomical—to underwrite the expense of all those double desserts and other little adjustments it must take to keep a place like this running smoothly. And the clientele probably preferred it that way, too—the high prices would keep the place from being listed in *Frommer's* or the *Rough Guide*.

"Yes," Jonathan said, later in the cab, "that's how it will be." He sounded dreamy and bemused, his eyes on some building and his fingers fiddling with the prickly little hairs on my cunt.

"It's an interesting feeling," he added, turning to me now. He moved a finger inside me, pulling me closer to him. "I'm not used to having to offer you when politeness demands it." He kissed my eyelids, my cheeks, he probed my mouth with his tongue, while his finger continued to tease my clit and his other hand traced the welts he'd put on me.

"You can come," he whispered. "Do it quietly."

As a mouse. A very greedy, hungry little one. Letting out each spasm as a deep, quiet sigh. I wasn't fooling the cab driver, but he was reasonably circumspect. Probably because Jonathan looked like a big tipper.

I leaned against his shoulder and closed my eyes, thinking of the park, the boy in the white pants, the green foliage and yellow blossoms. I wondered if there weren't areas like that in every city. Public venues that were invisible to those with untutored vision. Zones where an alternate world of ritual, exchange, and display coincided with the normal, everyday world—as though the stage lights had been turned up and you could see what was behind the scrim, if your eyes had been trained to see.

The cab stopped, and I gathered myself up, smoothing down my skirt as Jonathan paid the driver, who threw me a brief bright white toothy grin. I'd been surprised that I'd been permitted that orgasm. But it made sense, I thought now. Jonathan would spoil me on these holiday trips. There'd be movies and pretty dresses, ice cream and orgasms—he'd be like a guilty divorced father taking the kids to McDonalds on his custody weekends. Only he wouldn't have to feel guilty. He wouldn't do any permanent damage—not with Kate in charge of my day-to-day routines. We stepped into the hotel elevator.

"We're going to a party tonight," he said. "An acquaintance invited me, while the gentleman was using you. So you can rest this afternoon—well, you can in an hour or so, anyway. I have some errands I need to do. Oh, and I forgot to tell you. This is our last day. I mean, I've got plane reservations. We go home tomorrow."

JONATHAN

Had I truly meant to say that, you know, about its being our last day? Well, in retrospect there was definitely something valedictory about those last twenty-four hours together. But at the time—no, I wasn't conscious of any double meanings. She'd been a very good girl and I was pleased with her. I was looking forward to taking her home. To seeing Kate go to work on her. And I was looking forward to bringing her to the party that night, too.

I hadn't wanted to give her to the guy in the tea room. I'd always enjoyed sharing her with friends, but I'd resisted giving her to strangers—people I'd never seen before, whose only bond with me was a set of shared codes and rituals. But now, after the fact, I'd found it surprisingly sensible and gratifying. What else, I thought, do you base civility upon, besides shared codes and rituals, gifts and generous exchanges? I was glad I'd taken her on today's outing.

She was on the floor at my feet now, her face pressed into the carpet, her white dress up over her head and spread out around her ass. I smoked two slow cigarettes, surrounding her with smoke rings. I undid my pants, and then I knelt behind her, unfastening all the little buttons down her back, starting with the high neck and moving downward, tracing the bumps of her spine with my tongue. I reached up under the dress and squeezed her breasts, pulling myself back up, arching around her, until my cock was against her ass. "Open yourself up," I said. "Use your hands to spread yourself." I entered her, thinking of the guy in his unspeakable green jacket. I held her body close, pressing my belly against her.

"Kneel up," I said afterward, when I'd sat back in the armchair and she'd turned around to thank me. I took the crushed, wrinkled dress off her, pulling it gently over her head. And then I just looked at her for a while. I nodded, giving her permission to fix the garter that had come unfastened while I'd been fucking her.

"Bring me the whip," I told her. I love the moment when a slave lays an implement of discipline in your hand, with a soft, trained mouth. I love the trust in the gesture and the fear in their eyes. The hurried self-scrutiny—what have I done?

what *haven't* I done? The remorse, if they know that a punishment is coming. Or—like Carrie that day, who knew she'd behaved impeccably—the certainty that what was coming would be gratuitous, whimsical. Pain that had no purpose (no purpose!) but the master's pleasure. And finally, either way, the struggle to accept—to welcome—the pain.

But I didn't beat her. I prodded her through her repertoire of presentations. I nudged her into position with the whip; I used my fingers, my tongue, to trace the raised welts on her skin. I closed my eyes, pretended I was blind, tried to memorize her with my fingertips.

She'd be punished at the party tonight, I thought, after they found the demerit token she was bound to collect when, inevitably, someone would notice the spark of consciousness in her eye. The tiny light that would flash as she registered amusement or amazement, took note of some telling or outré detail. No wonder she was an expert on party punishments. And she was right, they do tend toward the funky. I'd enjoy that.

"Tonight," I said, "at the party, I'll arrange for the token master to give me all the tokens in your coinbox. After the ceremony, I mean. And I'll take them home with me, and when we get back here you'll tell me the story that goes along with each one. So remember all of them, everybody who uses you."

"Yes, Jonathan," she said it softly, but very clearly. "I'll remember everything."

"Just see that you do," I said.

My voice was hoarse, anxious. I reached down for her, holding her tightly while I kissed her. And then I got to my feet.

"Well," I said, "you'd better rest. And I'd better not put off my errands any longer."

So no, all in all I guess I wasn't really surprised, when I got back to our room a few hours later, around dusk, and found that she was gone, leaving this note:

> *Thanks for manufacturing a reason to leave me alone while I finally do what I need to. I love you for making it a little easier for me.*
> *And I will remember everything. Always.*
>
> *So long, Carrie*

She'd taken her clothes and a few pieces of the more soft-core paraphernalia. Whips that were more for show than punishment, things like that. Items I'd bought at the sex shop on Gaité, for guests. I was surprised. Wimpy stuff, I would have imagined her sneering inwardly, babyish stuff, for amateurs.

I wondered, briefly, if she was going back to California. I knew that her department at school would take her back in a flash. And she had that friend, that gangly boy I'd sometimes seen her with. She'd want to see him. I knew a little about what she did when she wasn't with me, you see. I'd spy on her from time to time, hanging around the Mission District, lurking in dark corners behind underground newspapers in grungy coffeehouses, to catch a glimpse of her in her real life, in her silly slacker clothes. Okay, now you know—keep it to yourself, okay? But I wouldn't do it again. Because it was too silly. And because, I thought, even if she did go back—to Berkeley, or San Francisco—I'd never manage to see her, never even run into her. When somebody's gone from your life, they're gone, into a separate, even if proximate, sphere.

I lit a cigarette. Stopping was going to be unpleasant, I thought, poking around the room some more, inventorying what else she'd taken. One of the corsets. And the little whisk. I suddenly had a flash of some guy who might be getting his own gift subscription to *On Our Backs*. He'd be young, I imagined, and I hoped he'd be crazy about her—wildly, and wholeheartedly, the whole nine yards, caring for her with a depth and a completeness that I'd never be able to match. I shrugged, a little surprised I'd had that thought. And a little touched and pleased with myself as well, if truth be told.

I figured I'd better call Kate and tell her the plan was off, that I'd be coming home alone tomorrow. Because, as it turns out, some things can't be arranged. So we'd just have to make do with each other. It was a tough life. Well, we'd have each other and Sylvie and Stephanie and Randy. And whoever else she'd collect. Like Ariel. Hmm, Ariel. Maybe I could use Ariel to help me stop smoking—as a deterrent, you know. Kate had suggested it once.

I picked up the wrinkled white dress from the floor and smoothed it out. *Vale,* Carrie. So long and farewell.

CARRIE

I had to write out my note three times. The first draft had lots of run-on sentences and meandering paragraphs that never got to the point—perhaps because I wasn't sure what the point exactly was. I wound up crossing out just about everything. Keep it simple. Well, I guess I'm not as afraid of simplicity as I once was.

And when I finished the second draft, I noticed that it was actually tear-stained, and that I was crying my eyes out. Partly, I was miserable about leaving him, of course, but partly, I was absurdly and sentimentally moved by the brave, chipper tone I'd pulled off in the letter. And partly, or perhaps especially, I was finally letting myself cry in hurt and rage, the tears I hadn't shed the night before commingling with a year's angry tears about the love letter he'd written when he hadn't really meant it, because he'd found it diverting (or therapeutic, perhaps) to imagine he was in love with me.

For the third draft, I kept my face far away from the paper. But I was still weeping, my eyes "portable and commodious oceans," as some entirely ditzed seventeenth century religious poet once wrote. Remembering the phrase made me smile a little as I sniffled. And then of course I was disappointed in myself: I had imagined that my grief would have been a little purer than it was turning out to be.

But why should it be, I thought. Nothing about this thing was purely one way or the other. I certainly wasn't being purely brave. Brave would have meant leaving to make it on my own, dazed and alone, and I'm not as brave as that. Perhaps you imagined me trudging off into the sunset, sadder but wiser for the experience—sighing and squaring my shoulders. Like the girl in *A Certain Smile*, the first grown-up book I'd read all the way through in French. "I was a woman," the book's final sentence goes, "who had loved a man." And *that*, I'd thought at twelve and a half, must be how you felt when you were really grown up.

But there were other ways to grow up, I thought now, and other ways to play out the story. Because it seemed that you could take one of those midlife-crisis-meets-youthful-confusion love affair stories (and Mr. Constant was right, this was really an old story) and put a whole new spin on it. As Kate had tried to do, dreaming up an arrangement so total, and so

231

challenging, that Jonathan would never have to leave, and I wouldn't have the strength to. Maybe at this very minute, they'd be leading me into Kate's parlor, and Jonathan would be sitting in an armchair, smiling at Kate, a drink in his hand. I'd kneel. I'd present to him. I'd barely be breathing, I'd be so excited, wanting to show him how she'd been training me, hoping that he'd be pleased, that he'd find me improved.

But none of that would ever happen. Because, and at the last minute, too, I'd lucked into an escape clause—the clause that contained my safe word. Well, there had been this other story, you see, that had slipped in—almost parenthetically—between my year with Mr. Constant and these five days with Jonathan. And I hadn't told Jonathan this story. I almost had, when he'd told me about the hacker. I might have, you know, if he'd noticed that I had something to tell him. But he hadn't, and I hadn't, and I was glad of that now.

Not that it was a story I could easily imagine telling him. It had a hero, for one thing—an unlikely one, who'd hacked through tangled vines of information to win an unobstructed view of the girl imprisoned in her tower. And who some-how—through the deliberateness and patience and innocence of his gaze—had broken the spell that held her thrall.

And I don't even like fairy tales, or swords or spells or sorcery, or any of that redundant archetypal stuff. But by that last day in Paris, I'd admitted to myself that—like it or not—it was mine, this ultimate, unfinished story. It had chosen me, and I would have to have a hand in shaping it, giving it a little more wit and originality. I knew that I didn't want to tell this story to Jonathan. I wanted to keep it, to live it—well, to see if I could make a life out of it, anyway. And that's how I knew it was time to go.

The First Day, Earlier

CARRIE'S STORY, TOO

I'd settled into the seat of the train from Paris to Avignon. I was glad I was next to the window, because I thought I might be too nervous to read. This is it, I thought. The first day of the rest of my life.

I hoped Jonathan would like the clothes I'd bought in Paris. I'd gone there directly from Greece, the day they'd taken off my collar and cuffs and Mr. Constant had given me the money—more than a hundred thousand dollars, including a credit card. He'd been nice that last day, removing his glasses and trying to having a real conversation with me in his office.

"I enjoyed the year," he said, "and I've always thought you were a nice girl. I'm not so sure about that Jonathan, though, you know."

"Well, I'll have to see," was all I said.

He supposed I would. He wished me luck, but unfortunately, he was a bit pressed for time at the moment. He had an interview scheduled—a new young economics genius he hoped to hire. It wouldn't be easy to replace Stefan, who was training at that very minute, happy at last in the dressage ring. Tony'd left two weeks ago, for New York, to try to make it as a dancer.

Well, I said, I wish you luck, too, Mr. Constant. He'd need it, I thought—or maybe it would be Annie who'd need it, to impose some form and discipline onto Stefan's fierce adoration. We shook hands, and I turned to go. Oh, just one more thing, I said. I'd borrowed a book from his library....

"Keep it," he said.

I wasn't sure I'd remember how to use money, but it didn't turn out to be a problem. I needed clothes to go see Jonathan in, and I started spending recklessly—going to snooty, ultra-hip shops that charged a thousand francs for a tiny black T-shirt that would leave a little line of skin above the top of your skirt. It had been fun the first few days, in a numb, giddy, slightly autistic way, and then I'd calmed down a little and realized how alone I was. I hadn't wanted to admit to myself how difficult it would be to be free and on my own, even in Paris with a virtually bottomless credit card.

I phoned my friend Stuart in Berkeley.

"I'll pay for your plane ticket, I'll pay for everything," I said. "Please, I need to see you."

He could tell, when I came to meet him at the airport, how overwrought and slightly hysterical I was, and how much I needed to talk. We must have hit every café in the city, talking nonstop for the five days he was there, and I could feel myself slowly calming down. I began with all my war stories from the year with Mr. Constant—but the conversation gradually evened out, because he had a lot of stuff to work through too. His boyfriend, Greg, had a job offer in Maine, and he was probably going to take it. And somehow, the two of them were determined to make this arrangement work. I was pretty impressed, though all the stuff about relationships was kind of a foreign language to me. And we spent hours, poring over Jonathan's letter together.

"Mr. Constant was right," Stuart said, for about the millionth time, his last day. "That's a spoiled, selfish letter. Look, you've had your adventures. It's time to come back to Berkeley. Come on. You can sleep on our couch. If you'll read the other chapter of my dissertation, you can have the bed and *we'll* sleep on the couch."

"I can't," I said. "You know I have to see this thing through. And anyhow, I've made so many corrections to the chapter I've been reading that it'll take you a year to get it into shape. Good, though."

It *was* good. And I'd enjoyed adding my opinions. It had been fun, all the arguments and discussions we'd been having. I'd miss him. I put my arm around him, and he squeezed my waist.

"So what'll we do this afternoon?" I asked. We had reservations for a fancy farewell dinner, and we'd figured we'd go dancing later in some clubs he knew about.

"I need notebooks," he said, "sexy French stationery. A good Waterman pen. I mean, we're in the world capital of office supplies, you know."

We wound up spending more in the *papeterie* than we would that night in the restaurant. And I cried when he kissed me good-bye at the train station early the next morning.

But, as the train started to fill up. I realized that I was actually feeling pretty good. I pulled out one of the new notebooks I'd bought, and the Waterman pen. And the book I was reading. I wanted to copy down some words whose eighteenth-century usages I wasn't sure of. Five days with Stuart had brought back some of my pedantic old habits.

It was an interesting book. *Clarissa,* by Samuel Richardson. All four volumes and two thousand unabridged pages of it, that somebody had left in Mr. Constant's library. I probably wouldn't have begun it, except that I'd been so sick of reading stacks of downloaded pages. But now that I was reading it, I was glad I'd picked it up. And surprised by what I'd found, too, and increasingly involved in the narrative alternations of female and male voice—eighteenth-century gender impersonation—the male voice a funhouse of narcissistic projection.

I had some breakfast in the dining car, my nose still in Volume IV, and stumbled back into my seat, overturning the open briefcase at the feet of the guy next to me. An English translation of Sade's *Justine* tumbled out, as well as a bunch of notebooks. I murmured that I was sorry, as he scrambled to put the books away, repeating several times that it was "no problem."

"That a good book?" he asked, in English. He was American. A student, maybe. I didn't know if I really felt like having a conversation right then. Yeah, and if you believe *that,* well, there's a bridge halfway across the Rhône that maybe I could sell you. The truth is I would have talked to anybody who'd listen—the last few days with Stuart had shown me how utterly starved for talking I was. Poor guy, I thought, turning toward him and taking a deep breath, he tries a cheesy pickup gambit, and in return he gets a lecture on Samuel Richardson and the Deconstruction of Gender. Tough, I thought. He asked for it.

He hung in, though, following my argument and even asking some good questions. He hadn't read much, but he had a logical mind, keeping me honest about stuff I was pretty much spouting off on-the-fly.

"And the female voice?" he asked. "What keeps it so grounded?"

I frowned. "Well," I said slowly, "Richardson would have given you a religious answer. But I'd say the opposite. I think she prefigures a kind of modern, secular autonomy. I mean, even though she couldn't legally own anything, she always owns her body and soul. You never doubt that."

"I think that she pissed off the Marquis de Sade, with her groundedness, her reasonableness," I added. "So when he parodied her in *Justine*"—I nodded toward his briefcase—"he did her voice, like the big bad wolf doing Little Red Riding Hood's grandma, in a kind of moral falsetto. He made her goody-goody, namby-pamby. And—this was a smart, deconstructive move—he gave her a narcissistic streak. I mean, Justine obeys more for effect than to save herself, or to save others. She gets off on what a good girl she is—she's as much an admiration junky as Richardson's Mr. Lovelace."

And I could understand *that,* I thought. But then, I seem to have an affinity for fables of domination, the ones that interrogate the dark side of what it means to be material, autonomous, and individual, and that career dizzily between Richardson's impossible pieties and Sade's equally impossible tableaux of total satiation. And I realized that I hadn't said anything for a while.

"Still," I continued, trying to pick up the thread of my argument, "Sade was a big fan of Richardson's, which might seem surprising, but...."

I wondered, suddenly, if I'd embarrassed him by bringing *Justine* into the discussion like that. I mean, some people are secretive about reading pornography. I hadn't meant it that way, of course. I'd just wanted to talk about the books, the writers. But you never know what people think is okay to talk about. And I'd been cut off from normal conversation for so long. My voice trailed off uncertainly.

"Yeah, you were saying?" he asked softly.

"Oh, nothing," I said. "Sorry if I was talking your ear off." I *had* embarrassed him, I guessed. He looked nervous. I smiled apologetically and made a show of turning back to my book.

"Oh, no," he said, "no, go on, it's interesting." He said it slowly, making it a four-syllable word. And then neither of us seemed to know what to say. The silence got a little unsettling, and he bit his lip, nervously.

I noticed it then, the space between his front teeth. The gold-rimmed glasses, wavy hair, aquiline nose. Cute, actually, in a nerdy kind of way....

"Oh, *no*," I gasped. "*You!*" And I'd been worried *I'd* embarrassed *him*.

"I'm sorry," he said quickly. "Really truly. God, I'm so sorry. I know there had to be a better way to do this, but you have to believe me, I've thought about it for a year and I haven't been able to figure one out."

How could I have not recognized him? The waiter, that first night, the one Mr. Constant had shown me off to, "next time, she's your tip." And we'd eaten in that restaurant a few other times, and he'd given me to the waiters (he'd often done that—once or twice to a chef, too, when the food was really special), but this waiter hadn't been there any of those times. I'd thought about him, too, I remembered. Yes, I'd even been a little disappointed, I realized now, shamefaced and angry.

"I suppose you think I owe you a fuck," I said sharply. "Well, okay, we can use the WC at the end of the car. Come on."

I must have spoken more loudly than I'd intended because the people in the seat ahead of us swiveled their heads around, looking eager and amused and curious. I guessed they understood English, or at least, what *fuck* meant.

Meanwhile, the guy, the waiter or whoever he was, was looking terrified. "Oh, no, *please,*" he whispered in a mortified voice. "Oh, god, *no,* that's not what I want. Oh, shit, well of course I *want* to, but...*please,* Carrie...."

He knew my name. Well, of course he did. I could hear Mr. Constant's voice, "It's nice to watch you, Carrie." And, yes, of course, "Avignon, March 15," too. He knew my name and he knew where I was going. And I could remember his hands, too, how they'd felt on my breasts, my ass.

"Okay," I said, doing my best to stay calm. "I'll ride the rest of the way in the dining car or in the WC or whatever. No, even better, I'll just get off at Lyon. But first, just tell me why you're following me, you creep."

"Listen," he said, softly, "working that private room is always an amazing experience. The tips are great and the women, well...I hadn't known there *were* women like that. And I especially wanted to work there that night, because I knew that Edouard Constant had reserved the room."

"You know who he is?" I asked stupidly.

He looked surprised. "Well, he's, uh, famous," he said, trying to cover up his astonishment that I didn't seem to know this. "Anyway…the women are amazing—but not like you were. I kept watching you—well, you know *that,* I knew you could tell, I wished I could be cooler about it, but…. And, well, by the end of the evening, I'd learned something. I mean I'd learned everything. Or it seemed that way to me anyhow. About this whole other dimension to sex. Things that had never made sense to me—perverse sex, fancy sex. It had always sounded stupid, redundant. But I knew you weren't stupid, and I watched you, and I got it. Like when I got calculus, maybe. I could see how sex could be like a story—one that built up slowly, and kept you guessing, and maybe had a trick ending. I could see the humor of it too, and the irony. The infinity of permutations, the endless redefinitions to one more point of precision, and the limit—well, I think if you know what you're doing, maybe you never reach the limit…" and he trailed off, seeing something, I thought, that I couldn't see. Maybe it was some complicated curve plotted against a pair of axes, or maybe it was me, in the restaurant, in my punk Roissy dress.

"It was an education," he continued. "I mean, I've been reading all this porn since then, but it just confirmed what I learned from you that night. Of course, the problem with that was that I also fell in love with you. It was the cognitive jolt, I suppose—I tend to get the physical stuff all scrambled up with important mindtrips—I mean the first woman I ever fell in love with was my seventh grade algebra teacher."

I laughed and he bit his lip again, amazed, I guess, at how much he'd told me without taking a breath.

"And I also thought you were incredibly beautiful," he added softly.

Oh dear. What was I going to do with this sweet nutcase?

He was nice though, I thought, he really was. And when you've lived a year in the land of Sylvie and Stephanie, it's sort of pleasant to hear yourself called "incredibly beautiful," even if you know it's arrant nonsense.

"Anyhow," he continued, "when Constant said 'Avignon, March 15,' it soldered a whole new set of connections into my brain. I've been planning this trip all year. I was gonna plant myself in the Place d'Horloge all day and maybe tomorrow and then I was gonna tell myself, 'Okay, Daniel, you can forget about her now.' I didn't think we'd be on the same train or anything. I didn't really believe you'd be here at all. And then I didn't get out of work last night until like two A.M. So I got to the station this morning figuring that if you had been here I'd already probably missed you and, my God, there you were, on line to buy your ticket. I got in line a few people behind you and then those people changed plans or something and got out of line and I was right behind you. I was really worried—I was afraid to be quite so close to you, you know. But you didn't notice, you didn't recognize me—well, you had your face buried in *Clarissa*, anyway—and I just held my breath and hung in there, and...and here I am. I guess they sell the tickets in order of seats. I'm sorry, Carrie, really. I didn't mean to scare you. But I've thought about you all year. I had to come. But I won't bother you after today. Please believe me. I promise."

"I believe you," I said. He's not a nutcase, I thought. He's just got his nerves a little too close to the skin. Like I do.

"Why'd you leave the restaurant?" I asked a little peevishly, as though I thought *he* owed *me* a fuck.

"Well, I had to go back to work," he said. "That wasn't really my job. I was just traveling, hanging out, working illegally before my real job started. I know people at that restaurant. The tips are great even if you don't get to work the private room. But that night, though—well, it turned out they really needed me that night. One guy was sick and another one was in a major crisis with his girlfriend. He was so grateful that I could take his shift. Anyhow, I work in Paris now. Research. Cognitive science. Neural networks."

Cognitive science and neural networks, I thought. And in his spare time, he seems to have worked out quite a fair understanding of my basic sexual modus operandi. Smart. No, not just smart. *Really* smart. I looked at him for a while. Except for Stuart, of course, he was the first person I'd really looked at since I'd left Mr. Constant's. Cute enough, I guessed, if you were willing to stretch your judgment a little—if you liked him, as I seemed to. Your basic okay male shoulders, hips and thighs in black jeans, white T-shirt, and a leather jacket. The jacket looked familiar. Not bad, I thought, but a little sloppy in the shoulder seams. And the zippers are too shiny, the whole thing a little too stiff and new looking. I realized it was sort of a knockoff of the one I was wearing. Well, after all, he hadn't been paid as well as I'd been this last year. Still, I was touched by its stiff, new look, thinking of him buying it to look tough in, for me. Anyhow, under the jacket everything seemed to be more or less in place and okay. Nothing special, though, except I liked the gap between his teeth.

We were pulling into Lyon now. I guessed I wasn't getting off the train. So I told him...well, I didn't have time to tell him everything, but I told him a lot. About my year, and about Jonathan. He nodded seriously from time to time. At first I was relieved that he wasn't horrified, but as my story continued, his lack of response began to trouble me a little.

242

I mean, even Stuart had looked a little green around the gills when I'd told him some of the heavier stuff. Daniel just didn't look surprised enough, and he didn't ask any questions either. Of course, now I know that he was afraid to say anything that might give away that he'd hacked the association's online system. He'd been a little ashamed of it (though pleased that he'd figured out how to—he'd never hacked anything before, it's not something he's interested in). And afraid of what I might think of him for knowing so much about my body—the association maintains amazing statistics, including closely calibrated measurements of how much pain and penetration you can tolerate. And he couldn't imagine how to tell me about some rather obsessive viewing of a seven-second clip of me crossing the finish line at the Hudson River Rainbow Races—he watched it something like four hundred times the night he broke in. Which he thought I might find a little weird (as though anything could have been weirder than actually running that race). And he worried about having violated my privacy, too, even if he'd intended the break-in as a labor of love, and an act of derring-do. So he just kept quiet until I finished what I had to tell him.

"So," he said, finally, "you're gonna go back to him, uh, Jonathan, huh?"

"Yeah," I said. "Well, I think so. One way, I guess, or another."

He was quiet.

"I don't know," I said.

"I have to see," I told him then, as it seemed I'd been telling everybody I'd spoken to for the last two weeks. "I'll know when...I know."

"Research," I finished, weakly.

"Look," he stammered a bit on it, "I know we don't really know each other or anything, but, uh, if it doesn't work out with him...well, here, take my address in Paris. But I'm going back to where I really work in a few weeks. Well, to where I go to school. You could come back with me though—I mean, if you wanted to."

"Back where?" I asked.

"Urbana, Illinois," he said, getting defensive when he saw the expression on my face. "They do really important research on cognition there. I mean, I got offered almost as much money by...."

He stopped himself, embarrassed that he'd felt the need to boast. "And, mostly really, I wanted to do this particular kind of research, and it included the year at the Institut in Paris, and it's not so bad to be away from the East Coast for a while—I mean, I grew up in New York...." (he shrugged, realizing that I'd probably already figured that out).

I nodded. Urbana's not the greatest place, but at least it's far enough from New York so that he could beg off from coming home for Thanksgiving dinner. I mean, Christmas—well, Hanukkah, I supposed, in his case—is okay, but Thanksgiving...I don't know, you just want to give it a rest for a few years. Even if your parents are really quite okay, like mine are.

Which was why, in my case, Urbana wasn't so good. "Well, see, I grew up in Bloomington, Indiana," I said.

So there'd be Thanksgiving. And Midwestern winters—I remembered how much I hated that first one, back home after the year in Montpellier. And it wasn't just the weather, it was the wholesomeness, the lack of edge. I'd come back to high school in Indiana and sworn to myself that this was *not* my life, even as I took my place with the rest of the faculty kids, hurrying off to swim teams and drama camp and flute competitions, Mom and Dad thoughtfully signing you up for summer college extension courses so that you could get a leg up in calculus or Italian. But I'd get out, I promised myself— if not back to France, than at least to California. Well, and I did, too, didn't I? Well beyond California, I thought, remembering my whitewashed room in the cliff rising from the sea. Far enough that maybe I could even stand a Thanksgiving dinner or two *en famille.*

"What would I do there, in Urbana?" I asked.

"Use my library card," he said, matter-of-factly. "Read, while you figure out how you get back into books and the stuff you're really interested in. Apply to schools, I guess."

He made it sound simple. Maybe it was, I thought. The stuff I was really interested in—hmm.

Read all the books. Write the big dissertation about sex and women and romance and pornography. I'd have to make it all sound a little more academic than it really was, of course. Tell my stories by retelling all those other profoundly erotic stories that somehow have passed into "literature." Disguise it all as disinterested scholarly discourse. Of course, I surprised myself by thinking, the vogue for that sort of thing might have passed by the time I finished the book (and I wondered where I'd kept that canny, careerist part of myself hidden these past years). Still, it would be fun to try to pull it all together. I even let myself fantasize a jacket blurb from Arthur Geist. And then get into line with all the other silly, book-crazed fools to apply for the elusive job.

And Daniel? Well, it was clear that we could talk to each other. And I knew that we shared some important spaces in the sexual imagination. He would be stunningly inexperienced, compared to the types I'd been hanging around with these past few years, but somehow I was confident that he'd turn out to be original, adventurous, on a day-to-day basis. And perhaps a little more than that, on the rare weekend when one of us didn't have a big paper due. Nerds' night out. And then I became amazed that I was having these thoughts at all. After all, I was going to see Jonathan. In less than an hour.

"Well," I said, "thanks for the offer." The train was nearing Avignon.

"I mean, this is all a little theoretical, isn't it?" I continued. "Talking about being together, I mean."

He was looking out the window, scowling at the gathering outskirts of the city. "Well," he muttered, "I guess so. I mean, 'theory' doesn't really cover it all that well, though I guess you're used to using it the way they do in English departments."

"Oh, right," I said angrily, "yeah, like you pocket protector types never use any buzzwords or jargon or anything. Great move, Daniel, correcting my language—*that'll* get me into bed for sure."

(And I wish I could say he never did any of that dumb humanities baiting again, but he still sometimes does it, when some of his friends from the lab start up. I think he does it less than he used to, though.)

"Sorry," he said, smiling a little as he opened his jacket to show me his perfectly normal, unprotected shirt pocket.

"But you're not going to bed with me anyway," he pointed out. "At least not today, and maybe not ever. And you can see how I'd be pretty depressed about that. I mean, I love to talk to you—to hear the lights and darks of your voice and to watch you bend your face out of shape when you talk about literature. But you know, tonight, this afternoon, when I turn around and take the return train to Paris, I'm going to wonder—I'm wondering right now—whether, long-term, what I should have done instead was take you up on your offer of fucking in the WC.

"I guess," he added sadly, "I'm really the first amateur you've run into in a long time."

Which was what, deep down, probably decided things for me, though I didn't know it at that moment. I mean, at that moment, I must have been thinking about half a dozen things. It's possible to do that, you know. When computers do it, it's called massively parallel processing, and it's what Daniel says is going to enable them to do real cognition one of these days. (Well, he says that on days when his work is going well, anyway.) Right now, of course, computers can't do mindtrips nearly as complicated as the ones people do, like when they meet somebody they like on the TGV from Paris to Avignon.

Anyway, at that moment, obviously, a lot of me was wondering what was going to happen with Jonathan. As well as wondering exactly how bent out of shape my face actually gets when I talk about literature. I was probably also still mulling over parts of *Clarissa*. And of *Justine*. I was deep into massively parallel mode—wondering and thinking all that stuff to myself at the same time. But I didn't say any of that stuff, because I said something else—which I was also thinking at that moment.

And what I said was, "You know, that's one of my favorite words in English. 'Amateur,' I mean."

I repeated it softly, giving it a French pronunciation, my tongue hitting the top of my front teeth and wanting to be in that little space between his.

"Amateur," I said again. I wasn't kidding either. It was one of my favorite words. Perhaps it was even a safe word. Or perhaps a dangerous one—because I wasn't sure exactly where it led.

"I mean, you know, people think it means beginner or something," I said. "And it does. But beginner, in the sense of being excited about something new. About having the guts to keep at it, because you love it, not because it's your profession or you have a license or something. It means enthusiast—passionate enthusiast. It means...well, think about it, its root. Amateur. Because, well, what it really means is *lover*."

Amateur.